flying jenny

a novel

theasa tuohy

Jug
6/18

KAYLIE JONES BOOKS

for Mom

~ ~ ~

Published by Akashic Books
©2018 Theasa Tuohy

ISBN: 978-1-61775-621-4
Library of Congress Control Number: 2017956878
First printing

Kaylie Jones Books
www.kayliejonesbooks.com

Akashic Books
Brooklyn, New York, USA
Ballydehob, Co. Cork, Ireland
Twitter: @AkashicBooks
Facebook: AkashicBooks
E-mail: info@akashicbooks.com
Website: www.akashicbooks.com

CHAPTER ONE
DEFYING THE ODDS
NEW YORK CITY, 1929

THE WILLIAMSBURG BRIDGE WAS ALREADY jammed with photographers, spectators, and newsreel cameras when Laura Bailey and Cheesy Clark arrived on the scene. They had a tough time shoving their way through to a good vantage at the railing so they could see all the way upriver toward the Queensboro Bridge.

"So," said Cheesy, removing the bulky flash attachment from his Speed Graphic as he set himself up for shooting, "here we is, me and you. A gal reporter and a cheesecake artist. Whaddaya think the deal is?"

"This whole thing doesn't make any sense." Laura frowned as she wriggled into a space between a steel post and Cheesy, and stepped up on a rung of the railing for a better view. A puff of breeze warned that she needed to hold as tightly to her little hat with one hand as she was gripping the railing with the other. "I bet that span isn't even two hundred feet above the water," she yelled to him over the noise of the crowd. "No one can fly under that. And look," she said, pointing west toward the Manhattan side of the bridge, clogged with Sunday traffic moving to and from Queens over the East River. "There are cables and stuff hanging down that could catch and rip a wing in a second."

Cheesy, the stub of a cigar clenched tight in his teeth, did no more than grunt. He was too busy jamming plates in and out of his Speed Graphic, turning one way for shots of the swelling crowd, whirling back, shooting the bridge up ahead, the barges, Sunday sailors, and other river traffic, then leaning back to get a dizzying shot of the soaring towers of the bridge they were on.

"Heck of a spread for the paper tomorrow," he finally said. "Don't wanna miss any angles. If the fool pilot gets hisself killed or not, still heck of a spread."

"Ouch, get your clodhopper off my foot," Laura yelped, as a Pathé newsreel cameraman backed into her.

Laura was at a distinct disadvantage jockeying among all these men, dressed as she was in a mid-calf-length skirt that hobbled her movement, the tiny hat with a veil perched atop her dark marcelled wave.

"Sorry, lady," the cameraman said. "But what are you doing here, anyway? You're in the way."

"So are you, buster," Laura snapped, giving him a shove and turning her attention back to the bridge ahead, scanning the horizon on the outlandish possibility that there could really be a little bi-wing airplane approaching. It was a perfect summer day, blue, cloudless sky. The rumor was, as hard as it was to comprehend, that some crazy barnstorming pilot from Roosevelt Field was planning to fly under all four bridges that crossed from Manhattan to Brooklyn and Queens.

People were doing all sorts of screwy things in 1929, as a glance at any newspaper would reveal. They called their era the Jazz Age, the Roaring Twenties. The Great War had been over for ten years, it was a time of boundless hope, optimism, and prosperity. "Blue Skies" was the song on everyone's lips. The tabloids were full of flagpole sitters, flappers doing the Charleston, and marathon dancers leaning on their partners through endless nights. The more serious journals had many readers believing that Herbert Hoover would put a chicken in every pot, a car in every garage, and that the bull market would run forever. But everyone agreed that these stunt pilots took the cake. Ever since Charles Lindbergh had flown the Atlantic solo two years before, the entire world had gone nuts over flying. Even women were doing it.

The traffic on the Williamsburg Bridge was light but growing; it didn't yet look as jammed as the Queensboro up ahead.

"Let's hope he flies north to south," Laura said to a reporter jammed next to her with an *Evening Graphic* press card stuck in his hat. "If he starts downriver from the Brooklyn Bridge, we won't be able to see him coming, only going."

The man laughed. "If he crashes into the Queensboro before he gets under it, we won't be able to see that either. Some guy I just talked to has binoculars; he says he can see a lot of press stationed up there. They'll get the good shots."

"We shudda had another shooter here," Cheesy grumbled. "I can catch action north, but with the bend in the river, I'm outta luck if he crashes into the Manhattan or the Brooklyn Bridge."

"You've got to crash doing this stunt," said a photographer Laura recognized from the *Evening Standard*. "There's hardly any clearance under most of those bridges."

At that moment a collective *"Ooh, ah"* rose from the growing crowd. Laura could make out a dark speck moving through the sky toward the Queensboro Bridge. "Can you see any better through your camera lens?" she turned to ask Cheesy. But the photographer was slamming plates with the staccato of a machine gun.

The black spot was coming closer. It wobbled, caught a sunray that flashed on the water, and headed straight for the dangling cables. Laura's chest tightened; she realized she was holding her breath. The poor guy was going to kill himself! She'd never seen anyone die before. She gritted her teeth. I suppose it's part of the job, she told herself. I can't be weak-kneed, I have to be strong. I have to prove myself. She watched the speck swerve, then merge with the shadowed waters beneath the bridge, her held breath turned to a gasp. The little spot popped up into the sun! A cheer went up from the bridge watchers.

"He made it."

"That was close."

"Wow."

The crowd roared. The expanding dot was clearly identifiable as a plane now, fast approaching, threading its way among the ships and barges in the harbor. It neared the Williamsburg, and the open-cockpit biplane rocked from side to side in greeting to the cheering, waving crowd. Laura could have sworn she caught a momentary glimpse of a grin under the cloth helmet and goggles of the figure in the cockpit. Bridge traffic was at a standstill.

The plane was heading straight for them, its nose pointing down. Laura elbowed and clawed her way back through the crowd and zigzagged past the stalled cars in what could only be described as a broken field run. The goal post was a view from the other side.

As she shoved one last person out of her way, she grabbed up a handful of skirt, yanked it above her knees, kicked off her high heels—Thank God they're not the ones with the strap across the instep, she thought—and hoisted her lithe five-foot-four frame up several rungs on the bridge's railing. Jeez, I hope Cheese has the good sense to be right behind me.

Cheesy Clarke, nicknamed for his penchant for pinup photos, was known in the trade as a cheesecake artist, but his talents went way beyond that. Before he was taken on as a staffer at the *Enterprise-Post*, the tabloid where he and

Laura worked, he'd continually scooped most of the staff photographers at the numerous newspapers in New York City. Always in the same black rumpled suit with no tie, he all but lived in his car with its police radio. Day or night, he was at a crime scene faster than anyone else, often beating the cops.

Cheesy was a swell guy, one of Laura's favorite photographers. He was a *deez* and *doze* type from the Bronx, with little education, and not the best table manners in the world, but he was funny and dedicated to his work.

Sure enough, there he was hanging over the bridge railing right beside Laura.

"You're pretty fast on your feet for a broad," he said with a grin.

"Darn right," Laura yelled into the wind. Mild though the weather was, there was more than a little breeze when you stuck your head out this far. "I was saving you a spot." She was already half over the rail leaning on her abdomen to help balance while she stretched for a better view of the water.

"Holy cow, here he comes." Laura could barely hear Cheesy over the sound of his camera's slide click as she caught sight of the first dark shadow of wings spread on the water.

At that same moment, she felt the wind tug at her hair. *Uh oh.* She didn't dare grab at her hat. She needed both hands on the rail, or she'd be in the drink as well. With something akin to seasickness, she watched the little veiled felt that represented a week's salary sail off. Borne by the fickle wind, it floated, then dipped, then glided down to the river far below.

She didn't have time to mourn, here came the plane. It did the very same kind of pop-up Laura had seen when it had come out from under the Queensboro Bridge mo-

ments before. I must ask someone how they do that, Laura
thought. If the pilot is too dead to talk, someone at an airfield or someplace like that will know. Must be like gunning
a car engine. Wow. I've never had a story like this before. It's
a real humdinger. She shifted her belly slightly on the railing
and peered down, straight into the hole of metal that passed
for a cockpit—a flutter of white.

A silk scarf flashed, blowing in the wind.

In a long-ago picture, it had been wrapped around the
woman's throat and a car's rear wheel. Isadora Duncan, her
mother's lover. It had broken Isadora's neck, and her mother's heart. But, nothing ever *really* touched her mother, Laura
had decided then. Just another moment of her narcissism.
Mother had wailed, "Poor Isadora, a part of me has died.
How shall I go on?" It always felt to Laura that everything
in the world except herself was a part of her mother's past;
Isadora had been her modern dance phase. It would take a
genius to ever predict what *phase* Mother would . . .

"Good grief," Laura screamed at Cheesy, "that was a
woman!" She knew it. She didn't know how, but she just
knew it! "A woman!"

The tiny biplane and its shadow were already skimming
through the sky and gliding along the choppy surface of the
water. The crowd behind Laura was cheering. Some people
were actually dancing around the stalled cars or doing jigs
on the roadway of the bridge.

"A woman!" Laura screamed again at Cheesy. "I've got
to get to a phone." As she dropped off the railing and scrambled into her shoes, she caught a view through the bridge's
lacy grillwork. The tiny dot of a plane was swinging slightly
to its left trying to avoid the smokestack of a river barge on
its way to the next bridge. I've got to file this story. I can't
stay to see what happens, Laura thought. Cheesy will get a
picture.

CHAPTER Two
FLYING JENNY

WHAT A LARK! JENNY FLYNN MOMENTARILY turned in the cockpit to watch a woman's tiny hat waft its way toward the choppy waters of the river below. Was the hat a salute or just some overzealous gawker losing her balance? Jenny raised a hand to her own cloth helmet in a loving salute to her hero brother. Look down, Bubba, from your home in the clouds, and watch me win this one for you.

A beautiful, cloudless day—she felt one with the sky. The wind whipped her face and stiffened her silk scarf into a flag flying in her wake. But why were the bridges packed with spectators and newsreel cameras? No one was supposed to know. Nosy reporters with their stupid questions. She hated the way they seemed to treat fliers as their own personal terrain. How did word get out she was doing this? She'd impulsively been drawn into a dare . . . Yikes, of course. That dadgum Mark had set her up, trying to entice her into accepting his job offer. She'd deal with him later!

Jenny squirmed a bit in her hard seat—not much more than a hole cut in the metal fuselage—to adjust the pillow she always kept wedged at her back against the risk of falling out when flying upside down. She hated chutes, rarely wore one. And seat belts in these old clunkers could be rusted and worn, and certainly too big for a ninety-pound teenager. She gripped the stick, looked around, and focused on what was ahead. The map spread on her knees, a corner tucked in her seat belt to keep it from blowing away, showed two bridges down and only two more to go—the Manhattan and the Brooklyn—around this bend of the river.

New York was an alien place. Flying under bridges packed with cars and people, past huge buildings that folks actually lived in! Skyscrapers. No yards, no grass, few trees. Soaring over billowing wheat, making forced landings in cornfields, was her way. She'd be in a dickens of a spot if she had engine trouble around here. For now, the steady drone of the new and souped-up Curtiss-Wright engine in this borrowed but familiar old Great War relic was sweeter than a concerto. Another Mark selling point: "Working for us, you'd have the best and latest equipment. Your incredible skill and our expertise—a winning combo." But she didn't want that. *This* was her life: moving on her own, just herself and the sky.

What a day. Glorious, skimming over the water, testing her mettle. That first bridge, what was it called? Its dangling cable caused her to drop so low, lose so much altitude before she could scoot under, that she'd nearly stalled—was close to being dunked. Her altimeter registering less than zero! She'd skirted so close to the river she could smell it, feel the spray hit her face as her propeller roiled the water. Then she'd gunned her, to pop up on the other side.

A slow grin spread up from Jenny's mouth to crinkle her eyes behind her goggles. She slapped her knee in glee. I bet that was the very spot where the so-called hot shot from the airfield took his dunking last week. The tale of that guy was how Mark goaded her into taking this dare. Once he'd started in on Jenny, a lot of the other hangar jockeys had chimed in. No *way* could a girl do it. Too many men had tried and failed.

Coming around the river's bend, Jenny gasped—two

looming suspension bridges one after the other, each a beauty. The first, the straight taut fingerboard of a violin, the next strung like creamy harp strings. Wow, they were really close together!

And something she hadn't counted on—open shipping channels. There were not only two bridges, but two *ships* as well. Big ones, each with several smokestacks: one going to and one coming from the open sea beyond. She tightened her grip on the stick—what to do? Stay level, calm, as she always did. The two behemoths were passing each other in the short space between the bridges.

She skimmed the water under the first bridge then sharply pulled back the stick to pop up and take quick stock of her situation.

She could most likely make it flying level in the space between the ships as they passed each other but, unsure about the wingspan of her borrowed plane compared to the smokestacks on each ship, she decided not to chance it. So she flipped a hard left rudder and the little biplane dutifully turned on its side and did a vertical slip under the Brooklyn Bridge. The faces of the seamen as she passed were a blur, but she could hear their cheers.

As she righted her plane, she pulled back on the stick and soared into the open bay of New York Harbor. There, straight ahead, was Lady Liberty smiling at Jenny's accomplishment, the white sails of weekend boaters dotted around.

"Hallelujah!" Jenny yelled to the open water.

She looked again, and the Lady's smile had vanished, just the same stern stone face so familiar from high school history books. I hope she's not mad at me, Jenny thought, everyone else is going to be. Her mother would have heart palpitations, call for the smelling salts, if any photos ran in the *Daily Oklahoman*. "My dear, how could you do this to me? Don't you know who we *are*? We have a standing to maintain in the community."

The Department of Commerce will probably be so angry they'll take away my license. But shoot, that's too much to worry about today. I just did something no one has ever done before, and now I'm going to buzz around Miss Serious Face over there and see if I can't get her to smile again.

Jenny remembered from those same school lessons that the symbolic broken chains on Miss Liberty's left foot could only be seen from the air. At the time, she'd thought what fun it would be to circle in an airplane to see them. Now was her chance. Probably never be frolicking around these parts again. Let's just hope the killjoys at Commerce don't yank my ticket and forever shackle me to the earth. She kicked her right rudder, made a sharp banking turn, and began circling for a better look. First around the torch. She dropped closer, spotted the broken chains and then tourists leaning sideways looking up from openings in the statue's crown at the sound of the buzzing plane. She waved and yelled, the spectators gleefully returning the greeting. She dipped her left wing, a favorite gesture of Bubba, her brother Charles.

As she made her final circle, Jenny wryly noted that Miss Liberty was wearing a dress. She could hear her mother's refrain, her mouth tight, her pince-nez set firmly in place for the stern admonition: "A lady is always properly attired." Jenny laughed into the wind. Demerits, though, for the Big Gal's stone sandals.

She glanced down at the map to refresh her memory of the return route to Roosevelt Field and wondered at the strangeness of the day. Had she accepted this dare because of her takeoff point, named for the fallen son of a president? Quentin, son of Teddy. He'd been in the same regiment as Charles. Was that it? Of course not! But Bubba would have been proud of his baby sister, not aghast like their parents. The Roosevelt heir had an airfield named for him. This would be *her* monument to Charles.

She touched a little finger to tight lips, smiled a child's smile, and the deal was sealed. Now her sense of accomplishment was thrilling. But with it came added determination to not let the joy of flying turn into work. She wanted to have fun, go to dances at the country club, play tennis. Not toil all the time at perfecting aerial stunts. Phooey!

"Oh lordy," Jenny said out loud, as she saw from the map that the spot to her right was Governors Island. She knew her aviation history. She had pored over all of Charles's books after he was shot down. This was the very place Wilbur Wright took off from way back in 1909 to fly around the Statue of Liberty in his old crate—that thing with all sorts of struts and him just sitting up there out in the open.

Jenny swooped down to check out the terrain. Sure enough, it was a spit of land with a grass runway and a row of buildings that might be hangars. She buzzed the field, but no one appeared. A ripple of excitement, of reverence, ran through her—feelings tinged with a vague sense of disappointment that there was no one around who might have noticed her bridge feat. But it didn't cross her mind that she herself was now part of aviation history. Instead she thought of the business at hand, finding her way back to Roosevelt Field.

C HAPTER THREE
RACING AGAINST DEADLINE

SEVERAL REPORTERS WERE RIGHT ON Laura's heels, charging for telephones. She had staked out a public booth in a drugstore just off the bridge on Delancey Street by paying a tough-looking street kid two bits to hold it for her. With a salary of only twelve dollars a week, a quarter was a big investment, but she wasn't about to risk losing precious minutes and be beat out filing this story. A half hour spent searching for an available phone was a lifetime in the tabloid news business—she had to prove that she was skilled at these breaking stories. And maybe, just maybe, if her story was good enough, she could get the money reimbursed on her expense account. Sure enough, the kid was standing guard in the booth's doorway, a grin on his face, his corduroy cap pushed back on his head, eating a Tootsie Roll that had obviously been purchased with his spoils.

When she got a rewrite man on the telephone, he told her the wires were already reporting that the pilot had tipped up and flown sideways under the Brooklyn Bridge to thread the plane between a tanker and a US Navy destroyer.

"Can you confirm he did that?" he barked.

"I don't have eyes in the back of my head," Laura snapped back. "I saw the plane go under two bridges, and that's it. But I swear to God that *he* was a *she!*"

"Whoa, what's that? Okay, kid, give me what you got."

When Laura had finished dictating, he said, "Barnes wants you and Cheese to lam it to Long Island and get a beat on whoever that pilot was."

"Will do," Laura said, and hung up.

Cheesy was waiting outside the booth at their prearranged spot. He had heard talk too that the pilot had flown sideways under the last bridge.

As they started to leave, the phone in the booth rang. Laura snatched it up, and heard Barnes, the city editor, bellow: "It definitely was a girl, kid. Get on it. Mac supposedly has Roosevelt Field covered, but you better get out there too, so we can have a sob sister number."

Roosevelt Field, some twenty miles from Manhattan on Long Island, was a flat, treeless plain where cattle had grazed in colonial times. Charles Lindbergh had taxied down its muddy ruts two years earlier on his way to Paris, wheels greased to help his lift, beginning the world's first successful transatlantic flight. Visionaries, daredevils, and drifters all came together there in the aircraft-company hangars that dotted the several thousand acres and housed the flying machines that would soar into the future, or crash and burn at the ragged edges of the unkempt acreage.

Presumably, it was also the spot from which the latest daredevil had taken off.

When Laura arrived with Cheesy in his battered DeSoto, the immense flying arena was swarming with people cheering and waving, hot dog vendors, cars, trucks, newsreel vans. Even a dirigible hovered overhead.

"How do we plow through this mess?" Laura asked after she and the photographer had parked some distance away and climbed a pasture fence to get nearer to the action.

"Nutin' to it," he replied. "The victim's gotta be at the center of the pile. Hang on," he offered her an elbow, "I'll bull my way in." He thrust his camera forward like a ramrod.

As they pushed their way through the circus atmosphere, a small plane would occasionally take off down one of the rutted roads that served as runways, the pilot hanging over the side of the plane waving to the crowd scattering out of his path. Some of the stunters would then buzz the excited onlookers, dipping their wings or even barrel-rolling over them.

"Holy smoke," Laura said to Cheesy when they'd gotten close enough to spot the star of the day, who was perched on the open rumble seat of a 1927 Chevy. "You've got to get a picture of that outlandish outfit." The tiny fair-haired young woman at the eye of the storm of reporters and photographers was wearing boys' knickers and argyle socks topped off by a beat-up leather flight jacket. She was merrily swinging a cloth helmet back and forth in her right hand.

"Those clothes should please Barnes since he wants all this gal reporter fluff," Laura said with a malicious grin. "He says my serious pieces read like *Stella Dallas*."

"Go get 'em, tiger. You got spunk," Chessy said. "You certainly throw yourself into things all right."

"Ah, Cheese, you know I think these kinds of stories are silly. I'd rather be working on more worthwhile stuff."

"Dis here's da business. You gotta realize that, kid."

She found this kind of assignment annoying. Barnes usually let her work on things that took time and some thought. She knew it was because he didn't trust her to work fast and handle breaking news. That suited her just fine. She could develop her own stories about issues or people in need— not just pander to the lowest common denominator. On the other hand, this was her job and she didn't want it thought around the newsroom that she couldn't handle whatever the desk threw at her.

As she and Cheesy pushed their way into the crowd,

a reporter at the center of a howling pack yelled up at the woman in the rumble seat: "Say, you got a license to fly that crate?"

The sparkly young woman, who had answered endless questions for the last twenty minutes and had long before identified herself as Jenny Flynn from Oklahoma City, frowned and squirmed. "Of course I do."

"So then," asked a guy in the front row, "aren't you worried you might lose that license? The Department of Commerce frowns on stunts like flying under bridges. You did four of 'em."

The tall, good-looking, middle-aged man who stood next to the pilot patted her shoulder reassuringly, and made motions that she should sit down so the car could move on.

Jenny shrugged away his hand and squared her shoulders. "We'll see," she said in a much louder voice. "I trust that won't happen. It's interesting to discover, don't you think, just what magic can be done with an airplane?"

Laura, still missing her hat, but with her marcel wave back to its original stylish perfection thanks to some intense work with a comb and her compact while Cheesy was driving, finally got a chance to shout from the crowd: "Why are you dressed in those clothes?"

Jenny looked stunned. She leaned forward, scanning the sea of faces, and did a double take when her pale gray eyes landed on the sole woman among the pack of reporters. "They were handy," she yelled, frowning and using her hands like a megaphone. "One can hardly fly in a skirt." She turned to her companion and, in a voice that carried over the crowd, said, "These New Yorkers really are rude, just like everyone at home says. What business is it of hers what I fly in?"

"But those look like boys' clothes," Laura persisted.

"They are. I borrowed them from the child of a friend,"

Jenny replied curtly. "Do you want his name and address so you can check?"

"Naw," Laura shouted over the din, "I doubt he's important to the story. But what about this license business? Do you have one or not? And why did that question make you so nervous?"

"I *said* I had one. Are you doubting my word?" Jenny turned and plopped down next to the tall man. He banged on the back window of the coupe, and it slowly pulled away, the driver tooting the Chevy's horn to clear a path through the reporters and well-wishers.

C HAPTER FOUR
THE LESSON

THERE WAS HELL TO PAY WHEN LAURA got back to the office with no more than what the pack had gleaned through the impromptu answers from the back of a rumble seat.

Laura finished her entire story in one shot instead of giving it in takes for a copy kid to run over to Barnes at the city desk. She knew Mac had already filed his, and she had a feeling that somehow hers might not compare too favorably. She hadn't quite understood what was wanted here. A mob of people, everyone shouting questions. No real answers, it seemed, to anything.

She took a deep breath, squared her shoulders, and wound her way through the cluttered desks to hand her story to Barnes.

He glanced it over, then threw the copy on the floor. "What's this nonsense? Didn't I ever teach you nothing? This is in Mac's story. It's on the wires." He was revving up to such an extent she thought he was going to swallow his cigar. "For damn's sake, it's even in the cutlines next to Cheesy's pictures."

Laura could see that Barnes was wanting to say something a lot heavier than *damn*. She knew she frustrated Barnes on a lot of levels. But why did he keep sending her out on silly stories like this hysteria over flying aces? "You didn't say anything about an interview when you sent me

out there." She tried to keep the defiance out of her voice.
She had a feeling this was a dumb thing to say, but it was
true.

"You knew Mac was already there!" Barnes yelled, his
face turning purple. "Do you think it takes two of you to
lift a pencil?"

"Whoa!" She thought she was only thinking it, but
she'd said it!

Barnes gave her a startled, enraged look. "*Whoa*? Kid,
you're the one who'd better *whoa*."

"Sorry boss," Laura mumbled, "I was just thinking out
loud."

Thinking was right. It hadn't crossed her mind before
now that they'd sent her to Roosevelt Field because she
was a woman—assuming that would somehow set her up
for special treatment to get an interview with Jenny Flynn.
Whoa. She said it to herself this time. She needed to think
about this, and keep her mouth shut. This was a confusing
world she found herself in, but like everything else in her
life she needed to just grit her teeth and find her own way
through the maze. Never let them see that you don't have
a clue how to do it. And this *sob sister* stuff, what exactly
did it mean? She had thought it was synonymous with *tear-
jerker*. Could it possibly mean any old thing written by a
woman?

How to recoup? Barnes was really in a rage. And he was
her lifeline in this place. He'd been stuck with teaching her
the ropes ever since she'd had the good luck to land the job
a few months earlier, after her English professor at Barnard,
a friend of the publisher, went to bat for her.

Not only had the job of trying to teach Laura how to
chase a breaking story fallen to the longsuffering city editor, but he'd had to instruct her on the simplest tasks that
one normally learned as a copyboy. Barnes had empowered

Laura with the knowledge of such things as slug, lead, graf, cutlines, takes, kicker, wood block, type size, how to signal the end of your story with -30-, and, most of all, how to tread lightly around men in the back shop, also known as printers. *And* he had not been shy about grumbling that Laura was yet another example of why publishers should keep their noses out of a newsroom.

"Say, boss . . ." Laura began tentatively, but knew she had to plow ahead into his rage. Otherwise she'd be worse than a wallflower in this joint. "I wanted to ask you about how to handle this license business. I did check for clips in the morgue . . ."

Barnes had already turned his back on Laura, and was screaming at a copyboy across the room: "Get those pages to me, NOW! What license, what about the morgue?" Barnes whirled back to Laura.

She quickly explained that Jenny Flynn had acted nervous when asked about the Department of Commerce and her license.

"I asked if she really had one, and she got huffy as a hornet. Took off right after. But when I checked the morgue, I found a story that she got her license when she was only seventeen. She doesn't look like she could be more than eighteen now."

Barnes's face lost its purple tone and seemed to be flirting with a grin. "So you did all that, did ya? Okay. So that's what she's afraid of, losing her license because of this bridge stunt." Barnes screwed up his mouth in thought, shook his head. "Hmm. Do you know what to do next?"

"Umm, uh, I checked, but of course the Department of Commerce isn't open on the weekend."

"It will be tomorrow. Keep after them to find out if they yank her ticket. Good girl. Mac didn't mention this." Barnes rolled his eyes in mock disgust, then gave Laura a stern, furrowed-brow command: "Now go back and write a story speculating how the winged lass's young hopes and dreams hang on the whim of the Commerce bureaucracy."

Laura frowned. "She's awfully irresponsible, I have to say. But isn't that hounding the girl?" She was being kind to say that. She had found a lot more about Jenny in the morgue clips than she was imparting to Barnes. The pilot appeared to be spoiled and rich like all those uppity girls in college with whom Laura had never been able to make friends. Several wire stories had taken note of Jenny's singularity in Oklahoma as a girl flier, but emphasis seemed to be more on her debutante status than anything else, and on the fact that her much older brother had been shot down over France during the war. The girl intrigued Laura. Why would she do such a silly, frivolous thing? She obviously didn't understand life was tough. Was she trying to copy her brother? And running around in men's clothes? Maybe in Greenwich Village, where anything goes, but—

"Hounding?" Barnes voice rose to a near screech. "Don't talk nonsense. We gotta keep pestering the feds or our readers will never get the answer."

CHAPTER FIVE
OXYGEN

JENNY FLYNN AND HER FRIEND MARK SNYDER were at Roosevelt Field the following afternoon. Wearing a cloche hat and a light summer frock of peach organza with an uneven ruffled hem, she was hard to recognize as the curly headed waif outfitted in boys' clothes who had accepted a dare from Mark the day before.

But the tension between them would have been readily apparent to anyone bothering to take notice in the boisterous, milling crowd of thousands who tramped around the field anticipating that another transcontinental speed record was about to be broken. All eyes were scanning the horizon for Frank Hawks, who was due in from Los Angeles. He had set a record getting there—nineteen hours, ten minutes—and was now on the return trip.

"I just can't believe you did that to me." Jenny had been fuming all morning. "You set me up, Mark. Alerted the press, just to get publicity for your darned company. And you know perfectly well that kind of notice could cause me to lose my license."

"Jenny, what you did was extraordinary. The world needs to know about it. You don't have to worry about your license. You'll be a household name."

"That's exactly what I don't want—notoriety. Easy for you to say not to worry, but they could ground me."

"Not with the Curtiss clout," Mark said, a grin losing its fight against an Eastern prep-school smugness that had always grated on Jenny's Western sensibilities. His pasty, too-pretty face needed more sun. He never was much of a flier, as far as Jenny was concerned, and logging most of his hours in closed cabins gave him an armchair pallor that was hardly her idea of handsome. "We're already working on it."

She blinked in disbelief. Mark was a Curtiss Aviation executive. "Working on what? My license? You're sure? I've been really scared."

"The government wants to promote aviation, not suppress it." Mark couldn't lose his smugness. "Why do you persist in hiding your talent? Doesn't make sense."

"I'm not interested in flying for hire." My lord, Jenny thought, how many times am I going to have to say this? "I won't work for you. That's it. I certainly appreciate it, if you can save my license, but I came to the field today only because Frank Hawks is a friend. I want to cheer him on. Then I'm going back to Oklahoma." She pursed her lips, jutted out her chin, and clenched a fist as though she were going to hit someone.

The crowd pressing around them was in a festive mood, watching and waiting. A two-seater Movietone biplane circled overhead with *Fox News* painted in huge letters on its side. In smaller script, *Mightiest of All* could only be read when the plane buzzed close to the ground, its photographers hanging out of the cockpits taking pictures of the spectators. In these heady flying days of the summer of 1929, records were made to be broken, and the press was agog with every lurch. The New York *Daily News* even had its own plane, its ace aerial photographer always scouting around the field for stories.

Now that she'd said her piece to Mark, Jenny decided

she must try to be more civil. She had been flown to New York as his guest, but she should have known better—no such thing as a free ride. He was an old friend, she a houseguest of his family, and he'd even lent her some of his teenage son's clothing for her stunt. But Mark had recently invested heavily in the corporation that merged Curtiss Field and its hangars and flying school with Roosevelt Field. Always on the lookout for ways to tout his products, he'd sent a company plane and pilot to pick her up from Oklahoma City. She should have known better.

"Mark, I like that Curtiss agreed to drop its name and keep Roosevelt," Jenny said, trying to keep her tone level and light. If he could solve the Department of Commerce problem, it wasn't smart to keep being snippy. She scanned the facilities along the north and west sides of the field that created a right-angled flight line, where planes parked and were serviced. "That was nice."

"No one wants to dishonor the memory of a dead war hero. Especially a president's son," Mark replied. "You're too young to remember, but Quentin was Peck's bad boy in the White House. He was only three when his father's term began, and the public loved the kid's antics. He threw spitballs at Andrew Jackson's portrait, took a pony into a White House elevator, and walked on stilts in its garden."

"And was shot down by a German Fokker." Jenny's face clouded.

"Yes."

"Ninety-fifth Aero Squadron," she said cryptically.

"How do you know that?" Mark asked.

"Just do."

Mark had flown her to New York in a closed-cabin Robin, a spiffy little blue-and-white monoplane, with two wicker passenger seats behind the pilot. It was that plane he'd first suggested for her bridge stunt, but she thwarted his hope of her showing off his new model by insisting on borrowing, instead, an old Curtiss JN-4, like her own at home.

"I don't see any thrill in flying in a cabin," she'd told him. "Might as well be on the train if you can't feel the wind on your face."

"But you said you loved the trip here in the Robin."

"Oh sure," she'd replied. "Sitting back and being chauffeured halfway across the country. Who wouldn't love that? I leave the long-distance stunts to people like Frank Hawks. He's a swell guy, you know that, but I don't care about setting records. I'm only in it for the fun."

Having fun was Jenny's signature mode. Her dignified and very conventional parents, who were horrified by her unladylike interest in flying, called her headstrong. Others called her cocky. But perhaps what distinguished Jenny most from the convention-defying flappers of an earlier era was her own secure sense in the rightness of her thinking. She shared her parents' core values of refined propriety, and was more than happy to impose those restrictions on others. Nonetheless, she had overlaid such constraints with the notion that she could do as she pleased as long as *she* defined it as having fun. "Oh, Mother," she often said, "don't be a spoilsport. It's perfectly acceptable to wear pants in the car when I'm only on my way to the airport."

Waiting now for Hawks to land, Mark again broached the subject of the new Robin as they stood in the field not far from the Curtiss hangar.

"Walter Beech has several Travel Airs in that upcoming women's race," he said. "So far, Curtiss has only one Robin entered, the pilot is barely out of flight school. You're ten times better than she is, Jenny. You would be perfect."

"Don't start that again!"

"This cross-country race is huge. A first for women.

Great for the industry and great for you gals." With the noise of planes taking off and landing, Mark leaned in closer. "My company would be the ideal sponsor for you. You're an instinctive pilot. Your looks, the Robin's pizzazz—a winning combination. We'll paint it whatever color you want. Look at how the press went crazy over your bridge thing. If you don't want the race, then you could do selling, plane demonstrations, whatever you want."

Jenny waved her hand in dismissal. "Get Amelia. She's into promotion. Besides, I decided yesterday that's the end of my stunts. No more. I'm not looking for notoriety *or* a job."

"How about a hot dog or ice cream," Mark offered. Roosevelt Field was laid out almost like a baseball diamond. With runways forming its outline, there were hangars, manufacturers, and flying-service offices where the bleachers and stands would be. Sitting in the middle of the infield was a hot dog shed advertising its wares, including ice cream. A huge sign painted in red on its white clapboard sides read, *FLY $5.*

Jenny laughed. "I can't be bought, Mark, but I can be appeased."

Mark trotted over to the spot in the middle where spectators, often with their cars, clustered for better views of whatever the daredevils might be trying next. It was jammed right now with those awaiting Hawks's arrival.

"Look at that outlandish garb," Jenny said, as Mark returned, pointing at a woman on the Curtiss apron preparing to climb into an open-cockpit biplane. She was wearing heavy clothing with a mask and plastic tubing hanging around her neck. "What's she up to?"

"Don't know," Mark replied. "I've heard talk someone was planning to challenge your friend Louise Thaden's altitude record. But Jenny, let's not get off the main subject

here. You need to be thinking about turning this into a career. Curtiss could *really* use you. We're just beginning to let
the American public know about the importance of flying,
and we need people with your talent and good looks to promote what is—not to sound melodramatic—the future!"

A number of spectators had begun moving away from
the area where Hawks was expected to land and were
watching the woman. Word was circulating that she, indeed, was going for a record.

"These endurance flights are so boring," Jenny said.
"Whether it's altitude or seeing how long you can stay in
the air. First one circles overhead for fifteen hours, then
someone else does it for twenty. Now twenty-six hours is
the record to beat. Why do they waste their energy?"

She was eating a hot dog and trying to adjust her footing
in the open field, even though she'd taken the precaution of
wearing low-heeled shoes. "I wish I had my jodhpur boots,"
she said. "But how silly would that look with a dress?"

Mark chuckled. "You women fliers are such a different
breed. I hate to sound so evangelical, but we've got to keep
aviation in the public eye to get facilities built, make ad-
vancements. And everyone finds it thrilling that even women
are doing it."

"Ah, Mark, you're the salesman. Not me." Jenny glanced
around for a moment at the gawking crowd, assuming this
was the "public" to which Mark referred. but quickly decided
she saw nothing of interest. So she turned her attention back
to the flight line. "Lordy," she said, indicating the woman flier
by waving her hot dog in Mark's direction and pointing with
her chin. "She's wearing fur-lined clothes in this heat."

"It'll be pretty cold up there," he said, "even if she
makes it to only twenty thousand feet. Probably twenty below zero. But that thing dangling around her neck looks like
an ether mask for a surgery patient."

"Isn't it about time for Frank to arrive?" Jenny asked impatiently. "What *he's* doing makes sense, it's worthwhile. He's getting from one place to another. By pushing the limits, he's proving what a flier can do. Gaining information for designing better planes."

"The same thing can be said for those setting endurance records," Mark countered.

Frank Hawks and Roscoe Turner had been jockeying back and forth for months setting new transcontinental speed records, first one then the other. Both were veterans of the Great War, and had since become well-known stunt and test pilots. Hawks had the distinction of having given Amelia Earhart her first airplane ride, charging her ten dollars in 1920 at a state fair in California. Earhart, billed as Lady Lindy and the first woman to fly the Atlantic, had been a passenger on the trip from Nova Scotia to South Wales in June 1928. She had immediately published a book titled *20 Hrs., 40 Min.* and become the aviation editor of *Cosmopolitan* magazine. Turner, a giant of a man with a waxed mustache, was an accomplished pilot who could easily be taken for a buffoon. When his old uniform had worn out, he fashioned a military-type costume of blue tweed that he wore with a cross-the-shoulder Sam Browne belt and high leather boots. He often flew with his pet lion, Gilmore.

"Frank's a friend," Jenny said. "I hope he sets a record Roscoe can't beat. From what I hear, Roscoe's okay and he's a brilliant flier, but lordy, he's such a showoff, it's embarrassing. I don't like the idea of fliers being viewed as circus clowns."

"I'd be happy to have either one flying for Curtiss," Mark said.

"Look over there," Jenny said, excitement tinged with disgust in her voice. "The flight crew is putting a tank in that woman's cockpit. Must be oxygen. The poor thing is going to need pliers to turn that valve on and off. That's just what Louise did back in December when she set the record."

A collective murmur of excitement was coming from the crowd as they surged en masse across the field, away from the hangar where Frank Hawks was expected and toward the woman pilot and her plane. Mark took Jenny's arm, steadying her as they were pushed forward in the wave. Ground attendants were attempting to hold people back from rushing the flight line. To add to the melee, a small Waco biplane touched down and was taxiing between the woman and the swirling mob. It nearly clipped a young man in a plaid cap who was trying to hurry across the runway. Gawkers could be bigger hazards to pilots than bad weather or faltering engines. They often rushed into the path of planes taking off or landing. Parked planes had their ribs cracked, their linen torn, and occasionally were even knocked over by swarms of people.

The woman pilot waved, climbed up on the wing flapping her fur-lined leather jacket trying to create a little breeze to cool herself off in the sticky heat, her plastic mask dangling from a cord around her neck. As she hoisted herself into the cockpit, her left leg momentarily hung over the side, revealing fur sticking out of the top of her high leather boots.

"Louise told me her instruments indicated she made it to twenty-nine thousand feet, but the official barograph in her plane only registered a little over twenty," Jenny told Mark. "I wish this woman luck whoever she is, but these endurance records are silly. And you have people butting into your life, reporters asking about your clothes. Ridiculous. It's unseemly."

"Jenny, you're flying for the thrill. Why can't you see that people flock to these exploits because it enhances their lives?" She rolled her eyes. Here comes another pitch, she thought. Mark's voice swelled in her mind as though there were a drumroll behind it. "Where else are they going to find thrills? Not sitting at home clustered around a radio listening to a dance band, or a sermon by some evangelist like Billy Sunday."

Jenny had heard all this before from the aviation missionaries. Her instructor, Roy, was one of the worst. But she just wanted to do what she wanted to do. Yet she *was* tempted by some of Mark's proposals. Make a little money to just fly around from time to time in that cute little Robin. Although its closed cabin wasn't very appealing. Maybe she could cut a deal to earn a little spare money flying her own Jenny. After all, it was a Curtiss product, even if an antique. She didn't know what was involved with all this. But it was a bit tempting to be able to at least pay for her fuel and flying lessons. She couldn't care less about promoting flying, setting records, or proving that she could fly a plane as well as any man. Things were advancing fast and fine of their own accord. Barnstormers and daredevils were continually breaking and setting records. Lindbergh and some businessmen had established Transcontinental Air Travel, a network of airports purposely situated near train stations, so passengers could cross the country by flight during the day, then take a train overnight. They charged $350 for the coast-to-coast trip, which took forty-eight hours. The line flew Ford Trimotor planes with *TAT* emblazoned on their sides and carried eight or nine passengers, plus a crew of three, including a steward. TAT planes were made of metal, which was very unusual, as most were still made of linen and balsa wood.

Jenny gave Mark her brightest smile. "You're a good friend, Mark. I appreciate the confidence you have in me. But yesterday's mad house was enough." She pointed in the direction of the Curtiss hangar. "I'll leave it to these other ladies to set the records and grab the headlines and get pawed over by the public."

"I don't care what you say," Mark replied. "I'm going to fill out an application for you and the Robin to enter the derby."

Jenny shook her head. "You're a super salesman, but this one won't take."

The pilot revved her engine and began taxiing down the field. There was a collective *oomph* from the crowd as thousands moved in unison, trying to help the vibrating little plane lift off.

"There she goes!" Jenny yelled, as her own small frame unconsciously straightened and lifted, choreographing the plane's rise.

The pilot made a nearly vertical climb into the cloudless sky and soon was no more than a speck of lint to those watching from the arid field. Two other planes were then spotted, both coming in from the west. Could one of them be Frank Hawks? Members of the milling crowd moved one way, then another, murmuring suggestions to each other about how to best position themselves for a good view.

Jenny and Mark, like everyone else, were doing their best to plane spot. "That closer one has double wings," Jenny finally said. "That can't be Frank."

The first plane landed, and as it taxied toward the Fairchild hangar, it was swarmed by much of the crowd. Those who had hung back for the landing of the second, an open-cockpit monoplane with *Texaco* emblazoned on its tail fin, watched in horror and fascination as it touched down and almost immediately went into a slow skid, eventually hitting a low-lying wooden fence at the field's edge. Jenny, running toward the plane with the rest of the crowd, saw with relief that it was upright and appeared to have suffered little damage. Frank Hawks stood up from the cockpit and, to a chorus of cheers, began to climb out. When the crowd reached him, he had fallen asleep on his feet, his head resting on the fuselage against the white lettering that read, *The Texas Company*. Other than exhaustion, he was unharmed. With his Los Angeles–to–New York round-trip, he had been on the road, so to speak, for forty-two hours and forty-eight minutes, with a six-hour layover in LA.

Frank Hawks had set a cross-country record of seventeen hours and forty-eight minutes in his souped-up Lockheed. It had an aluminum-alloy cowling that covered the engine for reduced drag, and a full array of gauges, panel instruments, and a radio. The latter wasn't a lot of help since there was no control tower at Roosevelt. But progress was being made to bring some system of order to air traffic. In St. Louis, the airport hired a stunt pilot named Archie League to stand on the field and direct pilots with a red flag to "hold" and a checkered flag to "go."

Jenny had just reached Frank and was trying to lend him support when she looked up and exclaimed, "Oh, good heavens."

"I'm okay," Frank mumbled.

"No," Jenny said, stiffening. "It's the oxygen lady, spinning out of control."

By this time, crowds were swarming Frank's plane. A ground crew had arrived and was trying to hold the spectators off, and lift his plane from the fence to shove or carry it toward the hangar.

"Oxygen?" Frank asked, suddenly coming fully alert.

"Altitude endurance. She's got on some kind of makeshift mask. She's spiraling straight in. Probably passed out."

Jenny watched, her right hand shading her eyes, her throat constricted, while the tiny object in the sky became bigger and bigger as it hurtled toward earth. For an instant, she could distinctly see the frightened face of her brother

Charles at the controls. The good die young. He was twenty-one. Jenny was six. And poppies grow in Flanders fields.

A thundering explosion competed with the sounds of planes on other runways taking off and landing, as a huge fireball erupted in the sky.

"These damned inexperienced kids," Frank growled, an anguished expression on his dirt-caked, sunburned face. He ripped off his leather helmet and flung it to the ground.

"Oh my God!" Jenny gasped. "I'm going back home."

"Jenny!" Mark yelled over the screams of the crowd and the clang of fire engines. "You can't do that!"

"Who says I can't!"

CHAPTER SIX
THE CITY ROOM

"DAMNATION!" LAURA YELPED TWO WEEKS later. "My story got bumped off Page One for Dietrich and her darned pants!" She slammed that day's *New York Enterprise-Post* down on one of the mounds of clutter fighting for space on her desk. "I thought Paris was supposed to be liberated! Don't they know this is the modern age?"

"Who you talking to, kid, the wind?" asked Joe Collins from the next desk over, a playful scowl on his weathered face. "People'll think you're batso, grumbling to yourself." Joe sat with his feet up on his desk, his snap-brimmed hat pushed back on his head, press card stuck in its band. He was chewing on a toothpick.

"Knock it off, Joe. You know I've had at least a blurb about this series on Page One for the last week. It's an important story—children in detention and how they're mistreated. I worked hard on it."

"Sure, kid, we all do. But everybody can't hit a home run every day."

"But for some stupid incident in France! If Marlene Dietrich wants to look silly wearing pants in Paris, fashion designers might care but the cops shouldn't be quizzing her about it. Whose business is it but hers? This is 1929, not the Dark Ages."

"Pants. The broad had on a man's suit! Look at that picture," he said, slapping his fist hard against the newspaper in his hand. "Pinstripes and a tie! You tough dames are all the same—no sense of propriety." Collins pulled his feet off his desk, pushed his hat back on his head, and began banging away with two fingers on his Underwood upright. The toothpick was moving faster than his fingers.

Collins is a jerk, Laura thought, always smelling of hops from having drunk his lunch, never an original thought in his bleary head. Even his desk was blank. No mounds, like hers, of all the odds and ends and tidbits she always meant to do a story on. Collins's desk looked like no one lived there.

This was, indeed, 1929. Prohibition was in full throttle with bathtub gin selling for as little as ten cents a bottle. Any Saturday, even the kiddies at their five-cent movie could see jerky black-and-white newsreels of Elliott Ness's G-men smashing stills with their axes as mobsters fought over territory in the streets of big cities. Al Capone was king of Chicago. Speakeasies were everywhere. Detroit authorities claimed that the city's version of the clandestine booze joints, colorfully known as blind pigs, were so numerous that revenue from illegal liquor was second only to the city's auto industry.

The Nineteenth Amendment had been ratified nine years before, giving women the right to vote, and it appeared there was no stopping them. They were moving into all sorts of male preserves that had previously been forbidden. They were even flying airplanes under bridges like that daredevil Jenny Flynn, whose exploits had been recorded by Pathé News and RKO, and spread across the front pages of all of New York's papers. And they were also crashing and burning, like that Gena Jones, who knew how to fly but didn't know what level of oxygen would keep her from blacking out. True, Dietrich, the glamorous German film star, had been stopped and questioned for wearing pants in public; but that was Paris, not America. Here in New York sat Laura Bailey, the *Enterprise-Post*'s first and only female reporter in the city room, with Collins and the other reporters grumbling that she had the temerity to sound off when her story didn't make the front page.

"Hey, Bailey," the city editor bellowed, "get over here, I got something for you!"

Laura unfolded herself from her desk, stubbed out her cigarette on the linoleum floor, patted into place any stray strands of her dark hair that might have escaped from her bob, straightened her calf-length skirt, grabbed a notebook and pencil from the mess on her desk, and headed toward the pulsating center of this tight little universe. She passed rows of cluttered desks, peopled by white-shirted men, their sleeves rolled up, banging away at typewriters or yelling into the mouthpieces of long-necked telephones. It's no wonder everyone shouts around here, Laura thought, we're so used to the continuous clacking of the wire machines we're not even conscious of the roar.

A stub of cigar in the grip of his stained teeth, Rufus Joshua Barnes mumbled, "Long Island, you grew up out that way, didn't you?"

"What are you talking about?" Laura replied. "I was born in Greenwich Village."

"Oh yeah," Barnes said. "A bohemian, I forgot."

Laura smiled to herself, thinking that this tough, gritty, fat man would be stunned to know just how bohemian her upbringing really had been. Like having no idea who her father was.

"Get on with it," Laura said tartly, circling her right wrist in a hurry-up motion. "What do you want me to do on Long Island?" None of them seemed to like her or want her around, so she saw no reason to try to be polite. She had learned quickly to give as good as she got.

"Nothing, actually," Barnes said with a cat-ate-the-canary smirk. "I was just thinking how you fouled up out there at Roosevelt Field and didn't get an interview with that stunt-flying dame. I was hoping the failure might have matured you a little as a reporter."

"Now just a minute—"

"Just a minute yourself. Here," Barnes said, studying a scribbled note in his big hand, "I've got another assignment that I trust you won't mess up."

"Yeah?" Laura couldn't keep the skepticism from her voice. It sounded like a trap—some back-of-the book rubbish, no doubt.

"So, you've done okay on the orphanage thing."

"Detention," Laura corrected.

Barnes looked at her and rubbed the stubble on his chin. "You really have a sassy mouth, kid. Didn't they teach you nothing in that college?"

This was an old refrain around here, and Laura got pretty tired of hearing it. As far as she could tell, most of these guys hadn't bothered to finish high school. Not wanting an education made no sense to her. She'd grown up in an atmosphere where intellectualism was everything. People in her mother's circle lived, breathed, ate, and slept with books, art, ideas—almost to the point of psychosis. They were poets and painters who always had to know everything, be on the cutting edge, test whatever theory was new, stretch the boundaries of convention way beyond anything that resembled everyday life. The poet William Carlos Williams and the writer Waldo Frank were just two of the legion of her mother's lovers who had hung around and pontificated to Laura on the spirituality of creativity. Laura's only escape from a bizarre childhood had been a full scholarship to Barnard College—which was a blessed 119 blocks uptown from her home. She took the IRT subway each day from the Christopher Street stop to 116th Street and Broadway, across from the large ironwork gates of Columbia University. It was light-years away from her chaotic home on Gay Street, just around the corner from another of her mother's friends, e.e. cummings, who was in revolt against the constraints of the rules of poetic punctuation.

Laura's mother was bereft that her daughter was consorting daily with such ill-read lowlifes, but took consolation in the thought that approval would have been forthcoming from another of her former lovers, the revolutionary journalist John Reed, who was now interred in the Kremlin Wall.

"I'd like you to let me do the talking for once," the city editor continued in exasperation. He frequently voiced his despair of ever being able to teach this highbrow kid anything. "I got something for you."

"So, what is it?"

"Here's the deal. Some stunt-flying women are in this cross-the-country air race—a first-time thing. Since you're such an expert now on flying dames, I've decided to send you out to the finish line. Your pal Jenny Flynn isn't on the roster, though. Her with enough pull not to lose her license. Curious thing. Anyway, I'm sending Riley to cover all the real races among the men, but you can cover the ladies."

"Out? Out where?" Laura was frowning.

But she'd already lost Barnes's attention, as he turned to pick up his ringing phone. The black cord dangling against his white shirt, he held the cup to his left ear and covered the mouthpiece with his right hand long enough to growl at Laura, "Don't just stand there. Get going. We need the sob-sister touch on this thing. There could be a bunch of 'em get killed. Damn sure if they can't fly any better than that Jones dame who buried herself in a fireball in Roosevelt Field."

Laura grimaced at the editor's callousness, but kept her

eye on the real ball. "Where am I going?" she asked again.

Barnes didn't bother to cover the mouthpiece this time. "Cleveland," he hissed, and Laura could hear someone on the other end saying, "What? Did they win the game today?"

"Cleveland—jeez, you mean out in Ohio?" Laura said to Barnes's back. "That's a long way. Takes days, doesn't it?" Laura had rarely been out of New York City, except, of course, the recent trip to Roosevelt Field on Long Island. And, she'd been in the country north of the city once and once to New Jersey.

As she walked in a daze back to her desk to pick up her hat and gloves, she thought, Maybe this business of chasing news isn't so bad after all. Going to the Midwest—maybe her own roots were there. She suspected that's where her mother came from. Laura had a picture of her mother that had been taken in St. Louis, although she could never get her to talk about any of that.

Ah, so what? She quickly came to her senses. She had nothing to go on. She didn't even know her mother's real name. Even her own was made up.

C HAPTER SEVEN
HOME SWEET HOME

INSTEAD OF TAKING THE SIXTH AVENUE EL as she normally would, Laura hopped in a cab at Park Row to head home and pack a bag.

As the taxi let her out, she glanced briefly up at the windows of her small room, perched like the afterthought that it was on the flat roof of the brick row house on Gay Street. She was put up there as a child so she would be out of the way of the adults, but it was a happenstance she had learned to cherish, being a short stairway's remove from the chaos of her mother's life and loves. She smiled as she looked up: that was her sanctuary, her spot, her place. She was even lucky in her fire escape. A number of houses on the block-long, crooked street between Waverly and Christopher in what was called the West Village were marred by clunky ironwork that ran down the front of the building. But hers was in back, and climbed to her window. On hot summer nights, she could fall asleep out there to the buzz of insects and the glow of fireflies stalking tall sunflowers and tomato plants in the garden that belonged to the tenants in the basement apartment. In the autumn, she would read in the waning light and, come winter, she had even been known to sit on her sill in muffler and cap practicing snowball pitches.

She took the steps to the stoop two at a time, unlocked the building door, then headed up the flight of carved wooden stairs to the apartment she and her mother shared on the second floor. Now that Laura had a job, she had thought of getting her own place, but decided her familiar garret room was just fine. And as much as her mother was a burden, she felt she needed to stick around to look after the child-woman who had never grown up, who was way too impractical to manage on her own.

"Why are you home so early? You haven't lost that dreadful job, have you?" Her mother's voice came from the tiny sitting room to the right of the stairs. On the left, at the front of the house, was her mother's bedroom. What passed for a kitchen (it had a tiny square wooden table and two chairs, a huge bucket for blocks of ice, and a single burner) was at the back, off the sitting room. Laura and her mother managed bathing and other tasks of personal hygiene with a bowl and pitcher in their respective bedrooms, with water heated on the burner. The little-better-than-a-ladder stairs to Laura's garret wound up through a space built in between the kitchen and the indoor toilet.

"Sorry to disappoint you, Evelyn, but I haven't lost my job yet," Laura said, moving to the doorway to address her mother, who was dressed, as usual, in a loose-fitting, airy garb that might have been Tibetan or Egyptian. One could never be sure, except that it would always be earth tones. The room was made even smaller by overflowing bookcases that lined the walls except for a break for a brick fireplace, containing a spit and a large black pot, where an occasional sumptuous meal was cooked. A colorful American Indian blanket with a child's handprints woven into it, for which Evelyn displayed an excessive attachment, served as a rug. No curtains hung at the two paned windows looking onto the street.

Laura, eager to move on, stayed in the doorway. "I won't be joining you in the ranks of the starving, writing for little *literary* journals. I have an *assignment* to go to Cleveland."

"What could possibly be of interest there? Everyone there is so repressed and boring."

"Repressed and boring might be good after the free-wheeling life you've led," Laura responded.

"Believe me, my dear, the Midwest is stultifying."

"That's interesting," Laura said, raising an eyebrow, a petulant tone creeping into her voice. "It's the first time you've ever admitted to me that you've even been there."

"One can know many things, my dear, without actually experiencing them." A sly smile flickered across her extraordinarily beautiful face. She was blue-eyed, and wore her long blond hair in a very non-revolutionary bun, pinned at the nape of her long neck. Most other countercultural women of the Village wore their hair bobbed, but Evelyn was quite frank about the fact that she liked the severity, to more prominently display the shape of her face.

"It would just be nice to know if the Midwest is where you came from," Laura replied. More to the point, she thought, who is my father and why do you revel in torturing me with unanswered questions?

"Your endless interest in questions of paternity are baffling, when what you should be doing is freeing your mind of constraints." It was her mother's mantra. Laura planned one day to have it immortalized in a cross-stitch sampler made as a wall hanging. "Conventions of the past are the enemy."

"You and your Freud and your free love." Laura's retort was fairly predictable too. "Mom, if you put your energy into writing about something sane, instead of beating that drum, you could be a very successful writer, like some of those friends of yours."

"*Mom*? Why do you insist on that? I don't call you *child*, why should you call me *Mom*? It's so impersonal."

"I've got to get packed." Laura started for her stairs. "I've got a train to catch."

"How long will you be gone?"

"I don't know, *Mom*. It depends on the story."

Evelyn's laugh was good-natured. "You can be so stubborn."

Laura turned with a grin. "Speaking of paternity, I wonder where I got *that*."

As she packed, Laura pondered the disparity in their looks, not to mention their outlooks. She tried to be serious and responsible, and did her best to conform to accepted standards of dress and behavior. She'd always watched her classmates, especially at college, to get clues as to how the rest of the world lived. Her mother, on the other hand, went out of her way to poke her finger in the world's eye. It was typically inconsistent, Laura thought, for Evelyn to disapprove of her tabloid job—the fellows in the newsroom didn't seem to fit anyone's idea of proper comportment. Laura yanked her new veiled hat off the closet shelf, and wondered if it was the right thing for an air show. She stopped herself. What a dumb thing to waste time thinking about. She had only one proper hat, and she couldn't very well wear a winter cap in the heat of the summer. As she took her comb and brush from the dressing table, she caught her glimpse in the mirror. She bent down to the low table and stared. "Whose little girl are you?" she asked the reflection. Dark hair and green eyes stared back, hardly a blue-eyed blonde. At five feet, four inches, she was considered average, no resemblance there either to the "statuesque" Evelyn, reed thin and nearly five-foot-nine. Without thinking about why she was doing it, Laura slipped off the gold chain she always wore. People had often asked if its tiny key was a charm or if it really opened something. She had learned early on to put them off by saying, "It's the key to my heart." It was no such thing, of course. A straightforward answer probably would have better satisfied her inquisitors: "It opens my childhood diary." But the heck with them. Whose business was it anyway but hers? She now pulled the scuffed leather-bound book from a bottom drawer and turned the key. The woman she called Aunt Edna had given her the diary for her twelfth birthday. The petite redhead was one of the few of her mother's friends with whom Laura got on well. Edna would play jacks and other children's games with her. They also seemed to have an affinity for each other because Laura was born in the same hospital from which her aunt had gotten her middle name.

Her mother always said that Edna St. Vincent Millay— whom her mother intimately called Vincent but would never allow Laura to—was her best friend in the whole world and was a devoted fan of her poetry. Had Evelyn and the poet been having a minor affair all these years? Laura doubted it, but with her mother one could never be sure. When Aunt Edna moved upstate to Steepletop, her country house, Laura had been allowed to go up only once; her mother left her behind for subsequent visits. No matter, for a short while, Laura's best and only friend had been Aunt Edna. By the time Edna married and moved away, she had long since put away her childish play with Laura, so Laura hadn't really expected to be allowed to go to Steepletop. Her mother would have dominated the poet's time there anyway. It wouldn't have been the same as having Edna all to herself on long stretches to write poems, do charades, invent guessing games, while her mother was off with some beau. Her mother, often jealous when she heard of their romps, would sniff, "Vincent is behaving like a child."

Laura had filled the little diary quickly, had even proudly shown her aunt some of her own poems. She hadn't read any of these entries for years, and had no particular curi-

osity about them now. She simply retrieved the faded, dog-
eared photo that Edna had secretly given her long ago and
dropped it into her purse. She snapped her handbag closed,
locked the diary, put the chain back around her neck, and
tucked the book back in its drawer.

Laura laughed to herself at the memory of her insistence
to her mother for years that she must surely be adopted. In
one of the few times that her mother had given in to Laura's
pleadings about her origins, Evelyn had finally produced a
birth certificate.

It said Laura was born February 6, 1906, in St. Vincent's, the hospital just up the street from their apartment. It
listed her as a female child weighing six pounds, eight ounces.
Mother: Evelyn T. Sampson, Father: Unknown. It told her
another thing: her mother was barely nineteen when Laura
was born. Pretty young to be stuck with a baby, she thought.
And New York is a tough town.

CHAPTER EIGHT
NOT QUITE THE 20TH CENTURY LIMITED

LAURA TROTTED DOWN THE LONG PLATFORM in her hobble skirt and high heels, one gloved hand up to her new hat, the other clutching her handbag. She was breathless trying to keep up with the redcap who was rolling ahead looking for her car, which seemed to be at the far end of the train.

He helped her up the two metal steps and showed her to her seat just as the conductor was yelling, "All aboard." The steam engine whistled and the cars jerked against their couplings as she dug into her pocket for the nickel she'd had the foresight to stick there. "Thanks, miss," the porter said with a wide grin, mopping his face with a huge checkered handkerchief. The car was stifling. The windows were open, but the overhead fans hung silent in the heat.

The porter put the valise marked with her mother's initials, *ETS*, on the brass overhead rack, and Laura settled in by the window, magazines and newspapers on the empty seat beside her.

The redcap had picked her up when her taxi pulled to the curb on the Vanderbilt side of Grand Central Terminal. He'd seemed amused by her lack of luggage. "Travelin' light, miss." It was a statement, not a question, as he put her vanity case, traveling hatbox, and the small satchel—all unearthed at the last minute by Evelyn—on his big rolling cart.

Laura, who had read stories of the red-carpet treatment and glamorous setting of the 20th Century Limited, had been disappointed and more than annoyed when the ticket clerk at one of the many windows in the cavernous marble hall informed her in a condescending tone that the super train was in quite a rush to get to Chicago. "Madame, one would hardly wish to debark in *Cleveland* at two o'clock in the morning."

"I might." Laura couldn't resist, and of course got little reaction other than a slight disapproving lift of the right eyebrow.

In some ways, though, Laura was just as happy not to be taking the special train. It really had been her mother's idea. Sure, it would have been grand to ride with the swells, but it would have been difficult to get her expense account past Barnes. And she certainly didn't want to have to admit to that big bozo that her mother had imperiously insisted on paying the all-Pullman train's eight-dollar surcharge because she was feeling flush from having sold an article to *Harper's Magazine*.

"Ticket, miss." The conductor was rolling like a sailor with the motion of the train as it picked up speed, moving north following the path of the Harlem River, before it turned left heading for the Hudson. The activity stirred up a fine breeze from the fans and the open windows, bringing relief from the August heat.

Laura peered out in wonder at the sheer cliffs of the New Jersey Palisades, and speculated how anything this near her birthplace could seem so strange and exotic. She knew the answer, of course. She had barely left the confines of Greenwich Village until she went north to Barnard College. And the encompassing atmosphere of her childhood around Gay Street was indeed a world unto itself. A world of art and poetry and philosophy and free love. A bohemian enclave that she realized at quite a young age was not the best environment for a child. She'd learned early on to mother herself and, as often as allowed, to do the same for Evelyn, the woman who didn't much like to be called Mom—the woman who was never too happy to acknowledge that she had a growing child. The woman who, in Laura's eyes, had never grown up. Laura had always thought how nice it would be to have a normal family life, and proper friends.

She felt hypnotized by the unfamiliar scene whizzing past. The Hudson River flowed far below, as the train cut through a lush forest filtering fleeting speckles of sunlight on its way toward Albany before it would turn west.

A white-coated waiter came through with a dinner gong announcing that the evening meal was now being served two cars forward. Amazing, these trains, Laura thought, a hot meal. But what is the proper etiquette? Should she put her hat and gloves back on to go to the dining car? Nothing in the purposely nonconformist life of the Village had prepared her for this. She waited until she saw other ladies heading in the direction of the dining car. One had her hat on, two others had none. The heck with the hat, she picked up her handbag and took the plunge.

After swaying her way through two coach cars and the couplings between, Laura entered a narrow passageway that fed into an actual restaurant. Her eyes popped with wonder. All along the windows, on each side of a slightly off-center aisle, there were tables. Waiters in white jackets glided smoothly among the tables taking orders. A maître d' wearing a black tie advanced toward Laura with a tight, practiced smile.

"One, miss?" he inquired. At her nod, he led her to a table for two, set with white linen. A small vase held a single tea rose. The hypnotizing trees were still whizzing by the window, although by now it was nearly dark and the

pines took on a menacing scarecrow aspect. After taking the
menu and seeing the prices, Laura gasped. The meal sounded
substantial, but it should be: it cost $1.50! Visions of Barnes
yelling when he saw the bill swam in her head. But the heck
with it, a girl had to eat. And this train ride was his idea.

She was just digging into her mashed potatoes and gravy
when a swell-looking guy with an unruly shock of red hair,
which even Brylcreem couldn't hold, appeared at the entry
of the car. He was tall and needed to bend down to share
a confidence with the maître d'. She had a funny feeling
they were talking about her, and she saw what looked like a
dollar bill change hands. Sure enough, they headed straight
for her.

"Miss," said the waiter, "would you mind if I seat this
gentleman at your table? It's customary for those traveling
alone."

I don't buy that for a minute, Laura thought, but she
gave a shrug of indifference. Let's see what this lug is up to.
Could be interesting. With my luck, he's probably selling
Good Housekeeping subscriptions.

As though on cue, he launched right in: "We're seated in
the same car, and I couldn't help but notice that you had a
number of New York newspapers."

"Good grief," she blurted out, "selling daily rags on a
train." Rude of me, she thought, but there is a limit, even
if he is kind of cute. Not bad, no face full of freckles that
usually goes with all that red hair. A little on the thin side,
but a strong square jaw. Maybe he's not so skinny after all,
just that his suit jacket hangs a little loose. Probably had to
get a size too big 'cause he's so tall.

The young man chuckled. "I suppose in a way you could
say that. I do work for a newspaper. I'm a reporter."

It was Laura's turn to laugh. "Yeah, sure, tell me another
one. That's a good pickup line if I ever heard one." Laura

was not very practiced with men, but she was excellent at fending them off, especially some of her mother's friends.

"Why is that so funny?" He seemed at a loss.

The waiter brought a menu to the young man, then took away Laura's plate and handed her a card with dessert suggestions. "Lovely hot apple pie today," he said.

"You must have guessed that I'm a reporter," Laura finally replied to the young man. "Work for the *Enterprise-Post*."

His blue eyes went wide. "I work for the *Trib* in Chicago, and we only have one woman. She's old as the hills and has nicotine stains on her fingers."

"I've heard it said," Laura gave him a broad grin, that New York is way ahead of Chicago. I'm on my way to Cleveland to cover the air races—the very first for women."

"You're kidding. The one they're calling the Powder Puff Derby? Wow."

Laura nodded, flipping open the dessert menu. "That pie sounds pretty good, doesn't it?"

He stretched his hand across the table. "Glad to meet you, I'm Joe Bailey."

Laura blanched. "This isn't funny anymore," she said, putting down the menu. "My name's Bailey too. Laura Bailey."

"You said you're from New York." Joe's smile melted to a slight blush. "I hope we're not related. My family all comes from Chicago. Where are your people from?"

"This is getting pretty silly." Laura signaled to the waiter for her check. "I really must go."

"I don't understand," Joe Bailey said plaintively as the waiter brought Laura's check and she hastily paid.

"Nice to meet you," she mumbled, and departed.

The startled young man followed her with his eyes as she left the car.

Laura's heart was pounding. Where are your people

from? she repeated to herself. That sounded like a challenge. Sure, Bailey was a common name, but the encounter somehow unnerved her.

As she wound through the train, past the restroom, past the rows of seats, and swayed between the cars as the couplings clanked, she thought of how she'd gone on her own that first day of school at P.S. 41. Her mother'd been off somewhere with who knew what man. Laura had heard about school opening for the semester, so she went and signed herself up. She'd washed and ironed her best blue gingham dress the night before.

The teacher looked a bit surprised to see this scrawny, big-eyed eight-year-old walk into her classroom saying she wanted to enlist herself in the first grade. A knowing woman with her hair in a severe knot and a gentle smile—her name was Mrs. Kominsky—she let Laura stay and only bothered with the particulars after class. When Laura was taken to the principal for the grand enrollment process, she told them her name was Bailey, that her parents were jugglers off with a touring show, and that she was home on her own. She learned a good many years later that the two women hadn't much believed her, but a child of eight who had yet to go to school spoke for itself, and they had obviously run into some strange tales from kids in those free-thinking days in the Village.

"Perhaps we'd better consider some testing by the district," Mrs. Kominsky had said in a low breathless voice to Miss Blear, the principal. "Laura here may need to move up a grade or two. She reads, and she writes without block letters. And," said her teacher, her breathlessness now so pronounced that Laura had to strain to hear her, "she also seems to have a passing acquaintance with Marcel Proust and Friedrich Nietzsche."

"My word," replied Miss Blear.

Laura peered through the train window into the dark. Instead of the river now, she could see only her own face reflected back by the overhead lights of the car. Taking herself off to school was one of the happiest things she'd ever done. School was nice. She liked the orderliness of it, the methodical way one subject came after another. And the time on the playground was frivolous and free. She did make friends there, but never saw them after school, never asked them to visit her home, although she *had* played hopscotch and jacks sometimes with one girl who lived on her street. She hadn't understood at the time that it was the structure that appealed to her, a time to study and a time to play. Her studies progressed in an orderly way, not the scattershot reading she'd done before she went to school. That was what was nice about a job. Just like school, you had to be there at a certain time each day, no matter what. And she was trying to learn fast just what was expected of her.

She opened her purse and took out the sepia-toned photo she'd dropped in there when she was packing. The image was difficult to make out, it was so faded and scratched. The old-fashioned clothes were from a different era. The pretty young blonde wore a large-brimmed lacy hat—perhaps straw or some kind of stiff organza. Short ringlets were tucked around her ears. Her demure chemise appeared to be silk and she wore a long single strand of pearls. Her smile was sweet and shy; she couldn't have been more than sixteen, the embodiment of flowering innocence.

Aunt Edna had given her the picture, but refused to answer any of Laura's questions. "Ask your mother," was all she would say.

"But how can I ask, if you won't let me tell her you gave it to me?"

"Tell her what you want about how you found it, just leave me out of it," Edna had replied.

Laura rarely saw Edna after that. The picture was her consolation prize. The poet was becoming better known and more people were making demands upon her time. Especially after the publication of the poem that gave her notoriety as something of a loose woman, and that she referred to as "Candle."

Laura mouthed it to herself softly as she looked out the window of the speeding train. *It will not last the night; but ah, my foes, and oh, my friends—it gives a lovely light.* Edna left for Paris shortly before Laura's fifteenth birthday.

She looked at the picture now with new eyes, at the tiny imprint on the lower left-hand corner: *Brown Hall Studios, St. Louis.*

St. Louis! Another world to Laura, and probably one her mother was from. Perhaps she could try to go there for a day, after she finished her work in Cleveland. But that was stupidly unrealistic! Barnes would never stand for it. Yet how would he know? He'd know; he'd want her in the office as soon as she could get back after filing her last story. The young woman in the picture had such a reticent air, such a lack of guile, that Laura had always found it hard to believe that it really was Evelyn. But there was no question since the older man standing next to her looked like Laura— coarse dark hair, the same broad cheekbones. He must be Evelyn's father, Laura's grandfather. The faded inscription on the back said, *Father Bernard.*

Sitting on the train, Laura mused about why in all these years she had rarely looked at the photo and never asked Evelyn about it. She'd told herself when she was a child that it was pointless, that Evelyn would either lie or refuse to answer, as she always did when asked about her past. With time now to ponder as an adult, staring at her own image reflected back at her as the miles clicked by, Laura felt comforted knowing who her grandfather was, knowing she looked like him. It gave her a tiny bit of her own history, and she didn't want Evelyn to try to take that away.

She had learned to take on a guarded, defensive posture at a young age, to tamp down worrying about questions that seemingly had no answers, and to just barrel along taking care of herself. She had no time for dwelling on the mysteries of life.

She didn't know what had prompted her to pick the name Bailey; when informed, her mother just laughed. "You changed *yours*," Laura had said defiantly.

"So I did," her mother replied with a firm and righteous nod. "I see no reason why you shouldn't do the same, if you want to. I believe in absolute freedom for everyone. *Nichts verdrängen,* repress nothing." And that was that. Henceforth, she was Laura Bailey. She'd never liked her mother's name, Evelyn T. Sampson, and could never worm out of her what her real name had been. Laura had always wondered if there was an actual Sampson, who might have been her father, but she didn't think so. The only sketchy details she knew of her mother's earlier life she'd gotten from children of her mother's friends who would eavesdrop when the so-called grown-ups were drunk or partying. The scuttlebutt on the kids' circuit was that Evelyn had run off to Germany with a much older married man when she was quite young and they both changed their names to avoid detection by the wronged wife. Where Evelyn had run off from was a matter of some difference of opinion. Some said St. Louis, others said Louisiana. From snide references that Evelyn had made from time to time, Laura felt that it was the *stultifying Midwest*, whatever that encompassed.

Now she was speeding through the dark on her way there. This seemed like fun, not a job. What else was she going to find out about this story-chasing business, which she'd always thought was so crass? Maybe she'd start learning some things about herself that she hadn't had time to think about before, always cramming and running to keep her scholarships. Who knows, she might even stumble on her father.

"I'm sorry you had to leave so abruptly." It was the young man again, swaying with the train, holding onto the seat back of the row in front of Laura. He smiled; Laura frowned. "I would like to sit down, find out more about you," he said. "I'm going all the way to Chicago, so we'd have plenty of time to talk."

The conductor walked through calling, "Albany, next stop!"

"I'm sorry," Laura said hesitantly, searching for a polite tone.

"Honest," he said, "I mean it. I mean, you're pretty and I like you." His face took on the color of his hair, though he rushed on in the gale of her continuing frown and the commotion of other passengers pulling down their bags and crowding into the aisles. "You're gutsy. I never met a young woman in my business before. It's a tough job." Now he was nearly out of breath in his headlong rush, but he plowed on as the train pulled into the Albany station. "It *is* tough, the job. You know what I mean. Dealing with cops and bureaucrats and rushing to fires."

"I know," she said crossly. Then stopped herself. He was sweet, a nice kid, she thought. Her mother kept asking why she had no boyfriends. "Seems unnatural to me, a pretty young girl with no beaus. All this studying is to be commended, but you haven't developed your personality enough."

"I'm sorry," Laura said, patting the papers on the empty seat beside her. "I've got to read, bone up on this race. I only got the assignment this afternoon."

And Joe Bailey was pushed toward the vestibule by those

rushing to exit the train. As the old wave left, a new wave entered, and a fat woman with large bags headed for the empty seat beside Laura.

CHAPTER NINE
CLEVELAND

LAURA, BLEARY-EYED FROM ONLY CATNAPS, dumped her bags at her Cleveland hotel Friday morning and headed for the pressroom at the National Air Show. She was anxious to find out what had happened to the flying ladies while she'd been stuck on a train for twelve hours. It was urgent that she hustle before the race ended Monday, when everyone would have the same information—who won. She also wanted to find Cheesy, who had been sent there earlier.

She found John Riley, the *Enterprise-Post* reporter who'd arrived the day before to cover the show and races that would terminate here at the city's municipal airport. He told her that the fliers remaining in the women's race had traveled across Texas on Thursday, making five stops including Fort Worth, where they'd been greeted by twenty thousand spectators before bedding down for the night. They would be in Tulsa and Wichita, Kansas, today. At every stop along the way, thousands were turning out to greet them. Louise Thaden, an ace with lots of endurance records, seemed the likely winner. Ruth Nichols, a Wellesley graduate and debutante, was among the frontrunners, as was Amelia Earhart.

"So are the women all okay?" Laura asked.

Riley's accounting was perfunctory. Of the nineteen women who had left Santa Monica the previous Sunday, one had crashed and been killed, another diagnosed the night before with typhoid fever. A twentieth pilot had started a day late because of engine problems, but was still counted in since their total time in each leg would be clocked. Several had been scratched because of seemingly unending mishaps or plane malfunctions. Just yesterday, a goofy colorful dame named Pancho Barnes, who smoked cigars, had landed on top of the car a spectator had pulled onto the runway for a better view, and Blanche Noyes had managed to make it down on one wheel after an earlier emergency landing caused by a fire. Another woman had run out of fuel as she was touching down, and had to push her own plane off the runway to avoid the incoming derbyites. Laura was intrigued by these stories, though Riley had no more information, other than to say that the wires had covered them.

"So what's your angle here, kid?" he asked. "Gonna do the sob number about all the dire misfortunes along the way?"

"This is a very exciting time, John," Laura said primly. "I guess the desk decided you aren't capable of taking what these pioneering women are doing quite seriously enough."

John Riley grinned. "Okay, kid, whatever you say. Gotta hand it to these dames, though. Quite a few of 'em have made it as far as Fort Worth. Will Rogers and Wiley Post are here. They seem serious enough about the lady pilots. I spoke to Rogers yesterday, told him the *Enterprise-Post* carries his column."

"Gee, you really met him?"

"Sure, a heck of a nice guy. And funny. He's the one calling this women's race the Powder Puff Derby."

"Oh yeah, Riley," Laura said, rolling her eyes. "So what else do you have as a scoop?" She walked off. She needed to file a story today—had to find something or someone to write about, a fan, a student pilot, something.

She wandered around the grandstands of the airfield, where

tens of thousands were watching stunts and formation-flying exhibitions. She bought a hot dog from a vendor. It feels like a ballpark, she thought. At a stop in the ladies' room, powdering her nose, she noticed a wisp of a thing wearing expensive-looking riding breeches and jodhpur boots running a comb through her short, curly, light-brown hair.

"You enjoying the races?" Laura asked.

The young woman turned to her with a smile. "Oh, they're swell, don't you think?"

"You look like you've just come from a riding stable."

"Oh, no," the woman said. "I've just flown up from Oklahoma City for a couple of days to see the end of the women's race. You can't fly in a skirt."

"Oh," Laura said with a startled look, realizing this was the spoiled little debutante she'd run into at Roosevelt Field. She fumbled for something to say; she hadn't exactly gotten a warm reception the last time. And she'd done those stories speculating on whether the errant pilot would lose her license, and then why she hadn't. Seemed some guy working for Curtiss-Wright at Roosevelt Field had pull in Washington. There was a lot of politics in this flying stuff—the government trying to push it as a national defense measure, whatever that meant. Wow, talk about stumbling onto something. "Uh, most of the women seem to have designed their own flying costumes."

"That's true. But since riding clothes are the one kind of pants you can just go and buy in a store, I decided that was a lot less trouble. My name's Jenny Flynn," she said, sticking out her hand. "What's yours? And where are you from?"

"I'm Laura. Why aren't you in the race?" She wanted to ask why the woman wasn't in knickers like the last time and what kind of pull she had with the Department of Commerce. Take it slow, one question at a time, she told herself.

"I just fly for the fun. They're all too serious, too dedicated for me," Jenny replied, then tinkled a happy, uncomplicated laugh.

Laura pulled her comb from her purse and swiped it lightly over her hair as she pondered how to start questioning this frivolous girl. What a contrasting pair they were, she thought, looking at their side-by-side reflections in the mirror. Jenny's almost-blond curls were tousled, actually unkempt to Laura's eye. It didn't cross her mind that her own tight, coal-black marcelled waves might look stiff to some.

Laura in a black print, crêpe de chine dress that was chic, but would have passed unnoticed in New York, was a standout here in the powder room in Cleveland as ladies came and went wearing their Sunday best—most with lace collars and lots of ruffles.

Jenny stuck out too, in her white short-sleeved shirt, open at the collar. And those riding breeches all bunched up at the knees and full at the hips held up by what looked almost like a cowboy belt to Laura; it was wide, of brown woven leather. Her ankle-top boots with a brass buckle on the side were polished, but scuffed. This didn't appear to Laura to be any kind of fashion statement like Marlene Dietrich in her man's suit. Topping it all off, Jenny had a very unladylike sunburn. Those white possum patches around her eyes were certainly the badges of aviator goggles.

"For fun?" Laura said, turning to Jenny, hoping she might elaborate. She didn't want to make this young woman bolt like she had from Roosevelt Field.

Jenny just smiled and stuck her comb back in her pants pocket.

Looking again into the mirror, Laura saw no common ground between her and the flying debutante. They couldn't be more different. And Jenny was just a kid. Laura knew from the bridge stories that she was only eighteen. Laura, of course, considered herself much more mature than her mere twenty-two years. After all, she had a responsible job, and had been fending for herself as long as she could remember. But she must figure out some way to bridge the gap.

"Let's go have a cup of coffee or root beer," Laura said, deciding on an indirect approach before taking one last go at her marcelled wave, then sticking her comb back into her patent-leather handbag. "I'm terribly interested in flying, and you seem just the person to explain how it all works."

"I'm sorry," Jenny replied, not sounding very sorry at all, and moving toward the door. "I have to run an errand for a friend." Several women crowded in, talking excitedly about an aerobatics display.

"Did you see that loop?"

"Could you believe how the plane twisted and twisted?"

"I thought he was going to crash."

Their entrance moved Jenny back in Laura's direction.

"Don't go yet," Laura said in a rush, "I have just a couple of quick questions. Like, I heard someone besides Amelia Earhart is the frontrunner here. How can that happen? She's the most famous. And this Crosson woman, the one who got *killed*. Did you know her? What was she like?"

"My goodness, that's a heap of questions. I wouldn't know anything about any of that."

"But you must know something," Laura said. "Is there a problem with Earhart's plane?"

"That big Lockheed Vega? Oh my, no," Jenny replied. "That's the fastest plane in the race. If Amelia's got a problem, it's controlling that monster." She tilted her head sideways and lifted her eyebrows ever so slightly. And again came her tinkling laugh. "Not the kind of maneuverability for three-point landings in front of judges. At least that big monoplane has brakes, a real luxury in this business.

"Ta ta." She gave Laura a wave with her fingers, and was lost in the crowd.

CHAPTER TEN
GET IT NOW!

LAURA ENDED UP GIVING RILEY A HAND with the day's coverage because there were so many things going on. She kept a sharp eye out for Jenny Flynn in the crowds, but with no luck. There were parachute jumps, pylon races, and a demonstration by a precision aerobatic team led by Lindbergh. A downtown exhibition hall was chock to the rafters with the latest in flight gear and equipment. Finally, Laura and Riley tossed—and he lost—for who would do a story about the plane on display in front of the city hall. It was Boeing's Model 80A that was being readied for commercial service. It could carry eighteen passengers in what the company described as *a spacious cabin appointed with leather upholstery, reading lamps, forced-air ventilation, and hot and cold running water.* The plane had a range of 460 miles and could fly at a top speed of 138 miles per hour. The final innovation: Boeing was hiring women, registered nurses, to serve as attendants on flights.

"Wow!" Laura exclaimed reading the press release from which Riley was working, seated at the Underwood across from her. "What will they think of next?" With Riley banging away, Laura did a quick story on Pancho Barnes, the derbyite who had landed on the car.

Then they heard talk of what their colleagues in the pressroom had dubbed the "Mystery Ship." It was rumored the plane had been built especially for the men's speed races that would end with the awarding of the Thompson Trophy. Military fliers had always won most speed races before, but there was great anticipation that Travel Air had built a craft that would beat them all.

"This has been a heck of a day," Laura moaned, rubbing her right elbow and shaking out her fingers, stiff from typing. "But while we wait to get the news on how the lady fliers did today, we better try to get a handle on what's so mysterious."

It turned out they couldn't find out any more than the other reporters, but they sent Cheesy to get a picture of where it was stored. Walter Beech, the president of Travel Air, had the plane spirited away to a special hangar he'd rented for the various craft his company had built for the races. Putting the plane under wraps was, of course, building excitement.

Laura dictated their four air-show stories to a rewrite man in New York. She and Riley decided not to bother with a story on the women's derby because reporters in Tulsa and Wichita were getting the details of what the ladies' day had been like. The wires were reporting that several made unexpected stops for such things as a dirty oil line, an overheated engine, and one who was lost because her map blew overboard. But there were also firsts. Leaving Tulsa, the racers were given wind charts drawn from balloon observations in anticipation of heavy rains they would encounter. The ladies reported being happy with a break from the unrelieved heat—those in open cockpits said they were not only drenched, but also kept busy using their silk scarves as windshield wipers. As they approached Wichita, the local newspaper sent a plane to greet the ladies, and an Army observer pilot used a short-wave radio as he accompanied them in. His transmitted description of the event was am-

plified and broadcast on the ground. It was also picked up
by telephone wires and sent to a local radio station. Cars
were bumper to bumper surrounding the field awaiting the
ladies' arrival. The crowds were estimated at twenty thousand, nearly one-fifth of the town's population.

Laura went back to her hotel and fell into bed exhausted. She thought she'd fallen asleep when she heard
church bells that sounded just like those near her old school,
P.S. 41 on West 11th Street. She hadn't noticed a church near
her hotel here in downtown Cleveland. She got up to look
out the window, but there was a chain-link fence blocking
her view. As she tried to peer through the chinks, she saw
Jenny Flynn skipping rope on the playground, laughing and
joking around with the children from Laura's class. Laura
put her hand through the fence and waved. "I'm here!" she
yelled, but no one paid any attention. Then Barnes came to
her rescue, swooping down from the air in a yellow checkered taxi. Laura climbed behind the steering wheel and they
had soared over the schoolyard before she remembered that
she didn't know how to drive. The taxi began to vibrate and
wobble so badly that she could hear her own teeth chattering. A wheel ripped off and clattered to earth with a loud
bang, the cab began listing to the left, Laura could see pedes-
trian ants walking the streets. She was losing altitude fast,
flying straight into the tower of the Jefferson Market Courthouse, the beautiful redbrick Victorian Gothic that sat in
the triangle between Greenwich and Sixth avenues. Its clock
hands were racing out of control, gyrating wildly, coming
straight at her—she was going to be impaled! Everyone was
screaming out the windows of the Women's Detention Center next door. The inmates had always shouted obscenities
from there. Laura would hear them when she got off the
el coming home from work, but now both her mother and
Barnes were adding to the chaos. "Get control and land this

crate!" the city editor yelled over and over. Her mother was
screaming for her to jump, but she could see no safety net
below. She heard the distant siren of the rescue ambulance
from St. Vincent's Hospital coming nearer, maybe it could
save her. She sat up abruptly in bed, and realized that her
bedside telephone was ringing.

As she fumbled for the receiver and put it to her ear, she
heard Barnes bark: "Aren't you watching the wires? Your
gal pal Jenny Flynn has stolen an airplane."

"Stolen?"

"Do I hear an echo? Stolen. Flew it straight out of a
barn where it was impounded. Stole it right out from under
a deputy's nose."

"I just talked to her yesterday." Laura was befuddled,
her mind still groggy with sleep. Whoa, she thought, Jenny
Flynn's voice ringing in her ear. *I have to run an errand for
a friend* seemed to take on a new significance. But Laura
certainly wasn't going to mention this to Barnes. It probably
didn't mean anything—Jenny could have been picking up
someone's laundry.

"There's a dead person somehow involved in all this!"
Barnes yelled. "Get over there!"

"Where?" Laura demanded, her annoyance rising.

"Let's see," Barnes said. Laura recognized the familiar
rustling of the long sheets of paper that rolled off the wires.
"AP says Kansas. Atchison, Kansas."

Laura sat up in bed and looked at her watch lying on
the bedside table. It was seven thirty in the morning. Things
would be humming in the city room. "That's not anywhere
near here, is it?"

"Must be."

"Must be what?" Laura snapped. "There's a Wichita on
the race route that's two days away. And a place called Kansas City that's not even in Kansas."

"Just get there. I don't have time for no geography lesson."

"I have stories lined up here. We'll know who the women's winner is Monday."

"So? The boys'll cover that. This is local—this kid's got a Long Island connection. Go."

"Listen, Barnes." Laura knew she shouldn't be so curt with her boss, but she'd had little sleep staying up late to file her stories. "You don't know how big this country is. I'm already out here where God threw His left shoe. How am I supposed to get to Kansas—call in Dorothy and Toto?"

"You've got an expense account, figure it out. Cripes," he exploded, "I never thought I'd hear myself saying that! I'm telling you, kid, that lip is gonna sink you one of these days." He slammed down the phone.

"Get there? Easy for you to say," Laura muttered to the silent phone in her hand.

As she rubbed the sleep from her eyes, she began to grin. After all, she thought, I *am* at an air show!

CHAPTER ELEVEN
THE WILD BLUE YONDER

LAURA GASPED AS SHE STRETCHED UP to look over the side of the plane. Turned earth, neat rows of plowed fields, puffy clouds that were lower than she was, tall waving green flags. I bet that's corn, she thought. She'd seen pictures of farms in *Collier's* magazine, but it all looked so organized, symmetrical from up here. How do they work out their coordinates? It appeared to this city girl that they all must have taken college geometry courses. Somehow that seemed unlikely.

Jenny Flynn had certainly been right about not being able to fly in a skirt. When Laura had gone out to the tiny Euclid Avenue airstrip on Cleveland's east side after making arrangements with some string-bean fellow she'd found hanging around the air show, he snickered when she'd asked, "How does one get in?"

"Not in them duds, lady," he'd said.

"I've paid you good money to take me," she replied stiffly.

"Lady, you got to hoist yourself up on the wing, then sling your'n leg over the cockpit there. I kin take your valise and stow it up forward with me, but I cain't do nuthin' 'bout *you*. And you're gonna have to manage that hatbox yourself." He gestured with distaste toward the offending object.

"Oh my," Laura said, following the arc of his arm toward the two gaping holes in the middle of the airplane. They had no lids. "There's no ladder or anything?"

"We might be able to locate some kind a ladder, but them heels on your'n shoes 'ud tear holes in the wings. That there linen fabric is fragile."

A rather long silence ensued, as the wind wrapped Laura's tight skirt even more tightly around her. She'd given up on her tiny veiled hat the moment she'd stepped from the taxi that had deposited her at the edge of this grassy expanse that contained only a large metal shed that she took to be the place where planes were garaged. Some sort of huge white sock blew from a pole atop the building.

The pilot cleared his throat. "Uh, ma'am, maybe there's a grease monkey in the hangar that might have a extra set a duds."

"Monkey?" Laura screeched, feeling very close to tears. Barnes would fire her if she lost this story, not to mention the twenty-five dollars she'd already paid the pilot.

She looked down at the world now whizzing beneath. *Barnes.* His name elicited a small shudder, thank goodness he'd never see her in these so-called monkey's clothes. She did love the goggles and cloth helmet; they made her feel quite dashing. She had a sudden image of herself flying the mail, the sleet pelting her face as she leaned into the wind. Heavens, though, there's not even a driver's wheel, she noticed, looking around at the uncomfortable and unadorned metal hole in which she sat. I wonder how they steer. She certainly didn't drive a car, but she'd ridden enough taxis to know that one had to somehow make the thing go in the right direction. She had a lot to learn, she decided, if she was going to be writing stories about girl fliers.

Her heart thumped. The world suddenly felt cockeyed. She looked to the right, and she was perpendicular to the neat rows of plowed fields that had been in a different place moments before. The pilot was waving from the front cockpit. Good heavens, we're dying. She could distinctly make out the back door of the caboose of a train that was chugging along, not quite keeping up with her. I'm going to land on the coal car or the engine, she thought, as she fell faster than the speeding train. Whoops, she was abruptly righted again, and the breakfast she hadn't had time to eat felt like it would make an appearance anyway. The pilot now turned full around in his seat, a wide grin on his face. "What in the world . . . ?" Laura yelled into the wind, which sent the words back to whistle in her own ears.

The little plane then rocked from right to left, as Laura watched in amazement while first one wing tipped toward the earth, then the other. He did that on purpose! How could anyone be so irresponsible! I will report him to the authorities. But just who in the world might that be?

Her head was swimming; she shook it to rid the dizziness. The lapel of the leather jacket she'd *borrowed* from the nice little kid the pilot had called a monkey was softly flapping against her cheek; she adjusted her goggles and a slow, serence smile spread across her face. She was floating through clouds, soaring above the world like a bird.

What a story. She could hardly wait to find a typewriter!

CHAPTER TWELVE
ATCHISON

LAURA'S DAYDREAMING FLOAT WAS suddenly shattered. She lurched forward and bumped her forehead against the metal of her encasing tube. It felt like a taxicab that had just made a sudden stop in a Manhattan traffic jam. Jenny Flynn had implied yesterday that most airplanes don't have brakes. Laura hadn't had time to ask how one slowed down or stopped. She vowed to learn more as soon as they got on the ground, *if* they made it in one piece. She looked over the side and could see another tiny airstrip with one of those big garages with a flying sock. The field was swarming with people. As they lost altitude and the pilot circled, Laura could make out barriers and tape strung around, the kind of stuff that police used to cordon off a crime scene. Where can the pilot land, she fretted, without crushing a bunch of people? He flew so low over their heads that Laura could read the markings on several cars: *Atchison Police* and *Atchison County Sheriff.*

Suddenly they swooped up and circled, then buzzed again over the crowd. This is what I would call a topsy-turvy ride, she thought. But it was exhilarating. Downright exciting. What fun! No wonder these crazy people do all these crazy things. As they soared up and left the tiny specks of humanity below on the ground, she felt the wonder of it all—above the world, riding the wings of an eagle.

They came around again, and it looked as though someone on the ground was beginning to push the crowds away
to make a small hole on what appeared to be a patch of
parched grass.

I guess I should be afraid, Laura thought, but she had
seen so many aerobatic stunts yesterday in Cleveland that
she figured these fliers could do whatever they wanted.

The pilot suddenly turned the plane sideways, and made
a steep descent, heading right for the open spot of grass.
Laura was so close to the ground she could make out the
round gold-framed spectacles on a fat woman in a faded
blue sunbonnet. The woman disappeared in a blur as
Laura was abruptly flipped back when the plane righted and
touched down with a soft bump. The crowd on the ground
let out a roar of approval, swarming around the plane as
police and deputy sheriffs unsuccessfully tried to hold them
back. Laura hoisted herself up from her metal seat with its
inadequate cushion to bask in the adulation of the cheering
throng. Good golly, she thought, as she waved and smiled
for the excited crowd, these goggles and helmet can work
wonders for a girl's self-esteem.

She hooked her right leg over the side of the hole of a
seat, and immediately realized that the awkwardness of trying to release herself from the confining and uncomfortable
metal box would detract from the glamour image she had a
moment before enjoyed. A barrel-chested young man with
a crop of yellow hair that looked like it had recently been
barbered with a bowl for a guide jumped up on the wing
and gallantly lifted her straight up out of her seat, and then
gently lowered her into the crush of admirers.

The police were not far behind.

As a blue-suited cop took a belligerent stance in front of
her, Laura decided to keep the helmet on and just lift a side
flap so she could hear. Clearly the helmet was some kind of

badge of honor in these parts, and besides, she could envision with horror how its weight had crushed her marcel.

"So, what are you doing here?" the cop yelled over the noise of the crowd. "This airfield is closed off." The words were gruff, but the officer had a peculiar, bemused look on his face.

"I'm a reporter from New York," Laura replied in as haughty a manner as she could muster, considering the flaming blush rising in her cheeks. She realized that not only was she standing there in men's clothing, but she was barefoot. She'd forgotten to retrieve the high-heeled shoes she'd removed when she boarded the plane.

"Now aren't we lucky," said the cop, the bemusement clearly fighting to overrule his sarcastic tone.

A fellow wearing a Sam Browne belt and a deputy sheriff's patch pushed his way through the crowd circling around Laura. "We don't need any more press, lady. You need to move along, go back wherever you came from. I've already told that to the fellow who piloted you in."

"Do you know Amelia Earhart?" asked a dark-eyed girl of about five, perched on her father's shoulders.

"Yeah, Amelia's from here. This here's her town," said a gray-haired woman in a cotton print dress with great pride in her voice.

Laura felt a tug at her sleeve. It was the pilot.

"I'm gassin' up and gittin' outta here," he said.

"But we can't go back yet. I've got to find out what's going on and call my office."

"I don't want no trouble with the cops," the pilot said, starting to move off.

The deputy nodded. "You better take his lead, lady."

"But I paid you for a round-trip," Laura called to the pilot's retreating back.

He turned. "No one stoppin' you from goin'. But I ain't waitin' around fer ya."

"Please," Laura said to the city cop, who seemed a little less stern than the deputy, "I have to know what happened before I can leave."

"It's a crime scene," he replied curtly, under the glare of the sheriff.

"Yes," Laura said, trying to hide her exasperation at the statement of the obvious. "What was the crime? That's all I want to know."

"A woman died yesterday. Then another woman showed up today and stole the plane the dead one had jumped from. Go talk to your fellow hacks. They're all over the place."

"Can't you help me with anything more?" Laura pleaded to the cop's answering shrug. She turned to the woman in the sunbonnet. "Can *you* help?"

"Of course," the woman said. "I don't know what you think you're hiding, Tom," she addressed the officer. "It's all over *The Daily Globe*. That's our paper," she said in an aside to Laura. Others in the crowd were all volunteering details at once.

"She flew right outta that barn yonder."

"The chute didn't open."

"Fell right there," another called out, "saw with my own eyes."

It was all a garble of voices and information.

"Will the pilot have to go far to buy gasoline?" Laura asked of no one in particular. "Is there a filling station nearby? I need time to get this straight, and find Western Union."

"Lady, you're not going to have time to get to town for Western Union," said the sheriff's deputy. "They have fuel pumps right there in the hangar. Now go on and leave with your pilot."

"The woman you're talking about, what was her name?" Laura asked the assemblage.

"We know the one from here," the lady in the cotton

print spoke up. "She's Sally Culpepper. Family has a farm just west a town. Hit the ground with a crack right over there." She pointed to the circle of police cars. "Terrible thing," she added, momentarily adopting a face of pious remorse, then her jaw hardened. "But she should have thought of her child before she did such a fool stunt."

"Child?"

"No one knows about t'other one who stole the plane," yelled someone Laura couldn't see at the edges of the crowd.

"Yes," piped in the dark-haired young father with the child on his shoulders. "She just landed in one plane, a guy on the ground jumped into hers, and she took off with the plane the district attorney had impounded."

"Oh my gosh," Laura said. "You mean someone really did steal a plane?"

"You betcha." The yellow-haired fellow who had helped Laura from the plane surveyed her with an approving grin. "Can I give you a ride to town, ma'am? My Model T is right over there. I could take you to Western Union."

Laura had never been much of what one would call a flirt. She had learned early on to duck and bob to avoid tight spots; first with her mother's many boyfriends and later in the city room where she was the only woman in a sea of men. She'd had a friend whom she met at a Barnard/Columbia mixer who encouraged her to write, but she hadn't seen him since he graduated and went off for an advanced degree at Stanford. There always seemed to be plenty of fellows around to open doors or hold coats, so she'd never bothered to perfect the coquette. But at this moment, she decided she needed all the help she could get, so she dredged up her most radiant smile.

"Thank you so much," she said to the young man, "but I really need my shoes. Do you think you might get them from the plane?"

A photographer with *The Globe* emblazoned across his camera bag pushed in and snapped a picture of Laura.

"Don't do that!" she shouted, sticking her hand flat out in the direction of his flash. "You don't want me, I'm a reporter." And heaven help me, she thought, no pictures in these outlandish clothes. I would be the laughing stock of the newsroom.

"So where you from?" he asked, lowering his camera.

"The *New York Enterprise-Post*, and I need a phone. Can you help?"

"Talk to the society editor, Mary Anderson. I saw her a few minutes ago in that clump of folks on the other side of the pasture. She's been talking to the dead woman's family." He gave a vague wave over the multitude to what looked like quite a distance to Laura, especially barefoot.

At that moment, Yellow Hair came pushing through the throng, holding high and waving Laura's shoes.

High heels with pants, she thought. Who would ever have guessed I'd be so grateful?

Shoes on, she explained her next two goals to Yellow Hair: get to the pilot and stop him from leaving; then find this Mary Anderson in the crowd; or short of that, get to Western Union.

"Quick as said, done," replied her savior. In no time, he had pulled her through the crowd, and she found herself in the hangar confronting the pilot just as he was handing cash over to a sweet-faced, curly headed young man in blue overalls.

"Chaz, my lady friend here has a problem," Yellow Hair said by way of introduction. "Do you think you could hold off a bit moving the plane in here to get gassed up? Might be hard to roll her through that crowd, don't ya think?"

Chaz looked from Laura to the pilot and smiled. "Sure, Billy Bob, whatever you say."

Gosh, thought Laura, I didn't even think to find out his name, and here he has two of them. "Hi, Billy Bob," she said, sticking out her hand. "My name is Laura."

Billy Bob nodded his head and turned red. "Pleased to meet ya, ma'am."

"Now wait a minute," said the pilot, "I already paid you for the gas."

"Sure you did," replied Chaz, "but Billy Bob here has a point about all them people out there. Wouldn't want anyone to get hurt."

"I'm not staying." The pilot glared at Laura. "All she has to do is take off them pointy shoes, and she can get in and we go."

"I can't leave yet," Laura said. "I have to get details from the cops then call my office. You can't leave me stranded here."

Chaz grinned. "Say, little lady, if all you need is a hop, we can arrange that any time you want. We got plenty of barnstormers looking to make a buck or two. If your pilot here has reason to fear the police, let him go on."

"Really?" Laura felt like hugging the mechanic. "I already paid him for a round-trip."

"I'm sure we can work that out." Chaz turned to the pilot. "I'd say before we roll the plane in here, wouldn't you think?"

That settled, they all headed for the plane. While Chaz recruited several men in the crowd to help shove, the pilot climbed up on the wing to retrieve Laura's satchel and hatbox. For a moment, it looked as though he was going to just heave them over. But a funny look appeared on his face as Billy Bob lifted up his arms to take the objects. The pilot then bent one knee down on the wing, and handed over the luggage with the care of someone transferring fine china.

C HAPTER THIRTEEN
GETTING THE LOWDOWN

WHEN BILLY BOB AND LAURA ARRIVED at the offices of the *Atchison Daily Globe,* they found Mary Anderson, hairpins flying from her salt-and-pepper bun, already banging out her story of the Culpepper family's loss. Mary was cordial enough. She waved Laura to a seat, told her to feel free to use her phone to call Barnes. But she couldn't talk, she said, as she typed and yelled, "Copy!" A kid came running to rip a page from her typewriter and sped with it to the composing room.

It was the same copyboy who had guided them to Mary's desk a few minutes earlier.

"We got to get this edition on the street," he'd said, with clear excitement and puffed-up pride in his voice. "United Press, AP, and the *Journal-Post* all sent reporters from Kansas City for yesterday's story, so they were Johnny-on-the-spot when today's thing broke. The *Journal*'s trucks've already dropped off their latest papers. They're our big competitor, you know."

Indeed, Laura had already spotted a copy of the *Kansas City Journal-Post* lying on the next desk over, and had begun to read while the kid droned on. She also found a *Kansas City Star* and a *St. Louis Globe-Democrat* that had bylined stories as well.

"You see," the kid said proudly, "nobody got to the Culpepper family but Mary."

With the last yell of "Copy!" and the final page ripped from her typewriter, Mary turned in her swivel chair to Laura with a businesslike, "And what can I do for you?"

Mary looked like the newswoman Joe Bailey had described to her on the train. She was a large, matronly woman whose skin was parched and deeply wrinkled from the Kansas sun, wearing heavy-duty lace-up shoes. She had a no-nonsense air, nicotine stains on her fingers, and was puffing on a small cigarillo.

"I need some information, and I'm told you're the society editor," Laura said.

"Now that's a joke," Mary replied with a quizzical squint, as though she were taking stock of Laura. "Do I look like the society type?"

"Oh, I . . ."

"Don't worry, just funning you," Mary said. "I do whatever needs to be done. This is a small town. I know most all the families."

"Okay, help me get this straight, if you would," Laura said. "As I understand it, this Sally Culpepper fell out of a plane . . ."

"She jumped. Paid a buck fifty for the privilege. An air show passing through town."

"Jumped?" Laura's eyebrows rose a notch.

"Parachute didn't open," Mary said. "Flying acts are big entertainment in these little towns. Barnstormers come through doing aerobatics, guys walking on wings. Had one daredevil pair, so help me God, played tennis, with a net and everything, strapped on the wing of a plane in flight."

"That's crazy, all right," Laura replied, "but what about Culpepper? What did her family say? And why did they impound the plane, was it *the* plane, and who stole it? I noticed some of the papers said it was the girl who flew under all the bridges in New York. Others said she hadn't been ID'd."

"Is this the way you get your news in New York? Ask other reporters?" Mary let out a loud guffaw, slapping her hand against her knee.

Laura's eyes blinked from the heat in her cheeks; she knew she'd gone beet red. "Look," she took a deep, calming breath, "I'm clearly running to catch up. But I can assure you that I will give full attribution to *The Globe*."

"*The Atchison Daily Globe*," Mary retorted.

"Absolutely."

Mary filled her in, and Laura then called Barnes in New York.

"A woman paid a dollar fifty to make a jump from an airplane!" she yelled into the phone in a rush, worrying about how much this call halfway across the country would cost and if the *Globe* would ask her to pay for it, "and the chute didn't open. The DA impounded the plane, and another woman came in the next day and flew off with it."

"I know all that," the city editor bellowed. "The wires have it. What do you think I'm paying you for?"

"I got plenty more," Laura said in a huff. "I'm just making sure you got the basics. This guy Chaz, at the airfield, described a woman who sounds to me like Jenny Flynn, and he suspects she was heading to Ponca City, Oklahoma, because that's where the stunter was planning his next show. DA says the guy's name is Roy Wiggens. Since it was his plane that was impounded, the guess is that he figured the guards would stop him from getting in it, but wouldn't notice a woman. Figured right. She moved so fast, they hardly had time to see her."

"Fine, then go to Oklahoma," Barnes said. "What else?"

"But say, boss, shouldn't I be getting back to Cleveland, instead of some wild goose chase?"

"Goose chase?" he bellowed. "When are you going to learn to do what you're told? I said what else!"

Laura filled him in briefly on the sad story of Sally Culpepper and the four-year-old tyke she'd left behind. With her story already on the way to press, Mary had given Laura all the intimate details of the family farm, where Sally had lived with her parents after her divorce.

"Plug her to rewrite!" Laura heard Barnes shout at the switchboard. There was the familiar click of the copper-tipped cords, the operator said, "We miss ya, kid," and Jimmy Murphy was on the line.

Laura laid the purple prose on thick. She began: "Quote, I want my mommy, close quote, cried the cherubic-faced four-year-old, tears running down his pink cheeks. Open quote, Mommy's with the angels . . ."

"So there's your headline," said Murphy, "'Mommy's with the Angels.'"

Of course, Laura thought, they love the color purple. When she finished, she put down the phone, thanked Mary, and asked, "Where can I buy riding boots and breeches?"

Chapter Fourteen
LOOPING THE LOOP

JENNY FLYNN HAD BEEN BY HERSELF in the Cleveland grandstand the day before, watching the first day of the National Air Races and Aeronautical Exposition under a hot August sky.

She was totally caught up along with the rest of the crowd in the excitement of a series of outside loops. The tail-skid dust of past landings hung in puffs over the field and smudged thousands of upturned faces. There was stone silence. Even the swish of hand-held palm fans had ceased. Then thunderous applause rolled through the stands as the pilot completed his third loop. The stunt had first been done two years earlier by the military ace Jimmy Doolittle. Until then, fliers had considered such a feat truly death defying because the G-forces acting on the plane could burst it apart, or yank the pilot from the cockpit, or cause him to black out. Now a number of people had become proficient at the loop that put the pilot on the outside of an imaginary circle instead of inside it. Roy, Jenny's instructor, had been trying to get her to perfect the stunt, but it wasn't easy.

"For starters," she'd told him, "it makes me dizzy as the dickens."

Jenny had an ambivalence about flying that seemed to confuse everyone but herself. She was fearless. She was an instinctive pilot, flying by the seat of her pants, as the saying went. But she backed away from perfecting her skills. She would tell the world and Roy, the mentor who kept pushing her to stretch herself, that flying was a lark, a once-in-a-while plaything. "I'm just doing it for fun," was always her response. She loved the escape of being in the air—being on her own. It was a luxury that didn't otherwise exist in her daily life. There were the constraints of family and friends, but most of all societal expectations so ingrained that it had never occurred to Jenny to question them. Besides, she was young—eighteen—and having fun was Number One.

Had it been suggested to her to envy Laura's independence, her lack of structure and inhibition in her home life, Jenny would have shuddered. She may have been young, but she was wise beyond her years in understanding the value of discretion and propriety in the world in which she lived.

Again, Jenny watched the silver plane climb high in the blue sky then drop off, forming a circle as it fell headlong, with the pilot upside down at the bottom of the circle, then climb up to complete the loop, right side up, at the point where he had begun. He did one after another, until he had completed seven loops. The crowd went wild. Jenny was on her feet jumping up and down, screaming along with the rest of them.

As she finally settled back in her seat to wait for the next performance, she pondered the discipline it would take to perfect such a difficult stunt. An inside loop is a breeze, she thought, you just throttle up, pull back on the stick, and around you go. True, you were upside down at the top of that circle, but forces pushed you back in your seat, not out of it. Easy peasy. So are rolls and dead-stick landings. No point in spending a lot of time trying to perfect something as difficult as an outside loop. If it's not easy, why bother? Easy is the way things should be.

This place is futuristic, she thought, looking around at

Cleveland's huge Municipal Airport. Recently built, it was the country's first airport owned by a city. It was so large that the grandstands for the air show were at the west side of the field and didn't affect traffic out of the passenger terminal at the other end. Several flights a day came in, including a daily from Detroit.

Jenny ordered a hot dog and a Dr Pepper from a vendor selling in the aisle. As she was passing her dime down the row, she spoke to the stout woman in the big sunhat sitting next to her. "Someone told me that there were a hundred thousand people here today," Jenny said. "That's nearly as much as the entire population of Oklahoma City."

"There were three hundred thousand at the parade," the woman replied. "That's a third of the size of Cleveland. People came from all over the world for this show. They even painted directional arrows for the planes on the roofs of buildings."

"Signs? I saw *people* perched on roofs when I flew in this morning," Jenny said. "Sometimes it looked like whole families, or even neighborhoods." She had flown here on her own and planned to stay until Monday to see the finish of the women's competition. Races for men would be culminating here all week from various cities, including Los Angeles, Philadelphia, Toronto, and Miami, but since this was the first year for the women, it was especially exciting.

She wondered who would win. Her guess was Louise Thaden, or perhaps Ruth Nichols. She was sure that poor Amelia didn't have a chance. She'd already busted up a propeller overshooting a runway in Arizona on an early leg of the race, and of course her press release had, as always, blamed it on plane malfunction or a rock or a ditch in her path. Amelia could be a good pilot, if she just applied herself. But instead of flying, she seemed to spend most of her time on the lecture circuit, which was hard for Jenny to comprehend. Why spend all your time either courting or dodging the press, and showing off for old ladies at rubber chicken lunches? Didn't make sense. Amelia was a nice woman, but seemed to be ensnared by her publicist and the idea of making money on endorsements. As a result, she was not at all qualified to be flying a fast, difficult plane like her Lockheed Vega. Many of the other contestants had sponsors, had been lent planes. Amelia bought hers because it was touted to be the fastest thing going. But fast wasn't going to do her any good if she was too inexperienced to handle the big bird. Everyone else in the race had logged countless hours in the air, while Amelia was off *talking* about flying. Jenny had heard rumors, too, that the hours Amelia had written in her logbook couldn't all be accounted for.

The woman in the big hat grabbed Jenny's arm. "Oh my," she said, "those Navy High Hats are next. It's said to be really something."

Jenny gasped as nine Navy fighter planes flew in formation, doing loops, rolls, and dives, with their wings tied together, strut to strut, with manila rope.

What would it feel like to be able to fly like that? she wondered. But she just as quickly pushed the thought away. Too much boring work.

The Navy planes had just swooped by close overhead— all nine of them—when the stout woman poked Jenny again. "Someone over there is waving at you."

It was a friend from the Curtiss hangar who, once he had gotten Jenny's attention, handed a paper to the first person on the aisle. The note was passed from hand to hand of the annoyed spectators who didn't want to take their eyes off the field even for a second.

What could it be? Jenny's fingers trembled as she unfolded the paper. She never liked to be away from home for very long. It was a message from her instructor saying to call immediately, it was an emergency.

After Jenny had struggled through the packed stands
and finally found a phone, she was grumpy with Roy for
frightening her over a problem that was nothing more than
his plane. She gave him a bunch of reasons why his plan
sounded like a bad idea. Even though she had flown his
closed-cockpit, five-seater Bellanca a few times before, she
wasn't really that familiar with the big plane. She'd never
been to Atchison, didn't know the field. What low-lying
power lines were around? Besides, she didn't want to leave
the air show—the end of the women's race was Monday,
three days away. She really got worried when he explained
just how low she would be on fuel. What if she couldn't
make it to Kansas City and had to touch down in some
farmer's cornfield, and then try to sweet talk him out of
tractor fuel? But Roy was a friend, as well as her instructor,
and he needed his plane to move on to a scheduled stunt
show in Ponca City.

So here she was, after flying until dark yesterday and with
an early start this morning, circling the Atchison airfield.
Roy was going to hide in some bushes near the hangar then
pop out and climb into her plane, while she ran and jumped
into his. They had closely choreographed this ahead of time.
Her Curtiss Jen4 was not a self-starter. If Jenny killed the
motor, someone on the ground would have to crank up the
plane's wooden propeller to get it going again. As she landed
and taxied down the field, she could already see someone in
overalls sprinting out of the hangar, wanting to be helpful,
coming with chocks to put behind her wheels for parking.
Jenny moved the little ship away from his path and idled her
engine, looking frantically around for Roy, seeing very few
close trees or bushes, wondering where he could be hiding.
She was also looking at the wind sock to see whether she or
Roy was going to have to take off into the wind. Seemingly

out of nowhere, Roy was suddenly climbing into the rear cockpit.

"Good luck!" Jenny yelled as she scrambled out and slid off the wing. "Take care of my baby!" The little plane was surplus from the Great War. She'd learned to fly in it, learned her first stunts, feeling dizzy and afraid she'd fall out when she first flew upside down. Even so, she'd refused to wear a parachute. Stunts were fine, she trusted the plane but never wanted to be on her own floating in the sky without it. She loved her baby, named after her, she always felt— everyone called the Jen4 a Jenny. It had seen her through many a scrape.

She peeked around the tail of her own plane, then scampered through an open side door of the hangar and headed for Roy's. She was happy to be helping him out of a jam. He was an ace, yet had taken her on as a student when other instructors dismissed the idea as a waste of time—she was a dilettante, a little rich girl incapable of being serious about much of anything. Her father had thought she should finally start developing some domestic skills, learn how to run a house properly. Her mother, who always had household help and wasn't too interested in cooking or needlework herself, thought Jenny should find a nice charity or civic project. She'd strongly recommended the garden club or the library board. Instead, Jenny was in a bustling hangar in Atchison, Kansas, hoisting herself up on the wing of the Bellanca, stealthily opening its cabin door, preparing to defy a sheriff's order that had impounded the plane because of an accident.

She smiled. "Twenty-three skidoo," she said.

Roy cleared the hangar just as she roared out of it in his Bellanca. The people on the ground were so startled to see a plane that had just landed take off that they had their backs turned to what Jenny was up to. She was glad she hadn't actually seen Roy's plane lift off. Jenny loved taking off herself, it always felt like a start, a new beginning. But watching friends or loved ones disappear into the clouds or beyond the horizon made her sad. It felt like an ending, as though, like Bubba, she might never see them again.

Jenny sped down the runway, pushing the throttle more than was really safe, wanting to lift as fast as possible to clear the trees at the end of the field. Under normal circumstances she would have taxied then turned back and taken off downwind to have a full runway as Roy had. But she just wanted to get in the air and say goodbye to Atchison. As the trees approached, coming at her way faster in this powerful plane than she was used to, she waited until the last possible second to pull back on the stick, and hope. She felt the lift she needed and relaxed as she watched the treetops recede beneath her.

She had saved the scariest for last. She finally peeked at her fuel gauge. Even worse than she had feared.

When she'd climbed to three thousand feet, she held the stick between her knees to keep her on course and pulled out the charts and map she'd stuck under her left leg. She realized with a start that her old habit of anchoring was unnecessary with no incoming wind in this closed-cockpit Bellanca. She could easily lay out a map on her lap to see the route she'd already marked to follow the Missouri River.

Atchison was in the northeastern corner of the state, so the quickest way out was to cross the river, then follow it south to Kansas City, Missouri. It was sixty or so miles away, and with good luck she had just enough fuel to get there. She looked down at a little frame house with a gabled roof, and wondered about its funny wooden walkway that ran from the front porch all the way around the side to its back door. Perhaps the river overflows its banks, she guessed, and that was Atchison's version of stilts. She flew over several three- and four-story buildings that no doubt were on the main street. Then she spotted the trestlework of a steel bridge and tipped her wings in a relieved sigh as she flew over the narrow span of the river that marked her exit from Kansas.

But taking even this much of a detour east would mean another refueling stop before she could reach her rendezvous with Roy in Oklahoma. She would certainly be happy when she could dump this big lumbering plane on him and retrieve her own Jenny. Shut up inside this covered bubble, she missed the feeling of being one with the sky. She decided to keep as low to the lush terrain along the river as she dared, both to save fuel and to more easily spot the next landmark on her map. She giggled—for once she didn't really need to worry about charting a course. The Missouri River was hard to lose, and that was her guide straight to her destination. It's not often you have landmarks as good as this, she thought. Rivers and railroad tracks, the pilot's navigational saviors.

Almost immediately, she spotted on her right the bend in the river that wound around the protruding thumb of land that held the sprawling military installation of Fort Leavenworth. She glanced over at the trees and green lawns and frame homes on the Army base, as well as the two-story dark blocks of the federal prison. She would love to dip the short distance across the Missouri to take a closer look at this world unto itself. That was one of the many things she loved about being in the air. You could just nip in and get a bird's-eye view of whatever struck you as interesting and then zoom on to the next thing. Jenny winced and tipped her left wing as she caught sight of the rows of white crosses in the base's cemetery. She thought of the president's son who had gone down behind enemy lines and been given a military burial with honors by the Germans. Her brother's body was never found. Several of the pursuit pilots of the 95th Aero had taken the trouble to make the trip to Oklahoma City to tell Jenny's parents they had seen Charles's plane disappear in a fiery ball near the Marne River. There was no hope that he could have survived. No hope that he could one day have a white cross like those below.

She so wanted to fly over, but didn't dare. Leavenworth was Kansas again. Where the sheriff was waiting. No sense in taking the chance of spurting out of fuel and landing back in the soup. Upcoming next on the Missouri side, she knew, would be the mouth of the Platte River with its muddy deltas. And sure enough, there it was.

She peered at the fuel gauge. Close. It was going to be a shaver, but she would probably make it. Running out of gas was usually no big problem. She was plenty used to that in Oklahoma, with its many flat spaces and cornfields. But she made a face as she looked down—an awful lot of trees along the river here. She could no doubt find plenty of open spaces if she moved a little to her east away from the water, but she would use up fuel doing that. Ah phooey, she decided, I'll just wing it. She could always glide along for a few miles with a dead stick. Then again, glancing at the map in her lap, she saw that the Kansas City airport looked like it was smack dab in the middle of town—not a good idea to count on gliding too much when you're on top of a lot of people.

Amelia had overshot the runway in her big red Vega, but Jenny knew that wouldn't happen to her. At least it wouldn't if she were in her own little plane. Heck, she thought, maybe I should start worrying a little. But that was usually a waste of time.

Jenny stared at the fuel gauge just as she flew through a puff of cloud. Red. Empty. But the engine was still putting along. What to do? She must veer left as soon as she could see where she was going. Then she was out of the cloud and back in the bright sunshine, and there, straight ahead, was what had to be Kansas City! Actually, two of them, right across the river from each other. She thought of cutting her motor now, but was afraid whatever fuel was left wouldn't be enough to crank her up again. So she began her slow descent on the Missouri side, banking to circle the town as she searched for a spot big enough to land, hoping that it would turn out to be the airport.

The engine sputtered. Jenny gripped the stick tighter between her legs to hold the ship steady as she prepared for her gliding descent.

CHAPTER FIFTEEN
GET A HORSE

THE ENGINE SUCKED UP ITS LAST DRAM of fuel, gave a little cough, and quit. Jenny frowned at the silence, so muted inside the closed cabin. Her face felt slightly hot, her heart began beating a little faster; she shifted in her seat and went into command mode. Automatically she tightened her seat belt and did her checks: altimeter, rudders, gas gauge. No point in that, it was definitely way beyond red. Still in automatic mode, she bumped her head on the cabin cover trying to look over the side for a sight check of the terrain. She laughed at her foolishness—there was no reason not to slide the top open, so she did. How much more fun flying is when you feel the wind in your face and hear the sound of the engine against the quietness of the sky, not the artificial lack of sound in this dumb little bubble. The wind rushed in, and with it her heart soared.

She and the plane were on their own. They were one. And she knew how to do this. Forced landings in farmers' cornfields were a dime a dozen, but the trick here was landing *on* a dime. Not a lot of leeway with all those cars and houses around. It was like threading a needle, but so much more fun. Her grandmother had long ago given up trying to teach Jenny to embroider. What kind of waste of time was that?

As Jenny moved the nose of the plane down in her glide,

she could see people the size of little ants moving below and felt a compassion for them that she never felt face to face: how dreary for them that they couldn't skim along the rim of the world the way she was doing.

The plane would always support you; just handle it right, and it would do as you said. She'd been guiding dancing partners around the floor since grade school with more effort than this.

Leaning over the side again, she set her path for what looked like an airport runway. The sweet silence was beginning to be broken by the muffled noises of the city below. She had to set her sight lines now, because she would have no front vision once she pulled her nose up to set her down. She grinned. That apparently was exactly what happened to Pancho Barnes during the derby when she'd landed on a car coming into the airport in Pecos. Dumb driver had pulled right under Pancho, and plop! Everyone had been talking about it in Cleveland before Jenny left.

She saw a line of cars that must be running on a highway. It was difficult to tell if they were moving because of her own speed, but surely they were. No reason for them to be in a line otherwise. As she drew nearer, looking over the side, she saw how close several cars were to the spot she was aiming for. She could also see people coming out of hangars on the field—at least *they* knew she was heading in. She hoped the motorists had the sense to see her and get out of her way. But with no noise from her shut-down engine, and the rattle of their own little traps, she knew they probably had no way of hearing her approach. She was swooping down with the silence of a large bird. She gripped her stick, lifted the plane's nose, and prepared to set down right in front of that middle hangar.

"Here I come, ready or not!" she yelled to the wind. She felt a slight bump, a glancing blow, just before she set the

Bellanca down on the spot she had picked out. Oops, hope my wheels didn't leave too big a dent in his car roof, she thought. At least she hadn't tapped the guy hard enough to tear off a wing like Pancho had done. But shoot, the driver ought to pay closer attention to road conditions.

As a hangar flier ran out with parking chocks to block her wheels, Jenny returned his smile and said, "There's some driver back there who ought to get a horse."

CHAPTER SIXTEEN
SEEING DOUBLE

JENNY COULDN'T BELIEVE HER EYES WHEN, after a long harrowing flight, she climbed out of the cockpit in a darkened field in Ponca City, Oklahoma, and saw the spitting image of herself come striding toward her—jodhpur breeches, boots, even the white short-sleeved shirt.

"Why did you steal this airplane?" the woman demanded.

"I didn't steal anything." Jenny moved off, searching for something large enough to chock her wheels.

The woman followed, wouldn't let up. "What about it?" she demanded again.

Jenny shoved a big rock under a Bellanca wheel before finally responding: "It's Roy's plane and he asked me to go get it."

"*I* got here hours ago. What took *you* so long?"

"I had to stop for gas a couple of times," Jenny replied. "Where's my plane?"

She took a good look around at what passed for the airstrip in Ponca City. She saw a rutty, weed-filled, windswept lot; a desolate-looking, apparently empty hangar; a limp wind sock; no planes; and this rude woman. "Three suitcases?" Jenny said, an incredulous look spreading across her face. "Of all the silly things."

"You must have done more than stop for gas," the woman persisted. "You had an eight-hour head start on me."

"So I had some engine trouble. I stopped to eat. And just who are *you*?" Jenny countered. But of course she knew. This was the woman who had been pumping her in the Cleveland restroom, and she suspected it was the same anonymous rude voice from Roosevelt Field, probably the same one who had kept writing speculative stories about her license. She'd never seen a woman reporter before, there couldn't suddenly be two, much less three. Strange, unladylike job.

"You know who I am. Laura Bailey, a reporter. We've met before. Didn't the authorities have that plane impounded?"

"Pooh." Jenny gave a barely discernible, dismissive shrug. "Roy said it was just some politician running for reelection."

"Someone died," Laura persisted.

"Yes, that was horrible—the poor woman." Jenny's face clouded before she squared her shoulders in a defiant stance. "That didn't have anything to do with the plane. Roy takes people up all the time for jumps, and gives them clear instructions. It was some sort of weird accident."

"Weren't you scared?" Laura asked.

"Of what?" Jenny's eyes were wide in innocence; she was laughing to herself. Of course there were things to have been afraid of in the last few hours. Like running out of gas, or handling a plane she wasn't familiar with, or finding her way across the Oklahoma border before it got dark. She'd known there were no fields nearby that had landing lights. The local politician surely was wrong, but it had still felt urgent to get out of Kansas. None of that would matter to this nosy woman whose big concern was clothes and snooping around other people's lives.

"You didn't worry you'd get in trouble?"

This person, Laura, was like a dog with a bone; she wouldn't let up. "I don't usually worry about things very much," Jenny said.

"I guess not. You already had your license suspended for a few days. Weren't you afraid that would happen again? I just can't believe you're that frivolous."

Jenny laughed. "Well I'll be. You go running around all over the country writing stories about ordinary things I've done, making something out of nothing. And you're calling *me* frivolous? That's rich."

"You call flying under bridges ordinary?"

"It seems pretty natural to me—more normal than prying into other people's lives. But I'm sick of this stupid conversation, when the important question is *where is my plane?*"

The pilot's voice sounded almost panicky. "What plane?" Laura asked, instinctively looking around even though she knew perfectly well that there was no plane on the field except the one Jenny had just landed.

"My Jenny. Roy should've gotten here before me." The pilot's voice was high-pitched, skirting the edge of panic. A hot August wind blew her words around in circles.

"Aren't *you* Jenny? What are you talking about?" She's finally losing her devil-may-care attitude, Laura thought with satisfaction. Now we're getting someplace—I can get under her skin and figure out what her real story is.

"My plane! That's what it's called. Don't you know anything?"

Laura could feel her face reddening, although she hoped that it wasn't discernible in the waning light. "You're expecting another plane, one of those old trainers? I've been meaning to ask if that's where your name came from. I've got to get out of here, there's no phone. Why can't we just leave in that plane you flew in?"

"That's a mouthful," Jenny responded. "Is that what reporters do, scatter out a whole bunch of questions and hope that one will get answered?"

"Why are you so hostile toward me?" Laura asked. "You've been angry ever since I asked you on Long Island about flying in men's clothes. I didn't understand because I'd never been in an airplane. I had to find out the hard way. Okay?" Maybe if she fessed up her ignorance about this business, it would help. She realized she was at this woman's mercy, stuck out here in the middle of nowhere. How would she get out without Jenny's help?

"Is that why you're dressed like me?" Jenny said, her tone hard.

"Look," Laura said in a reasonable voice, but determined not to back down, "I bought a white shirt and those riding things that you said were the only pants around. I'm just doing my job."

"Yeah? Well, I don't get it. It's beyond me why people would want to snoop into other people's lives."

The wind played with an old newspaper, skipping it across the field and wrapping it around Laura's legs. The little dance she was doing to disengage herself caused her voice to come out breathless and much harsher than she intended. "Don't you understand at all that the public is fascinated by people who have the nerve to go into the air without anything holding them up? Especially a woman. It's more exciting than being a movie star. People want to know what makes you tick."

Jenny blushed. "Well, it's embarrassing. I once had a reporter try to follow me around when I was grocery shopping."

Laura bent down and busied herself unwinding the paper. So, she thought, that's her problem—already got the celebrity disease. Put my picture in the paper, but otherwise leave me alone. All the glory with no pain. No way to fight that, I've just got to plow ahead. She paused, trying to decide how to tackle Jenny, and began folding the paper to use as a fan against the heat. It didn't work. The gusts of wind kept breaking up the folds, or blowing it back into her face. "So who's this Roy, your boyfriend?" she asked, finally tossing the paper away.

"My instructor," Jenny replied. "He holds several loop records—taught me what I know about stunt flying. He was in a jam. I helped him out, that's what friends do." She frowned as she smoothed out her cloth helmet and stuck it in her pants pocket. "I can't imagine where he is with my Jenny. I'm worried sick."

"About him or the plane?"

"Both. Don't be stupid. That sounds like a typical reporter's question. Then you can write a headline that says I care more about a silly airplane than a human being."

Laura grinned. "Sad to say, you kinda got that right. But just for the record, reporters don't write the headlines. Listen, you're the only one who knows where we are. Let's just hop in that plane of yours and get out of here."

"I told you, it's not my plane. It's Roy's. I'm not going anywhere until he shows up." She put her right hand up to shade her eyes as she scanned the horizon, then looked around her once more with a troubled expression. "I read a story that they were building an airport in Ponca City. I guess the news reports are wrong again." She gave Laura a hard look. "And I think you ought to leave the same way you came."

"I've got to find a phone." Laura ignored Jenny's remark. She had decided the best plan was to let Jenny get used to the idea that she was stuck with her. "Do you think there's a diner or something around?"

"Why didn't you make whoever brought you stay?"

"No choice. He said he had to get right back, couldn't fly in unknown terrain in the dark. Since I had to talk to you, I had to wait."

Jenny's tinkling laugh came back. "And *you* call *me* a daredevil!"

"Yeah, well, okay." Laura grinned. "Meanwhile, know any place where I can find a phone?"

CHAPTER SEVENTEEN
DELIVERANCE

LAURA LOOKED AT HER WATCH, it was past eight o'clock. The sun was still awake, but just barely. Dusk was moving in, night wouldn't be far behind. Her geography schoolbooks hadn't exaggerated about the wide-open, windswept plains. This remote spot that apparently passed for an airfield was desolate, deserted. Huge chunks of weeds or some sort of vegetation were being picked up and tumbled about in spurts and gusts. She was stranded in a big way. It gave her some satisfaction, though, that at least this smarty girl Jenny was too.

"We've got to do something, we can't just stand around," Laura said. "What's that metal building over there?"

"It's a hangar," Jenny replied irritably. "There won't be anything there."

"Let's check it out anyway," Laura said.

And so they did, and Jenny was right. After inspecting it all the way round, they found it locked. There weren't even any windows to peak into.

They both paced a bit more then finally sat down glumly on Laura's luggage. Ten minutes must have gone by and neither had said a word.

Suddenly Jenny leaped up from her hatbox perch and pointed at a distant speck in the sky. "I bet that's Roy!" She seemed close to jumping up and down in her excitement.

They watched as the plane approached, then flipped, flying over them upside down.

"My gosh," Laura yelled, "he's close enough that I can see the color of his scarf! It's bright red!"

"Fun, isn't it?" Jenny turned to her with a serene look on her face.

It's as though she were in church, Laura thought.

The plane flipped again, and dropped to a spot right in front of them. The pilot climbed from his cockpit, stepped on the wing, took a quick look around the field, then jumped to the ground.

"Good girl," he said to Jenny. "I see you've brought the Bellanca. I knew I could count on you."

Then, with a wide sweep of his arm, he bowed slightly as he pulled off his cloth helmet and swung it as though it were the plumed hat of a cavalier. "Sorry to keep you ladies waiting. I had to stop for gas."

"That must be the catchphrase in this business," Laura said.

"I haven't had the pleasure." The man turned to her with a smile. He was short, barely taller than Laura, with a dark, debonair mustache and a cowboy bandanna tied around his throat. He was shrugging out of a leather jacket. "Do you mind if I remove my coat? It's hot here, even at night."

"Laura, Roy," Jenny said with a wave of her arm that encompassed the two. "So what do we do now?" she asked him. "It's too late for me to fly home."

"I made arrangements for a fellow I know to give us a lift into town. Or at least to the roadhouse that's nearby. You'll clearly have to spend the night."

"Oh dear," Laura said, visions in her head of Barnes yelling. "When do you think your friend will be coming? I've got to get to a phone."

Jenny turned to Roy. "This woman's a reporter, and she wants to blab about everything we've done."

Roy raised his eyebrows. "You're serious? How did you end up here?"

"It's a long story," Laura said. "We'll fill you in another time if you think it's worth the bother." She turned to Jenny. "Now look, I'm going to have to call my story in. Do you want to tell me your side of this, or shall I just go with whatever I can surmise from the fact that you're here with someone else's plane?"

Jenny rolled her eyes. "That's what I'd call blackmail."

"So," Laura said with a grin, "what'll it be?"

"I told you, Roy's my instructor. Why don't we let him tell you what a great student I am?"

"That sounds good for over dinner. It'll give me a follow-up. Right now I need the details on the jumper's death, and why you took the plane."

"I've nothing to hide," Roy said. "I can give you that fast and easy. Two other pilots and myself have been going from town to town in two planes for the last several weeks. Doing some exhibition stunts, and then taking folks up for rides or jumps, whichever they preferred. A buck and a half a ride and two bucks fifty to use the chutes."

Laura pulled the stub of a pencil and a slim notebook from the pocket of her riding pants. She flipped the cover. "Go on," she said.

"Sure." Roy looked over at Jenny with a shrug. "An attractive young woman, probably in her midtwenties, showed up. Said she'd watched shows before and always envied the sense of sky-floating with a white parasol overhead. Those were her words, *white parasol*. We gave her the usual instructions, harnessed her chute properly." He lifted his arms, made two fists, and gave a hard tug back as though tightening a harness on someone. "We took all the precautions, and she never pulled the cord to open the chute. It was awful, we felt so darned helpless. We were yelling at her, even dove down to keep screaming at her as she fell. But she didn't do anything. Just had a smile on her face as she hurtled down."

"She didn't look frightened or anything?" Laura lifted her head from her notebook.

"Nope. Damnedest thing I've ever seen."

"She had a four-year-old son," Laura said, looking at Roy in disbelief.

"So I've heard from the DA. But so help me God, she made no attempt to open that chute. And I saw her face, she didn't look scared. Just happy. Probably a heart attack. They're doing an autopsy."

Headlights suddenly played across the field. "Hey, I bet that's Clem Donohue coming to get us," Roy said, starting to walk in the direction of the lights.

Laura grabbed his arm. "Sorry, but we've got to finish this. Didn't the DA impound your plane?"

Roy's eyes widened, startled. He looked at Laura with a smile that slowly took over his face, clearly making a decision to stop and answer. "Right, impounded. With no reason. They checked over the Bellanca, which had nothing to do anyway with whether the chute was proper. It was; they checked that too. The guy was running for office, what can I tell you? I needed the plane to meet a commitment for a show here tomorrow. If I'd gone near the plane, they would have stopped me. I knew they'd be watching Jenny fly in, and not expecting her to fly right back out."

CHAPTER EIGHTEEN
SEND MONEY STOP

LAURA STOOD AT THE WESTERN UNION counter in downtown Ponca City trying to write—in the briefest stop-start telegramese she could devise—her story of tracking down Jenny. The sparsely furnished, barren office was deserted, except for a pimply faced clerk who seemed as dim as the single bulb dangling from a cord overhead. She thought of her increasingly perilous situation: dubious friends, no bed for the night, little money. And she could lose her job if she didn't produce something here pretty quick that would pass Barnes's muster. *SEND MONEY STOP.* That would be a good start. Naw, be serious, she admonished herself. Get this story written and sent. She was probably already past deadline for the morning street editions. She'd decided she was better off not talking to her office. Barnes was just liable to tell her to get home fast. Not a good idea. She felt there were plenty more excellent stories here. But *SEND MONEY* was serious. She had almost none left after paying for jodhpurs, plane rides, and hotels.

Jenny had made it quite clear that she didn't like the idea of Laura following her around and writing about it. But was she so hostile she would leave her stranded in this one-horse town? Laura wasn't sure. Just in case, she'd already asked the counter kid about the nearest hotel and where the train station was.

Laura bore down with her pencil, getting close to the end. She had finished with the details wormed out of Jenny about her flight from Kansas in the "stolen" plane, how she'd had to glide with no gas into Kansas City, her wheels just missing treetops and thumping a car on the road, and she'd described how the two of them had met at a deserted airfield here in Ponca City. Trying to cram such a complex set of circumstances onto these little telegram sheets wasn't easy. Fortunately, Barnes had explained before she left that the entire story didn't need to be written, just chunks of the new information. A rewrite man could quickly fill in from the wires all the background and any later developments.

She had to move it along. The others were waiting, not too patiently, in Clem's car outside. If she dawdled, they'd come inside. Or worse yet, drive off without her. It felt like a fishbowl, this tiny office with its glass storefront and the yellow light burning against the dark outside. They were probably sitting out there in the car laughing. People always seemed to be hostile toward tabloid reporters. Including Laura's mother, who felt it was hardly a poetic way to live. And Jenny had a special superior air, which Laura tried to ignore just as she had the snootiness of those rich girls at Barnard. She'd finally realized at school that she was wasting her time fretting about it since most of her classmates weren't even aware of her existence, a day student who came and went from home on the subway.

Laura finished up her story with Roy's firsthand account of the jumping death in Kansas and handed it to the vacant-eyed clerk. "It's getting late," he groused. "You want me to send all them pages?"

"Yes, please." At least she wouldn't have to deal with Barnes tonight, and who knew what good stories tomorrow would bring?

As she was digging in her purse for money, she glanced out the plate glass and saw Clem's car pulling away from the curb. She dropped the stubby lead pencil she had laboriously been printing with and headed for the door. As she got to the street, she made a feeble wave and called out, "Wait." Clearly it was pointless; she could see the big car's taillights bobbing along a block away.

"Damn." Laura stamped her foot. She looked down at what she'd stepped on, weeds growing up between the cracks in the sidewalk. "I'm stuck in this nowhere place," she said aloud as she instinctively stooped down to pick a fluffy dandelion ball. They were a lucky charm, if you could blow all the seeds off at once, just like the candles on a birthday cake. She closed her eyes, took a mighty huff, and blew. "Please make them come back," she said to the dark and empty street.

Clem, at the wheel, turned slightly to Jenny in the backseat. "Not sure I think this is very funny. That poor kid is going to be worried sick. It's late. Where would she go?"

"She's so wrapped up in her precious story, we'll be back before she notices," Jenny said. "I want to get ahold of John. He'll be worried. No reason why her story needs to take priority over everything else."

Roy, sitting in the front passenger seat, laughed. "Aw, Jenny, she's a cute little thing. For some reason you seem to be jealous of that girl. I don't know why." He turned to her in the back, giving her a hard look. "Don't like competition, do you? Used to holding center stage."

"That's ridiculous, and you know it. She's just annoying. No manners, *three* suitcases, chasing me around, butting in. Good Lord, a hatbox!"

"So, here we are at my mother's house," Clem said as he pulled into the circular driveway of a sprawling, gabled two-story mansion. "You can run in and use the telephone, Jenny. We do need to get back though. That poor girl is probably already out looking for a hotel."

As Jenny ran up the broad front steps, the porch light came on and a liveried butler opened the massive carved door.

Laura stood there watching the car disappear, her shoulders sagging, pondering her situation. What a strange bunch of reckless people. Clem didn't seem to quite fit; he was even weirder—a tall, sunburned string bean, dressed in overalls and snap-button shirt, with warm brown eyes and a lopsided smile. When he laughed, only the left half of his mouth seemed to open up, giving one the feeling that the other half was reserving judgment or enjoying a private joke. And he drove the biggest, most expensive sedan Laura had ever seen, wood on the dashboard, leather seats. When she had inquired about it earlier, she'd been told it was a Pierce-Arrow. They had all laughed when she asked how to spell it. She didn't even know if Clem lived here; they could be headed for another town. She squared her shoulders. Nothing for it except to go back, get the telegram sent, and then find a hotel.

As she opened her two-sided coin purse she saw with a sinking feeling how little money she had left. After folding out several crumpled bills for the clerk, she had exactly nine dollars and twenty-seven cents.

"What time do you open tomorrow?" She would have to come back here before she checked out of the hotel, and hope Barnes had wired her money.

The clerk informed her that he opened at seven, and that the Arcade Hotel was just down the street.

"Fine," she said.

As she reached to pick up her bags, she let out a yelp.

"Oh, good grief, I forgot! My bags are in that car. They've got to come back!"

The slack-jawed clerk came halfway to life with a startled look. "Someone done steal your bags?"

"Yes, those people who drove me here. Did you see them? Do you know them?" Laura couldn't really hope that this dead-eyed fellow would know anything, but it was worth a try.

"Nope. And nope," he replied, his Adam's apple bobbing as though he'd just said something quite clever. He was probably delighted that he remembered there were two parts to the question, Laura thought.

"The man's name is Clem, and he's tall and thin and drives a huge brown-and-black car." Laura spoke each word carefully and slowly, in the forlorn hope that would somehow help.

"That there's Clem Donohue, he's the city attorney. He ain't gonna steal nuthin'." The kid's face brightened as though he'd passed still another test.

"City attorney?"

"Lady, I'm sorry but you're gonna have to wait outside for your friends," the clerk said. "You've already kept me way past my closing time."

Now what? She didn't dare go to the hotel and chance missing them. And surely they would return. No city official was going to steal her suitcases. Or was he? Maybe that explained the private smile. *Can't wait to get my hands on your hatbox, ma'am.* Her imagination was turning nutty. Laura trudged outside to wait. The curbs were quite high, with something like a step up to the sidewalk. Easy for sitting. She looked around and noticed heavy metal rings in the concrete every few hundred feet. She chuckled as she caught on. Of course, high enough to easily get off a horse and a ring to tether it.

She sat for a while, hoping a car, a horse, anything would come by. It crossed her mind that she always felt left out—at home, at college, at work, sitting on a curb, waiting for . . . what? Someone to give her a lift? Love her? Let her in?

Her heart raced when she finally saw headlights coming her way.

CHAPTER NINETEEN
ROADHOUSE

CLEM WAS GREETED AS AN OLD FRIEND by the owner of the roadhouse as the four of them entered for dinner. Laura noticed right away that each table had setups: glasses and bottles of soda and ginger ale. Just slip a flask from a purse or coat pocket and you had a lively drink. It made her think of Chumley's, a speakeasy a couple of blocks west of Christopher Square, near her home. She'd been there many a time as a kid, trailing along after Mother and one of her boyfriends. You found it by going through an innocent-looking courtyard off Barrow Street, or through an unmarked door around the corner on Bedford. When she got to high school, she was surprised to find that other students talked in excited whispers about sneaking off to Bedford Street as though it were some big thing. This place was certainly visible, neon sign out front.

Laura was still pondering the behavior of her new companions. Jenny had acted as though driving off and leaving her was nothing. Very breezy, she was. "Just had to make a phone call," she'd said. When they'd driven up to retrieve Laura they were all smiles. Roy had gotten out of the car and moved to the back. Clem had patted the creamy brown leather of the passenger seat and said, "Sit here, little lady, and I'll get you to some dinner in no time. You've had a long hard day."

"To say the least," was the only snideness Laura had allowed herself. She knew she was in hostile territory and had darn well better watch her step until she could get on a train. She certainly wasn't going to ask what kind of phone call could have been so important to leave a stranger stranded on a dark street corner without her luggage.

Jenny and Roy had been chattering about flying and friends ever since.

"I've got commitments all around here for a two-plane show," Roy said to Jenny as he sat down at their scarred table and poured from a pocket flask all in one fluid motion. "I really need you to come along." He waved the flask in Jenny's direction, but she shook her head.

"What nonsense. You know I can't do that."

Laura looked from one to the other, puzzled. This seemed to be continuation of a conversation she'd missed. Or was Jenny just refusing the booze? She couldn't be sure she'd heard quite right over the noise of the player piano cranking out a cowboy song at the other end of the drafty barnlike room. But Roy didn't add anything to the ginger ale in Jenny's glass, so when he held the flask high in Laura's direction, she took the cue and also shook her head.

A woman sporting badly dyed red hair, dressed in a black-and-red flouncy print dress, appeared with a pad and pencil in her hand. "We got chicken-fried steak with mashed potatoes 'n' gravy, or fried chicken with collards 'n' biscuits. What'll it be?"

Laura started to ask how you could fry a steak like a chicken, then thought better of it. She needed to get color-ful details about this strange country, but decided to just rely on observation. She hated to appear stupid. Perhaps she would get a chance to see both of these culinary wonders. Fried chicken, okay, but *collards?* What in the world could that be?

The other three ordered chicken so Laura decided to be adventuresome and go with the so-called steak. At least she could rely on filling up with mashed potatoes.

"Come on, Jenny, you can do it," Roy badgered. "It's only a few days."

Clem laughed, displaying his crooked half-smile. "You're a persistent kind of fella. Never give up, do you?" It was difficult to believe he was some kind of public official. Laura had pondered that question as she watched him fling his cowboy hat on the backseat of his car before they'd gotten out to enter this rowdy joint. And that expensive car? None of this made any sense.

"What are you two talking about?" Laura could stand the guesswork no longer.

"Well, if it's any of your business, James, the other pilot, dropped out on Roy," Jenny said. "He was so upset about the jumper's death he took his plane and went home, and his pal went with him."

"The show I've promised is supposed to have two . . ." Roy stopped, squinted his eyes at Laura, then his face broke into a radiant smile. "Two! Of course! I need two planes. What could be better—two *ladies* in that second plane." He placed his hand over Laura's and squeezed. "Sweetheart, you would be perfect."

"What?" There was indignation in Jenny's voice and written all over her face. "Don't be absurd."

"Aw, sweet child, be a sport. It's a great plan." Roy was cajoling and smooth.

"I'm not a child. Damnit, Roy. All of you, my parents, John, everybody treats me like some kind of doll."

Laura couldn't believe what she was hearing. What a break, if she could ride around in an air show! But she feared Jenny would never agree. Laura looked across the table at Clem. His smile was noncommittal, but his eyes flickered almost imperceptibly, and he may have been shaking his head ever so slightly. She read him as, *Keep out of it.*

"You're a flier, Jenny, and a darn good one." Roy took a long swallow from his drink then set his glass back down with careful deliberation, never taking his eyes off Jenny's face. "Go up there and show us what you can do."

Laura let out her held breath slowly, fearing it would explode and slice through the heavy silent air hanging in the tiny table space separating the four of them. She looked again at Clem. A flicker of his eyes still said no. She picked up her knife and fork and cut furiously into the chicken-fried steak. "Amazing," she said. "I guess it's as advertised—shoe-leather meat with thick batter. But say, it's tasty! Delicious, even." Her voice ran down, she didn't dare look at anyone or anything but her plate. "Milky cream gravy. Good."

Jenny's tinkly laugh erupted. Laura looked up to see her cock her head and smile at Roy. "My dear instructor, you're always trying to force me into a challenge, aren't you? Stunting with a greenhorn? What next—pressuring me again to try your precious outside loops that can yank you out of the cockpit or make you black out and crash?"

Roy turned solemn. "Sorry, no letup, Jenny. I'm serious, you've got to keep at it."

Jenny heaved a sigh of resignation and looked at Laura, her eyebrows arched. "Do you think you could hold onto your breakfast tomorrow and keep yourself in the plane if we fly upside down?"

Laura opened her mouth but no words came out. No message of any kind was being transmitted. All neurons seemed to have shut down. Was she really being invited to join this bunch?

Jenny laughed. "Okay, I give up. I'll call John back again and see if it's all right with him."

Finally Laura's brain kicked into action—Jenny's mysterious phone call was to someone named John. "Who's John?" she asked.

"Oh lordy," moaned Jenny. "Here we go again with the questions. He's my husband. Anything else personal you want to nose into?"

CHAPTER TWENTY
SOOTHING MINT TEA

LAURA LOST NO TIME, AS SOON AS THEY were alone, probing Jenny about John. "Why are you married so young?" This wasn't a reporter's question, as far as she was concerned, just a human one. Hardly anyone of her adult acquaintance bothered with such formalities. Sure, she had discerned that most of her schoolmates had two-parent households, but she'd never been close enough with any of them to figure out why they were so different. Her mother's friends all disdained what they termed *the conventions.* Jenny, with her frivolity, was no doubt conventional. "But you're only eighteen," Laura blurted out. "Surely . . ."

Jenny flashed with indignation. "I never heard of anyone who thought being married was strange. You're too nosy for your own good."

They were in a small dining nook off the grand hall of Clem's mother's home. Its walls a creamy off-white, with a hodgepodge of hand-painted French provincial and cozy flowered chintz, the room had an airy feel compared to the heavy furnishings throughout the rest of the antique-laden house. A Negro maid, wearing a white apron edged in lace with a matching frill in her hair, had just served them tiny cucumber sandwiches and tea from an ornate silver pot, despite the late hour and the fact that they'd already had dinner. Laura had asked earlier about staying at a hotel, but

Clem had insisted it was much easier to stay at his mother's.

Mrs. Donohue, a heavyset woman in flowing, multicolored garb with straight black hair pulled into a tight bun, had insisted they have some soothing mint tea before going to bed. "Now that I'm sure you girls are settled—Thomas has shown you your rooms and carried your luggage there—I'm going to excuse myself. You must have a lot to discuss from such a long, busy day."

The woman had barely said good night when Laura went right back to her questions: "Is being married what keeps you from flying very much? I can see Roy tries to challenge you. You told me at the Powder Puff Derby that you hadn't entered because it was too much work."

Jenny's voice rose: "I did *not* say that. You can see why no one ever wants to talk to reporters. I said that I just fly for fun. What in that sentence is so difficult to grasp? And why is it any of your business, anyway?" She banged her fragile Limoges cup back in its saucer with such a clang that Laura jumped.

"I don't mean to upset you." Laura's tone was sincere and intense as she nibbled at one of the delicate sandwiches made of store-bought white bread with the crust cut off. "It's just a curious thing that you seem so devil-may-care, so unafraid, and at the same time, you back off from everything."

"I'm not afraid." Jenny's response was so loud and harsh, it seemed as though she had channeled someone else. After a deep, exasperated breath, her tinkly voice came back. But still, she bit down on the words. "I just am *not* interested in being away from home and hanging out with a bunch of women all the time working on airplane engines, which always need maintenance. My mother grouses at me whenever she sees me in pants. I like to go up and buzz around a bit, then go home and go dancing with my husband."

For Jenny, this grilling was a variation on the same old

refrain. Only the week before, her mother, pince-nez dangling across her lavaliere-strewn bosom, had suggested once again that a civic activity such as a seat on the library board would "settle you down. Running around all the time in riding breeches, *really*. My dear, you're not fooling anyone. The neighbors all know you're *not* on your way to the stables. They know we sold your thoroughbred when you neglected the poor thing and never rode it."

"It wouldn't surprise me if you were afraid," Laura said now, with what she hoped was a sympathetic voice. "I read that your brother was killed in a plane."

"Charles was killed by a bullet in a war, not by an airplane." Jenny stood up abruptly. "Planes are safe. You can depend on them."

Laura put her hand out with a calming, almost shushing kind of gesture. "Please don't go, I didn't mean to upset you. I'm sure it's painful to think about. You must miss your brother."

"Of course I miss him." Jenny sank back down into the chintz cushion of the hand-painted chair. Her voice deepened, took on a ghostly, almost hollow tone: "That was a long time ago." Her eyes went far away. "I was only six."

"It's interesting, don't you think," Laura probed, "that you've chosen the same profession he did?"

"It's *not* my profession. I'm a housewife. I didn't start flying because of Charles, I started flying because of John. Besides, I just told you, I don't want to hang out with a bunch of women working as mechanics on engines. You have to learn about physics and aerodynamics and all those things. It's too much trouble." She banged her cup again. "It's so frustrating. You take up a hobby that's swell, just a lark, and everyone wants to turn you into something you aren't."

Laura wouldn't let up. "But why don't you want to get good at what you do?"

"I *am* good at it! I flew under all those bridges in New York, didn't I?"

"Why stop?" Laura was genuinely perplexed. "People have to stretch themselves to accomplish anything."

"Oh shoot. Look at you. Out here running around, butting your nose in . . . for what? You don't even know how you're going to get back home. I'm not interested in living on the edge like that. It's a silly thing you're doing. You're aggressive, pushy. And you're so intense about everything." Her voice took on a petulant tone. "Why won't people let me fly the way I want to fly? My parents think it's too much and you and Roy and others like you think it's not enough."

"You're so I-don't-give-a-darn." The implied criticism was harsh in Laura's voice. This was an attitude that was incomprehensible to her, a woman who'd had to find her own way to school as a child, scour for college scholarships, make her way through the thicket of a rough-and-tumble newsroom.

Jenny opened her mouth to speak, but stopped when the maid came back with a cut-crystal pitcher of ice water with floating lemon slices, and placed it on the high gloss of the inlaid table.

"You were saying?" Laura prodded after the woman had cleared away their empty plates and left.

"I just don't understand why you see something wrong with having fun." Jenny's tone became defiant. "My husband and all his friends fly. So I don't see why I shouldn't too. That way I know what they're talking about."

Laura frowned, trying to comprehend what she was hearing. "I'm not the one you need to convince that you should be flying. It sounds to me like it might be yourself."

"What nonsense. I'm going to bed. *I* have a show to do tomorrow." Jenny rose from her chair. "I'm sure if you ask the maid to wash and iron that crumpled blouse, she'd be glad to. Since you got outfitted up to look like me, I assume it's the only one you have."

Laura drew in a sharp breath. "I guess I was wrong about you. You just fly to hang out with the boys, to get male attention. They all think it's cute that you fly. Is that it? No wonder they all treat you like a doll. That's what you are. And with me here, you're not the only doll around."

CHAPTER TWENTY-ONE
SKETCHING THE ACTION

LAURA STILL COULDN'T BELIEVE she was really doing this, but here she was flying along, riding in the cockpit behind Jenny in her curious-looking old plane left over from the Great War. It had four wings, two on top of each other on each side, or maybe it was considered only two wings. She would have to ask. One wing was across the top of the plane's body, what they called the fuselage, and the other two wings were on each side at the bottom. There were supporting poles and wires running between the top and bottom wings, and some of the poles went directly from the top set of wings to the fuselage.

As Laura, with a pad in her lap, made a sketch of the plane, Jenny periodically turned around and stared with a quizzical look. Laura would give a slight shake of her head and shrug. *That girl's view of the world is so narrow that she can't comprehend someone else's curiosity,* she decided, and continued her sketch. There were two wheels at the end of poles about four feet long stuck out in front like a kid's go-cart. These made the plane's front, or nose, stick up in the air several feet, while its tail rested on the ground. But once the plane got in the air, then the whole fuselage stayed in a straight line, the nose no longer pointed upward. This was certainly a time she could use Cheesy and his camera. She had to see about trying to get him here.

Clem had helped them get going by pushing the wooden propeller around and around until it cranked up the engine. They had rolled along on the ground for quite a while, Laura waving to Roy and Clem, who stood in the dusty patch of grass, watching. Then miraculously they were in the air and she was looking down at treetops and cornfields. Of course, she had done this getting-in-the-air thing twice, coming here from Cleveland, but with men who flew for a living. She hadn't paid much more attention to the process than she would with a taxi driver, yet seeing Jenny do it somehow made her proud. She'd have to think later about what the difference was.

Right now she was worried about Barnes. She still hadn't called him, nor checked with Western Union to see if he had sent money. But how could he object when she'd already filed stories about Roy and the jumper and Jenny and the stolen plane, and would soon have one about her own exploits with a flying circus?

Surely she would get some wonderful stories—*if* she could keep the problems with Jenny from exploding. It seemed quite clear that Jenny wasn't used to sharing the spotlight.

Laura had gotten in the plane this morning anticipating that Jenny would do some extra dips and turns to try to scare her or make her sick, but she wasn't worried; she had ridden the Loop the Loop at Coney Island several times when she was a kid. Besides, she was determined not to let this pampered prima donna get the better of her.

Jenny was signaling her from the front cockpit. With her back to Laura, she was making a large circle with her right arm extended straight out. Laura gripped her notebook, trying to figure out where she could stick it so as not to lose it. If the plane started rolling around, she didn't want her notes flying out. Nor herself! She had a pillow at her back to give her a tighter fit in the cockpit. Despite the animosity between them, Jenny had explained that she always stuffed something behind her when she flew. Laura pushed her pencil in her pocket, sat on her notebook, and grabbed some metal pieces that were part of the exposed interior of the fuselage. And her head started to spin.

Their assignment was to fly upside down a couple of times and do a few barrel rolls—whatever they were. The idea was that the women were to pass over the crowd to warm them up then they were to land and sit in the stands for the rest of the show. Today was special. They were part of a rodeo and other acts, different from the barnstorming plan Roy had set up for the next several days.

And suddenly, Laura *was* nearly upside down and could see what was probably the stands. Tiny dots of people waving and cheering. And just as quickly they were gone. The plane was spiraling. Perhaps rotating was a better word because they seemed to stay in the same place, not moving forward. The stands came in view again, then were gone. And around and around they went.

"A barrel roll, indeed. It's called what it is! I should have been smart enough to figure that on my own." Laura said this out loud, speaking to the passing wind, trying to get back some equilibrium, some sense of orientation, by hearing the sound of her own voice. We're rolling over and over, like a barrel. Once again, once again. How many of these things could they do? Laura had lost count at four. She wasn't worried about her breakfast, but she was getting very dizzy. When the dots of people came into view this time, it looked as though they were on their feet and screaming.

When had she heard screaming like that? Laura searched her memory. It was a dream. Yes, the dream she'd had in the hotel room in Cleveland. She was driving an airplane that

looked like a taxi. She also remembered that the dream began with Jenny not letting her get on the school grounds to
play with the other kids. Laura smiled to herself, thinking
how her mother always wanted to inject Freudian theory
into everything. "You exhibit a father fixation even when
you don't know who he is." Mother would love the fact that
Laura's subconscious had pegged Jenny a lot quicker than
her conscious mind had.

Laura was shocked at herself for having had such an
argument last night. She'd never had a fight with a woman
before, except with her mother. And for a time, those fights
were so constant and so debilitating that Laura had finally
vowed to just quit having them. She never won, she never
got anywhere with them, could never get information about
her father, so why not just stop? She found that stoic ac-
ceptance of her home life worked much better for her. She
discovered the word *détente* in one of her college political
science classes, and decided that was the perfect way to describe her situation. *Détente*. She liked the concept: call off
hostilities and get on with life. Throw your energies into
school, into work, finding your *own* place in the world. She
was ferocious at that, which made it so hard for her to comprehend Jenny's laziness toward everything.

So what, Laura wondered, had caused the big commotion with Jenny? Laura had never had a boyfriend to fight
over; she assumed that was the bottom line with Jenny. She
wanted the men all to herself. Somehow this felt familiar.
She'd always known her mother didn't like female competition from any quarter, but it had never occurred to Laura
that her mother would see her own daughter as a competitor. Maybe that was it—with both her mother and Jenny!
What a strange revelation to be having here in the middle of
the air. Perhaps something about Jenny, or even just being
in close contact with another woman, was putting her life

in some sort of context. Laura had never really had friends. Her mother was her window on the world. She'd always known her upbringing had been what a lot of people called bohemian; perhaps it was even stranger than she'd ever realized.

An image flashed in her mind of her mother's poet friend, the baroness, walking around the Village with pink postage stamps stuck to her face and a coal shuttle on her head to make a Dadaist statement. Evelyn made fun of the male poets who complained that Baroness Else von Freytag-Loringhoven was too sexually aggressive.

"That's the way women *should* be—getting what they want and doing what they want to do," Evelyn retorted. One of her mother's lovers, William Carlos Williams, admitted that he'd finally had Else arrested for pursuing him so vigorously, and another poet, Wallace Stevens, claimed he was afraid to go below 14th Street for fear of her rapaciousness.

But heavens, if all those proper girls at Barnard were as shallow as Jenny, Laura was just as happy not to know how to lead a conventional life. Being, as her mother called her, "a déclassé reporter," suited her just fine. Which made her think of Barnes. She'd better get in touch with him soon. And she had better start lining up ideas for more stories. Describing riding in a plane upside down was probably not good for more than one day's edition. Luckily, today's flying stunts were part of a Wild West show. They were performing now at someplace they said was famous, called the Hundred and One Ranch. John, Jenny's husband, was even coming up from Oklahoma City to see it. She was eager to meet him and see what kind of strange bird he was. And what about this Clem? Maybe there was a story in that. Why was a guy in coveralls driving such a fancy car and brought up in a mansion?

Laura blinked into the Sunday-morning sun; her dizziness seemed to have subsided. The plane was flying level, and Jenny was waving, or signaling something again. Actually, she had turned in her seat and was yelling and pointing, but Laura shook her head. She couldn't hear a thing over the sounds of the motor and the wind. Jenny finally hung her arm over the side and pointed down. Laura leaned out and looked. Wow, they had gotten much closer to the ground. It was a huge crowd. Huge, huge crowd. Roy had said last night that they expected ten thousand people at the ranch today, and it looked like he was right. He said a story in yesterday's paper claimed that a hundred and fifty Rotarians from New England were arriving by train as guests of the local Rotary Club.

The plane swooped down and Laura could see, indeed, that the stands were filled with people waving at them. She could also see animals, probably bulls and horses, in pens around the main arena. She suddenly realized what Jenny's gesturing had been about. She was indicating it was now okay for them to fly low, the arena was clear of animals— they were all in their pens. Clem had warned last night not to buzz over while the roundup part of the show was going on. A cowboy trying to tame a bull or rope a steer could be stomped or mauled if the animals were spooked by the noise of an airplane.

As they dipped over the arena, Laura could hear a strange echoing boom reverberating around them—the public address system. An announcer was supposed to be hyping the crowd with the news that there were two "little ladies" in the plane. Next, Roy would do what they all said were his difficult and celebrated outside loops. Then they were going to watch the headliner of the day: some crazy was going to jump from a plane and land on an animal. It was unclear to Laura just what was involved in this stunt, but she knew New York readers would love it! She'd already checked that news photographers would be here, and she felt certain she could arrange to get shots sent to the *Enterprise-Post*.

Jenny gave another wave from the front cockpit, and this time they did a few last gentle rolls. The grandstands and dusty cornfields and a cowboy with a lariat all revolved in seeming slow motion before Laura's eyes. What a strange kaleidoscopic view of the world. She felt she could see the earth's curve. The land looked parched, dry and sandy, with only spots here and there of green, but a lovely breeze skipped along Laura's face. The cowboy was twirling his rope in ever-widening circles above his head. Cheering came and went in waves—at times it would nearly drown out the sound of the engine. And then with a roll, as they turned upright to the sky, it would recede like Coney Island breakers going back to the sea.

The noise got louder and the engine stopped. Laura looked around, startled, realizing she had lost herself in the immense beyond, and saw that they were on the ground with cheering crowds surrounding the plane. It was difficult to come out of her dream state of clouds and sky and cornfields suffused with the smell of exhaust fumes. She was dazed as she looked out and smiled at the masses of friendly faces. Her eyes seemed to have gone frighteningly bad, everything dim and blurry. Perhaps she was dizzy again. Suddenly Roy was there to help her out of the cockpit and onto the wing. Clutching her reporter's notebook, she was still straining to see clearly when she realized it was her celluloid goggles that were making her view dim and scratchy. As soon as she yanked off her shades, she saw Jenny on the ground kissing an older man. Must be her husband, but why did Laura think she knew him? Of course! The man seated next to Jenny in the rumble seat at Roosevelt Field. That's a surprise, Laura thought. This guy really does travel around with Jenny when she's doing her stunts.

"Is that John?" Laura asked Roy, taking his arm and leaning in close to his ear.

"Yep, a great guy. We flew together in the Lafayette Escadrille."

"The what?" Laura held herself back from asking how to spell it.

"Group of Americans who went over before the US got into the war. We were attached to a French squadron taking pot shots at the Red Baron and his boys." He gave her a smug grin. "We made mincemeat out of the Huns."

Another possible story. Laura was stopped from asking more questions when Clem came loping up to tell them he had saved them seats to watch Roy's upcoming exhibition. She noticed with relief that the stands—built in an L shape along two sides of the arena—were covered, providing some protection from the relentless sun. The crowd was so large that hundreds of people were standing on the field all around the bleachers. A border along the top of the stands read, *Miller Bros. 101 Ranch*. In the excited shoving and pushing to get to their seats, Laura got a chance to say no more than hello to Jenny's husband, a handsome man with a firm handshake who looked to be in his early thirties, considerably older than Jenny. Clem seemed to go out of his way to make sure he seated himself next to Laura. Jenny was on her other side.

"Not bad," Jenny said, turning to Laura with a cocky smile. "You didn't lose your breakfast."

Laura could feel a slight blush. Why should she care about compliments from such a superficial girl?

Roy was going to do an exhibition of the outside loops for which he and Jimmy Doolittle were famous. As he climbed high in his Bellanca cruiser, Jenny, with a superior air that again reminded Laura of her mother, gave a running commentary of what he was doing and the risks involved in this maneuver.

"He'll go to about five thousand feet . . . Watch, now, see, he's leveled off. He'll drop from, wow, see, there he goes, he's pushing his stick to bring the nose up a bit so he can make an imaginary circle rather than just dropping straight down. Being on the outside of the loop makes it very dangerous, not at all like doing it inside—the force against him is trying to yank him out of his seat. It's so strong he could stall, or worse, black out."

The crowd was going wild as the plane accelerated toward the ground. People were on their feet screaming, men waving their cowboy hats and stomping their boots.

"See, he's at the bottom of the arc upside down," Jenny continued. "He's throttling up, climbing to repeat the circle."

Laura could barely catch her breath. What a brave, exciting man, she thought. Most of the adult males of her acquaintance were the bleating poet friends of her mother or the gruff Neanderthals in the newsroom.

The little silver plane with its enclosed cabin was moving back up through the bright blue, cloudless sky. Laura searched the horizon for the cornfields she'd spotted from the air a few minutes before, but saw no more than dust rising up from the rodeo grounds and encircling animal pens. The strong smell of manure hung in the flat, oppressive heat. Only the silver bird completing its top arc and again heading down provided an out-of-body escape for the hot, sticky, earthbound souls cheering its descent.

Laura heard Jenny's gasp and felt her stiffen long before the audience went deathly silent as they saw that the plane was falling, not following the set circular pattern.

"Oh, please God," she heard someone say over the silence. She looked at Jenny, hoping for some kind of reassurance. There was none. Her soft features were rigid, her mouth tightly set, her hand a fist held up to shade her eyes. The only sound was the bawling of cattle. Laura could see

cowboys astride the wooden pens, motionless in silhou-
ette against the heavy sun. Her heart was pounding in her
throat. She was afraid she was going to throw up. It's the
heat, she thought. How can I get home? I want my windowsill overlooking the quiet backyard gardens on Gay Street.

The plane was spiraling, turning in tight twists as it
plummeted toward a spot that looked to be just beyond
the cattle pens directly across from Laura on the west side
of the rodeo grounds. The wooden pen gates, which were
about twelve feet high, provided Laura's horizon. As the
nose of the silver plane came within what seemed inches of
their tops, it leveled off and soared upward.

The roar from the audience was deafening, and Laura
clambered down from the stands with no awareness of what
she was doing. She pushed through the exuberant crowd
and made her way to the place where she and Jenny had
landed a half hour before, and sure enough, Roy was just
taxiing to a spot out of the way of the third plane that was
to be used by the other stunters.

Jenny and Clem and John were not far behind.

As Roy climbed out on the wing and leaped to the
ground, Laura was jumping up and down with her arms
outstretched. Roy whisked her off her feet and whirled her
around. When he put her down, the other three were there
with congratulatory hugs.

"You blacked out, didn't you?" John said.

"Damned if I didn't," Roy replied. "The grayness came
on first, you know. Just couldn't see. Then, next thing I
know, I'm looking at those cow pens coming straight for
me."

"I was so frightened," Laura said, her face so close to
Roy's she could see the beads of moisture on his mustache,
the pulsing beat of his temples. His arm was still around her
shoulder. "I can't believe you made it."

Jenny leaned in and with a stern look pulled Laura to one side. "If you're going to be shining up to anybody," she said in a harsh voice, "it should be Clem. He's not married, and he's Osage and has lots of headrights."

Laura was too excited to take in this unintelligible bit of information, although the married part did register somewhere in the back of her mind. Her mother always said married men were safer, they didn't make too many unreasonable demands on your time.

CHAPTER TWENTY-TWO
THE BULL RIDER

THE FIVE OF THEM WERE BACK in the hot stands waiting for the next act. It wasn't lost on Laura that Jenny had seated herself in the middle, with John and Roy on the other side of her. Clem, next to Laura at the end of the row, was regaling her with stories of cowboys, cowgirls, the Wild West, the famous Hundred and One Ranch, and the major attraction of the day.

"This flying stunt will be nuts. It's hard enough to bull-dog a steer under the best of circumstances, but jumping from a rope ladder hanging from an airplane? Ridiculous."

"Bulldog?" said Laura.

"You jump from a horse onto a bull or a steer's back, and twist his horns till you subdue him. Make him fall to the ground. It was invented by a cowboy named Bill Pickett. Look," Clem pointed, "he's standing right over there, near that far cow pen."

Laura followed his hand and saw an elderly dark-skinned man wearing a broad-brimmed white hat.

"Yeah," said Clem. "The son of slaves, and part Cherokee. Guy's nearly sixty, but he's still the best."

As a cowboy in the arena jumped from his horse and tied together the legs of a calf he had just roped, Clem went on: "This place is a shadow of what it once was. Twenty-five years ago they ran one of the world's most famous touring shows out of this place. When I was five, I saw Geronimo shoot a buffalo from a moving motorcar right here. The show had a team of cowgirls, fifteen or twenty strong, who could shoot, ride, and rope with the best of 'em. Will Rogers perfected a lot of his lariat tricks here."

His last words were nearly drowned out by the booming announcement of the upcoming event: "*Ladies and gentlemen, the next death-defying event will be Mr. Ted 'Suicide' Elder, who will ride astride two galloping horses as he jumps them over an open automobile filled with people.*" The daredevil, dressed in a fringed, one-piece yellow suit and a black cowboy hat, was standing erect with a booted foot planted in a strange-looking saddle on the back of each of the horses. They were yoked together by a large piece of wood. He held the reins in both hands, the same way one would drive a team.

"You saw Geronimo?" Laura exclaimed. "Honestly? That's really the Wild West."

Clem laughed. "The Wild West was gone long ago. These roundup shows have been a parody since the turn of the century."

"People in New York still think it's wild out here," Laura said. "Look! He's in the air, over the car." A hoof of one of Suicide's jumping horses pinged on the hood of the auto it was leaping over. The horses and their rider landed safely on the other side, but the several people in the car had taken the precaution of ducking. "Wow, that was close."

"The Wild West," Clem said with a wry grin. "Yeah, when I was at Harvard, a lot of people seemed to think I lived in a teepee."

"Harvard? That was a long way from home."

"I had the sense to come back for law school. People in these parts are not about to hire an attorney who doesn't know the terrain."

The announcer came on again, this time even more booming. "*And now, ladies and gentlemen, the death-defying stunt of the day: Tex MacPhearson will attempt to bulldog a steer while descending a rope ladder from the wings of an airplane.*"

"The only thing missing is the drum roll," Laura quipped.

Jenny glared. "This isn't exactly easy. Shush."

Damn her, Laura thought, a tight frown clearly giving away what she was thinking. Why does she have to be so superior and prissy?

Clem nudged her with his elbow and gave her a conspiratorial wink. Strange man, Laura thought, East Coast education and sitting here in twill pants and blue work shirt. He made the rogues in the newsroom look like sartorial wonders. At least he wasn't wearing his coveralls today. His mother's house was elegant, if overstuffed. Big mahogany furniture, crystal chandeliers, large gold-framed oils, heavy silk drapes—doilies and antimacassars everywhere. Jenny had said there was even a chapel for circuit-riding priests. What a mystery this all was. Rich Catholic Indians? She'd grown up thinking they all wore head feathers, carried tomahawks, and danced with a medicine man.

Clem broke into her thoughts: "This fella will do anything for attention. He recently tried to pull an automobile across a dance floor with his teeth."

"A flagpole-sitter type, huh?" Laura said. "And the cameramen are coming out in force. I noticed earlier there were photogs spread around the field. But look, several guys with motion picture equipment are setting up."

A small plane with an enclosed cabin flew low and slow over the field, dipping its wings left and right in greeting.

"How does a pilot make his wings dip like that?" Laura asked Jenny.

"Easy," she replied. "Two pedals on the floor, like a

car. Left rudder pedal dips the plane that way. Right to the right."

The plane banked and turned, and came back; this time the audience gasped, noticing a man waving from one of the wings. At this point, an angry bull came roaring out of a pen and began ranging around the enclosed arena.

"The plane is going to have to land once that guy has gotten to the end of the rope ladder," Jenny said. "The pilot will have to get his air speed so slow to drop Tex, he won't be able to pull up to gain altitude."

"How slow?" Laura noticed for the first time that what she'd thought was the open end of the arena to her left had, in fact, a sturdy-looking wooden fence. Just high enough to pen in a steer trying to escape, she realized, but still tall enough that it could catch a wheel of a plane trying to land.

"At about forty-five miles an hour he'll stall and drop like a rock."

A look of disbelief crossed Laura's face. "That's still awfully fast for jumping, even to the ground, isn't it?"

Clem chuckled. "You got that right, little lady. This stunt couldn't carry a bucket to the well."

"Why's he doing it? I don't get it." Laura looked from one to the other, both of whom shrugged.

The plane passed overhead once more, this time with a rope dangling from the cabin, with the man still on the wing close to the fuselage.

The announcer, again booming about death-defying acts, was drowned out by the crowd roaring its approval while the bull snorted and pawed at the ground. Two cowboys on horses were trying to maneuver the animal to a round circle branded in the arena dirt.

As the plane circled back around, the daredevil was clearly visible, descending the rungs of the rope ladder, which was swaying in the sharp drafts created by the movement of the plane. The bull was pawing the ground, throwing its head around as though trying to avoid a buzzing bee. Neither of the cowboys could control their horses, which were whinnying and rearing and backing away from the bull.

"That bull's never going to let anyone on him," Clem said. "The noise of the plane is enraging him and terrifying the horses."

A hot, dry breeze suddenly kicked up and swung the stunter, MacPhearson, parallel over the upraised horns of the bull, as the plane wobbled, then headed for the fence. MacPhearson was trying to swing his legs down toward the bull, but the wind and the plane were dragging him sideways. Laura could see the man clearly, he and the plane were so close to the ground. The ubiquitous high boots, the bunched-up pants, cloth helmet, goggles, and huge leather gauntlets that reached halfway up his arms. All of it topped off by a comic red polka-dot bowtie. He seemed tiny, swaying as he was. But to Laura's surprise he didn't look frightened. He seemed simply to be frowning in intense concentration as he repeatedly tried to swing his legs toward the ground. Laura was frightened for him. Her breathing was coming in gasps, and she was definitely fast reaching the conclusion that this flying stuff was dangerous business.

"The pilot can't pull up," Jenny said, "no way. MacPhearson's going to be smashed into the fence."

The crowd went deathly quiet.

"Oh lordy," Jenny gasped, "I think the plane's going to clear but . . ."

MacPhearson suddenly made a wild swing with his legs like a broad jumper clearing a hurdle and sailed over the fence and let go of the ladder. The plane disappeared from sight behind the fence, followed by the sound of cloth ripping.

"Must of made some kind of soft landing," Jenny said,

jumping up from her seat. "That's the quietest crash I ever heard. Both of 'em probably fine."

People were rushing from the stands, filling up the arena field, as cowboys and their horses tried to wrangle the steer back to a pen. Then with a flying leap, Bill Pickett wrestled the runaway animal to the ground; spectators stumbling and dodging to avoid running over man and bull.

Laura, who was trying to take in the scene as she scribbled notes on the run, hesitated for an instant wondering if she should get a quote from Pickett, but decided the plane crash was more important. Someone could be dead!

She followed Jenny at a dead run now, Clem loping along beside her as hundreds of people thundered past. After Laura rounded the cow pens, she stopped in her tracks. The little plane was tipped sideways among a field of huge green leaves, resting on a wing and its tail. The air was electric with flashing cameras.

"A sweet potato patch!" Clem exclaimed. "I'll be durned."

CHAPTER TWENTY-THREE
NEWS FROM HOME

LAURA PLUNGED INTO THE FIELD OF GREEN leaves and immediately sank up to her knees. As she tried to take a step forward, her feet were caught in a tangled mass of vines and she nearly lost her balance.

Clem grabbed her and pulled her back. "Tubers about to be picked, not much good for walking. You're liable not to ever get anywhere."

Laura turned to Jenny, who had stopped short of the patch. "What's that dangling from the plane?"

"That's the pilot. He's hanging from his seat belt," Jenny said with a nervous giggle. "Looks like he's all right, though. And there's MacPhearson over there, trying to make his way through the tangle of potatoes. No damage. The plane looks pretty much okay. Made a soft landing, and just sort of tipped over."

"Good grief," Laura said. "Everyone seems to crash, or nearly crash, and pay no attention. I think I'm going to stay out of airplanes from now on."

"You can't do that," Jenny replied with a stern look. "You agreed to fly with us for several days."

"That's before I realized how risky it is. This day has certainly opened my eyes." Laura looked down at her dusty jodhpurs and limp, wrinkled shirt.

"That's pretty dumb," Jenny said. "What did you think it was?"

"Sort of like taxis, I guess. You get in for a ride and you don't expect *them* to crash every few minutes."

"You *cannot* quit now. I gave up a dinner dance at the country club to do this."

"Where the dickens have you been?" someone shouted from behind her. Laura whirled around to see Cheesy, up to his knees in potato plants, his camera dangling from his left hand. "I've been looking for you everywhere. Only two hotels in town and you not in either of 'em. Barnes is worse than a hornet."

"Oh!" Laura's hand flew to her mouth as she stared at Cheesy. She was happy to see him, of course. She had so wanted him to come. Was that only yesterday? But now, she couldn't seem to form her thoughts. She was watching Roy high-step through the thick growth on his way to help the stranded pilot. He had a blue checked bandanna at his throat instead of the red he was wearing yesterday.

"Fer jeez sake, say something. It's me." Cheesy snapped his fingers in front of Laura's eyes to get her attention. "I can tell it's you, even in dose clothes."

"Oh, Cheesy, I'm so glad you're here." She grabbed his free hand and gave it a squeeze, her words coming out in a rush. "Is Barnes really angry with me? You can't imagine what it's like here. We need pictures."

Cheesy patted his camera. "I got plenty. Just gotta get to a post office to mail 'em. And you better call Barnes. *Now!*"

"You need a shot of that," she said, pointing. "The man at the plane helping to rescue the pilot is Roy Wiggens. He's an important flier."

"Who? The flier or the rescue guy?" Cheesy asked. "I sure got one of the pilot hanging upside down by his seat belt. It's a winner. Front page, I'll lay odds."

"Cheese, isn't this stuff unbelievable? I've been riding

around in these things without a worry. I guess I thought about them as sort of taxicabs."

"You can get hurt in a hack," Cheesy responded.

"Yeah, well, you know, you don't have horrible examples right in front of your eyes like this."

"All I know is ya better call Barnes."

"Problems?" Clem asked, interrupting. "I'll be glad to take you to a phone."

"That would be swell," Laura said. "This is Cheesy, my photographer. Talk to him while I go interview the guy who fell off the rope ladder."

C HAPTER TWENTY-FOUR
THE MOTHER LODE

"DON'T WORRY ABOUT THE CHARGES," Laura said, as she and Clem walked into the big house. "I'll reverse them."

Clem laughed. "That won't be necessary, my mother won't notice the difference. She's a very wealthy woman."

"No matter, it isn't right for her to pay for my work call."

"You seem very nervous about talking to your boss." Clem's voice was easy and soothing. "Perhaps it would be better not to call collect."

He placed the call for her. "Hello, Central," he said, "I want a connection to New York."

"Hey, boss." Laura's voice was shaky, tentative.

Barnes's explosion could be heard around the room. "So, it's the dead come back to life! We were preparing your obit!"

"I filed you a great story last night with the pilot's version of the death jump." Laura's snappiness had returned. "None of the wires had that, I betcha. And no one had Jenny's version of the stolen plane. Now we got a stunt guy trying to jump on a steer. Cheese has pictures of that."

"Gotta hand it to you, kid. You landed a couple of originals. But I'm not used to sending girls out to handle cowboys and Indians. And when a reporter doesn't pick up his advances, it's time to worry. I checked with Western Union, they said you were a no-show. Figured you for dead."

"I'm glad you thought I was worth missing."

"Don't go sentimental, kid. There's lots a money riding on this trip. And Cheesy reports there's more good stuff coming up."

"Naw, I'm not sure it's worth it anymore. We've got the crash in the potato patch for you." Laura tried to make her voice self-assured, a little brass for a sharp edge. "This aerobatic stuff is dangerous. I think I'll just come on home."

Another explosion resounded through the room. "What are you, nuts? Of course it's dangerous. Makes it exciting. No story, if it wasn't dangerous. Go get your advance and get back to work." *Bang.* The line went dead. Laura stood there looking at the empty receiver. Clem was shifting uneasily from one foot to the other, clearing his throat. He had moved into a far corner of the big room, clearly having heard her city editor. Laura searched for something to say.

"So, are you really an Indian?" She was embarrassed the moment she blurted the question. She wasn't sure, but perhaps this was a very personal matter. She'd never thought of Indians being mixed with the rest of society. In her schoolbooks, the land had been theirs and the government had kept moving them around to make room for white farmers. But she'd thought the Indians all stuck together, stayed on reservations, and—as Clem had said his classmates at Harvard imagined—lived in teepees. She felt embarrassed not to know more.

Clem smiled. "Sure am. Lots of folks in these parts are. Probably lots in New York are too, slipping past you." He peered more closely at her. "In fact, you could be part Indian with those high cheekbones. Most here in Ponca City are Cherokee. I'm from the next county, Osage. Discovered a huge pool of oil there. Made us all rich."

"But your name is Donohue."

"Yep. Lots of smart Irishmen came in and married rich Indian women. My grandmother was Osage, she married an Irishman. So did my mother. French explorers were marrying Indian women and trading furs with the Osage way before the Irish arrived. The Jesuits brought in religion and were well established in St. Louis by the late 1700s."

St. Louis again. Barnes. Plane crashes. Clem's gentle, lopsided grin filled the void of Laura's silence. She couldn't really focus on what he was saying. A huge grandfather clock bonged the hour in the hush of the heavily carpeted rooms. Laura noticed that in this bookcase-lined study, with its massive mahogany desk, there seemed to be several places where one Oriental carpet was lying on top of another. She counted the bongs, one . . . two . . . three . . . four. She had to make a decision about flying soon; she was supposed to meet Roy and Jenny at four thirty to go over their stunts for tomorrow.

"My parents moved here, away from Pawhuska, a few miles over," Clem said, "because things were getting a little ugly there. People being killed—dying mysteriously—over headrights. That's what they call the Osage oil allotments."

"Oh." It was all Laura could think to say. Her own head was crammed with scrambled thoughts. Clem had mentioned Jesuits in St. Louis. What did that mean? And what were the mystery killings? She should follow up on all this, but she felt a strange inertia. St. Louis had something to do with her mother, yet it was easier to let that worry go than try to figure it out. She knew who her grandfather was, and that was enough. There was just too much happening at once—Barnes now insisting she must stick with the air show. "What luck, firsthand accounts of those crazy stunts," he'd said, before she'd told him she was scared and didn't want to do it. Now that she'd seen the dangers, Laura never wanted to get in an airplane again. Jenny was mad at her for saying she wanted to back out, reminding Laura that she'd promised to fly in Roy's barnstorming act until he could find some kind of replacement. He would probably be furious. Strangely enough, Roy was the one Laura most wanted to please. Cheesy would probably be upset with her too. He was ecstatic with the pictures of that daredevil's crash. When they had dropped him off to mail his pictures, he'd said he couldn't wait to get to the next air show. Lucky me—Laura nearly got the shakes just thinking about it—I'll probably be his next picture of someone hanging upside down from a cockpit.

"I don't mean to be prying," Clem's soft drawl moved in slow waves across the room, "but you look lost. Maybe it would help to talk about it. These pilots don't seem to give any of this a thought. They don't worry about much."

"I thought Roy was going to be killed." Laura's words exploded out of her as two bright red spots appeared on her cheeks. "How can everyone take it so calmly?" She lowered her voice in the hushed room, but it was still husky with emotion. "I think he should stop doing these foolish tricks."

Clem gave her a slow, thoughtful look. "You don't want to be worrying too much about Roy, ma'am." He shook his head slightly. His voice was soft but firm. "Wouldn't do you any good."

The red spots in Laura's cheeks deepened. "I . . . ah, just mean, it seems so dangerous."

"He's a daredevil through and through. My older brother went to college with him—him and John. Both of 'em crazy to fly since they were boys."

"Was that St. Louis?"

"Yes, why do you ask?"

Laura frowned. "Just curious."

"Roy can be fierce, even mean sometimes," Clem continued. "You don't want to get crossways of him. His life is flying, and he thinks Jenny's should be too."

"Why pick Jenny? I don't quite get that part."

"Not sure, ma'am." Clem sat down in a huge leather armchair and waved Laura to a gilt brocade seat beside him. "Guess he's frustrated. Went out of his way to take her on as a student, did it as a favor to John. He claims she's turned out to be the best pupil he's ever had, fearless. Doesn't seem to worry about much of anything. But she won't take herself seriously enough to compete."

"I'm the opposite." Laura felt her throat tighten, her voice coming out high-pitched, nearly a screech. "I've always been serious." She could feel the scrambled thoughts taking over, rushing unformed out of her mouth. "I don't think about competing, I just *do* what's there." She stopped, looked at Clem without appearing to see him, shook her head slightly as though trying to recall where she was. Then, with a deep breath, she spoke more slowly, frowning, picking her way through unexplored territory. "I was never scared before, not of anything that I can remember." She had long ago learned to guard against asking herself the endless emotional/philosophical questions that never seemed to take her mother and her friends anywhere but in a circle. Abstractions—the meaning of life, riddles of time and space, of art and love. Can psychiatry redefine war? Or better yet, can poetry eliminate it? All things that could distract Laura from the here and now. She had kept herself too busy to stop and ponder. With no one to lean on for guidance or answers, she had hurtled forward with no time for questions.

"I've essentially been on my own since I was very little. Perhaps I had to struggle, but I wasn't conscious of it." She paused, looked again at Clem, more focused on him now, moved her eyes around his mother's library. Her words took on speed. "I guess I just put one foot in front of the other and tried to plow ahead. Now all of a sudden, things feel like they're changing. But I don't quite know what it means. Makes for a good reporter, I guess—just plow ahead. I'll lose my job if I don't fly with Jenny. But it's all been in such a headlong rush, I feel like I need to take a breather. Think about things for once."

"Seems like you need to sort a lot of things out." Clem's voice was quiet, reassuring. It flashed through Laura's head that these men in the West spoke this way out of habit of calming wild horses or angry bulls. No rat-a-tat-tat like New York. "How important is this job to you?"

Laura looked at Clem, startled. "Important? That's silly. I have no other choice. Do you have any idea how hard it was to get that job?" She took a deep breath, closed her eyes, squared her shoulders, and then smiled at Clem.

"We've got to get going," she said with a breathless urgency that suggested she had no memory of their previous conversation. "We've got to pick up Cheesy before we see Roy and Jenny. I'm supposed to meet them at four thirty to practice stunts."

CHAPTER TWENTY-FIVE
THE LOVEBIRDS

"WHAT A MESS." JENNY WAS LOOKING at the field littered with the debris of the afternoon's rodeo and aerobatic events, but she was thinking of Roy's insistence on their upcoming trip to Pawhuska. The three of them had just driven up in John's yellow Duesenberg with its huge wire wheels and spare whitewall attached to the side of its elongated radiator. Roy's closed-cabined Bellanca was there, parked alongside Jenny's open two-seater. He had already paid some locals to find fuel and gas up the two planes.

The trio stepped out of the car into Baby Ruth and Milky Way candy wrappers, Nehi soda bottles of every colorful flavor, and crumpled paper cups reeking of bathtub gin and bootleg beer. Shreds of dried grass competed with weeds in the rutted field.

Jenny could envision that the next few days wouldn't be much fun. Laura was sure to cause trouble one way or the other. Despite trying to insinuate herself into all their lives, she was probably going to back out of the air shows now that Jenny had made the commitment. Jenny would rather be going back home with John. She had meant it when she complained about missing an upcoming country club dance. She smiled to herself. John wouldn't mind, though, he hated what he called *those stuffed-shirt, dowager affairs*. No matter how it unfolded, she suspected this situation was going to get messy. Laura didn't seem to have any kind of proper moral compass and was ogling Roy, while poor Clem seemed to be smitten with her.

"Johnny boy, why don't you come fly along with me?" Roy cut into her thoughts. "The girls have their own plane. You might as well be taking part in this fine adventure."

"Thanks, but no thanks." John already looked dressed for the office in his vested, pale linen suit of a soft gray that almost matched the streaks at his temples. "I really need to be getting back to work." Unlike most men of the day, he chose to wear a wedding ring, a simple gold band on his left hand. Jenny and Roy were in their flying togs, he in tall leather boots.

"Breaking up the old gang to play with your darned cars." Roy wrinkled his nose in feigned disgust. "I can't imagine why you waste your time."

"Makes me a living. And we're developing some really exciting new things: front-wheel drive, retractable headlamps."

"Exactly. Stuck on the ground." Roy touched his trademark checkered flying scarf, this one a bright blue. "I'll never understand how you could give up the air."

"You know I haven't quit. That's bunk."

"He just finds other things more interesting." Jenny's voice had a slight edge. "Designing a car without running boards. Can you imagine the thrill?"

"Somebody's got to pay for your flying lessons," John replied with a grin.

"This isn't a joke." Roy's voice was unexpectedly stern. "She's got a real talent, John. You ought to encourage her more. Your boss at Cord auto owns a big interest in Stinson Aircraft. You should get Stinson to sponsor her. Lots of endorsement money could come her way."

"What's gotten into you? I don't discourage her." John narrowed his eyes at Roy.

"Don't pay any attention to him, darling." Jenny gave a dismissive wave of her hand. "He's just miffed because I'm not overly eager to learn outside loops."

John looked from one to the other in bewilderment. "What are you two talking about? My girl here always does as she pleases." He turned to Jenny, warmth in his ever-so-slightly solicitous tone. "Now, didn't you take off on your own and go flying up to Cleveland to see the races? I warned you it would be long hard days in your little bi-plane, having to stop every few miles for gas."

"And you were absolutely right," Jenny replied, fairly cooing at her husband. "It was grueling. I was certainly glad I hadn't been foolish enough to enter that derby, going all the way from San Diego to Cleveland. Oklahoma City was far enough."

"That's nonsense, Jenny, and you know it." Roy's rising anger startled her. It was rare for the devil-may-care bon vivant to step out of character. A sudden gust of Oklahoma wind swept across the flat plain of the airfield, kicking up dust and debris, but Roy met the competing roar, lifting his voice to a shout. "With proper sponsorship and the right mechanics, racing's a very different ball game from limping along on your own, refueling in one little town after another."

"*You* don't need a sponsor," Jenny shot back. "*You* just buzz around as you please."

"Not the same thing. I've already built my reputation and skills." Roy's angry tone dissipated; he was back to his evangelical stance for all things touching aviation. "I've been flying for twenty years, from the time when planes weren't much more than bicycles with flippers instead of handle-bars. Now we have these fantastic fast planes, commercial airlines that have established routes. Manufacturers hiring stunters to show off their new wares. All those women in the derby had sponsors and teams of backup people."

"Oh my." Jenny gave them both an innocent smile. "I didn't mean to touch a nerve. Let's get on with tomorrow's agenda and not just stand around talking."

"Jenny, babe, what's going on here?" John asked. "When we were in New York, you turned down Mark Snyder's offer for a sponsorship from Curtiss. You said you didn't want it."

"Oh lordy, sweetheart, you're right." She gave her tinkly laugh, but this time it had a distinctly nervous edge. "I just didn't tell Roy, that's all. He seems to want me to end up being just like that pushy reporter."

John responded with a quizzical frown.

"Well, I'll be damned." Roy turned on his heel, his shiny leather boots squeaking with the abruptness of the move. "I'm heading over to check out the plane," he yelled over his shoulder, moving away from the Deusenberg and toward his Bellanca.

As he strode off, Jenny and John watched Clem's Pierce-Arrow stirring up a cloud of dust as it headed their way.

CHAPTER TWENTY-SIX
A LION IN WAITING

JENNY LOOKED ON IN SURPRISE as Roy gushed over Laura, who along with Cheesy and Clem had just filed out of the Pierce-Arrow into the dusty field blowing with debris.

"Now don't you have a wonderful spirit," Roy said, standing next to his plane and bestowing a magnificent smile on the reporter. "Real spunk. You said you were frightened, but here you are." He waved his arm in the broad gesture of the cavalier that he had first exhibited when he rescued Laura and Jenny the night before at the Ponca City airport.

Cheesy, lugging his camera equipment, did a double take. "Her? Never saw her scared of anything."

Laura reddened. "We got the local news on the way over. It has the story I wrote in Atchison that was picked up off the wires."

Roy took the paper. "That's terrific, kid. Look at that," he said, hitting the newspaper with his hand. "You've got to admire a woman with that kind of spirit. Look at that. The whole story right there. Even spelled my name right. You're a real wonder, my girl." He put his arm around her shoulders and gave her a hug. "So," he said in a low voice, patting Laura on the shoulder, "I want to have a little talk with you about your fears." He pointedly turned away from the others.

As Laura blushed even deeper, Jenny lifted her brows

and rolled her eyes at John, who put a hand up to his face to hide his answering grin. Jenny knew her husband could see the play Roy was making for Laura, his smile that was almost a smirk told her that. But he didn't seem to have a glimmer about the way her instructor was trying to shame Jenny into competetive flying by praising the reporter's *spunk*.

"But first the big news," Roy continued. "Roscoe Turner is going to join us for a day, as soon as the show's over in Cleveland. And he'll have Gilmore, his lion. That will really bring out the crowds. Turner is one heck of a pilot. He'll put on a real show." Roy still had his arm across Laura's shoulder.

"Oh lordy," Jenny said, "he's one of those flamboyant fliers who cause us all to be viewed like circus clowns." The situation, she feared, was getting messier by the minute.

"Come on, babe, Roscoe is great fun," John said. "I was planning to go back to Oklahoma City today and leave you fellas to sort out your details, but I've got to hang around to see *him*. The crazy coot's an old friend."

Jenny immediately perked up, and gave her husband a dazzling smile. With John around, things were always fine, and he would diffuse tension if Laura's behavior got out of hand. He gave her a wink. Amazing how he could always read her mood.

John chuckled, turning to Roy. "I read recently Roscoe was made an honorary colonel by the governor of Nevada. Whatever the devil that means."

"Hell of a guy. Up in Cleveland for the races," Roy replied. "Flying a Vega. As fast as those things are and as good as he is, he could win the Thompson Trophy."

"Good gravy," said Jenny, slapping her forehead. "With all that's going on I forgot about the derby. Amelia's flying a Lockheed Vega too."

The tricky-to-handle Vega was a sleek single-wing plane that sat up high off the ground and was built for speed with laminated sheets of plywood stretched and glued over the wooden ribs of the fuselage. Vegas had won every speed award in the 1928 National Air Races in Los Angeles. Earlier this year, Lockheed had added Pratt & Whitney engines with 450 horsepower that enabled the Vega to hit speeds up to 165 miles per hour.

"We'll know tomorrow who wins," Roy said with a pointed look at Jenny. "That's when the women are due in. Too bad you didn't give it a shot, you could have won. Amelia's got the fastest plane, but she's not competent enough to handle it."

Jenny felt her jaw stiffen, and John noticed.

"I see," he said, almost to himself, as he moved over to put his hand on her arm. He lifted his voice and took on a jovial tone. "Last I heard of Roscoe, he was working as a stunt pilot for Howard Hughes, and flying women who wanted to get a divorce back and forth from Los Angeles to Reno."

"That's how he got the *colonel* title," Roy said.

"Hmm," said John, giving Roy a hard look. "An honorary title for stunting around."

Roy whirled, startled. "What's that supposed to mean?"

Jenny tensed. She had feared this was going to be a rocky trip, but it was taking a turn she hadn't expected. John and Roy had known each for so long that a shift in tone or of an eyebrow could put either on alert that something was up with the other.

"Lay off goading Jenny about how or when she flies," John replied. "She can do what she wants, just as you can. You're running around from town to town doing little air circuses? Come on."

"You got a problem with that?" Roy didn't lift his fists,

but he might as well have. His legs were planted, rigid, his stance that of a man ready to square off, basically to hide the fact that he was cut to the quick. He had been hit where it counted most and, Jenny knew too well, by the person whose opinion he most cherished.

"You know damned well what I'm talking about." John's voice lost its sarcastic edge, took on almost a soothing, sympathetic tone. "Others move on from the war and grow up. Your buddy Wiley Post has managed to hold down real jobs—test pilot for Lockheed, flying for rich oil men."

"Wiley and the war?" Roy adopted the sarcasm. "He spent it as a mechanic at Fort Sill."

"That's enough, you two. Now just stop it," Jenny scolded.

John's voice got back its edge. "If he's going to badger you about doing something serious, he should take his own advice. Wiley is talking about trying a trip around the world. Not a continual loop from Atchison to Ponca City to Pawhuska and back."

"Back off," Roy was nearly yelling at this point, "you know damned well what those jobs for rich oil men can entail."

John shrugged, but didn't respond.

"What? What does it entail?" Laura's question broke the spell. She, Cheesy, and Clem had stood silently by, nearly holding their breath, watching the argument unfold between the two old friends.

John nodded his head and pursed his lips in what amounted to a shrug. "Just lay off Jenny. Okay?"

Roy reddened. "Fine. You ease off, and let's get back to the business at hand." He turned to Laura with a wide grin, as though nothing unusual had just transpired. "Now back to you, my dear. Just a little lesson in aerodynamics. There is no need to fear flying. Of course there are occasional mishaps. But whenever we need to make a forced landing, it's no problem. The planes are light and can just glide to the ground if we have engine problems. It's what we call a dead-stick landing, and every licensed pilot knows how to do them."

"But why—"

"Time for more questions later, we have to get a move on." Roy turned to address the others. "So who's driving and who's flying to the next stop? I'll take Laura with me. I want to give her a couple of quick lessons, so she'll see how easy and safe this all is."

"I think I'll just bow out," Clem said, looking at Laura. "I've got work to do tomorrow."

"Hey," said Cheesy, "hate to impose, but I was hoping you could give me a ride. I had a heck of a time getting down here from Cleveland. The trains don't exactly go from here to there."

Clem looked around at the expectent faces. "John, I assume you're going to leave your car here and fly with Jenny. Cheese, I guess we're the odd men out." He circled the toe of his cowboy boot in the dirt, looked hard a Roy, then said, "Okay, let's do it. Pawhuska's about forty miles. There's a good hotel on Main Street, the Duncan. It's a quick walk from that grass patch Roy uses." He waved Cheesy toward the passenger seat then yelled over to Jenny. "The field's easy to spot from the air 'cause it's right behind the courthouse, which is on a big hill. See you at the hotel."

CHAPTER TWENTY-SEVEN
THE DUNCAN

JENNY DUMPED HER SMALL TRAVELING satchel at the front desk and said, "Hi, we're going to need several rooms. My husband's outside looking for some friends."

"You're traveling with a party, ma'am?" asked the clerk, a stiff young man in a dark three-piece suit and round owl glasses.

"Yes," John said, walking up, "there are four, no, wait . . ."

"Five," said Jenny, "We need five rooms. Clem, Cheesy, Laura, Roy, and us." She held up her right hand, rolling off each finger. "That's it, five."

"Perhaps your party has already checked in, ma'am," the clerk replied. "A couple fellas are over there in the dining room eating. The lady and gentleman haven't come downstairs yet."

Jenny looked at John, a question on her face. *The lady and gentleman haven't come downstairs yet? What in heaven's name could that mean?*

John laughed. "You've got a slow plane, my dear. And with your stunt exhibition for my benefit, we took quite a bit longer."

"I love showing off for you," she said with a blush. "I love it even more when you tell me what a superior pilot I am."

He put his arm around her shoulder and brushed her

forehead with a kiss. "Not only the best, but my favorite." He then bent down to whisper in her ear, give it a nibble. "And you know what else I told you. Roy's right. You probably should be stretching yourself more. But it's totally up to you."

The clerk cleared his throat, slight color moving up his neck at the display of affection. "You'd like to register, sir?" He shoved a pen and white card across the marble desktop toward John, who grinned and reached for the pen.

"Let's see who's in the dining room," Jenny said. "You'll have the bellhop take up our luggage?"

She looked around the lobby—tiled floor, a few comfortable leather chairs, a writing desk. Fairly spare and plain. Hardly Oklahoma City's Skirvin, she decided, with its crystal chandeliers and paneled walls with gold-leaf busts of Bacchus surveying the scene from on high. Velvet carpeting in the bedrooms. Jenny's cheeks turned rosy remembering her honeymoon there. The hotel had been made even grander shortly before her wedding reception last year when colored glass and artwork had been added, inspired by the 1925 Paris exhibit.

Jenny smiled thinking about the elaborate party her parents had finally put on, but only after they'd given up trying to dissuade her from marrying John.

Her mother was horrified, her lavaliere heaving, her eyes wide behind the pince-nez. "You're only a child. You haven't even finished high school."

Her father's objections were much more opaque, but had a sinister tone. "A man who has had John's experiences is not a suitable husband for a young woman such as yourself. The Army. France. He's seen the world and, I suspect, has the habits to prove it."

"Papa, whatever does that mean?" Jenny had asked, trying to tease her father out of his dour mood.

"He is much older than you, my dear."

"We all know that," Jenny had replied. "So what of it? That doesn't mean anything."

"I do believe he drinks. More than the occasional cocktail. And his friends all seem to be war buddies. Fliers. Not a very stable group." Her banker father had adjusted the gold collar pin at his throat. His face couldn't have been more stern if he were turning down a client for a loan.

Jenny crossed the lobby of the Duncan and looked into the dining room. It seemed passable. Linen on the tables, at least. A bustle of waiters and six or so groups of diners. She spotted Cheesy and Clem in a far corner with tall water glasses in front of them, accompanied by a bowl of ice and a bottle of soda.

"We found a way to amuse ourselves while waiting." Clem's lopsided smile was warm. "You fly a pretty slow old bucket, my girl. Laura and Roy haven't come down yet."

"How long have they been up there?" Jenny asked sharply.

"A while," Clem said, his smile evaporating. "Have a seat. Want a glass of ginger ale?"

"Yes," Jenny said with a laugh. "*Just* ginger ale, thank you."

"Not me," said John, joining the group. "I trust you've got something a bit stronger."

A bit stronger were the bywords of the day. With Prohibition in full swing, it was the rare man who traveled without a flask. Clem and John were both equipped. It was unclear just what gear Cheesy carried in his camera bag. But with his rumpled clothes, disheveled hair, and ever-present tail of a cigar, he didn't appear to have the price of a drink, much less one carried by pocket in a sterling-silver container.

Jenny momentarily studied the disreputable-looking lout lounging there, elbows on the white linen cloth, his shoes overrun at the heels, and once again wondered at the strange beings that populated journalism. She smiled her best Miss-Grace-Finishing-School smile and extended her hand. "I'm Jenny Flynn, we don't seem to have been properly introduced."

"Pleased," Cheesy said, nodding his head slightly in acknowledgment, and that was it.

Jenny was sipping her soft drink when she spotted Roy, appearing quite jaunty, enter the dining room. Laura, hesitant and looking slightly flustered, was trailing behind.

"Not good," Jenny mumbled under her breath to John.

Her husband's dismissive shake of the head said, *Don't be silly.*

"So what'll we do?" Roy's question was jovial. "A quick drink, then move on?"

"I'm hungry," Jenny said.

"Me too," agreed Cheesy.

"Then let's go eat," Roy said. "How about that fantastic barbeque joint Clem mentioned? An old Negro's place with a pit in the yard and some tables under the trees."

"Yep, and beer in his wife's kitchen ice box," Clem said. "Best eats in Oklahoma."

Chapter Twenty-Eight

MOONSHINE

JENNY AND HER TRAVELING COMPANIONS settled in at a picnic table shaded by oak trees, with several children playing and yapping dogs running around the yard. The sun had set, but the wide sky was still bright with light. Sweet-smelling smoke mingling with the scent of the sizzling meat curled up from the pit and wafted over the table.

The beer was in frosty pitchers in the center. The heavyset, grizzled owner named Jim was passing around dripping barbeque sandwiches wrapped in pieces of waxed paper. Jenny had chosen spare ribs, which came on a cracked china plate. She knew from experience how difficult it was to manage such sandwiches without sticky sauce dribbling down her chin. Although she'd never been here before, it was a familiar type. There were several such places dotting the little towns on the outskirts of Oklahoma City. Small enterprises in meager homes. After meeting John, visiting these culinary wonders was one of her many new experiences.

"I'd like a Nehi soda, Jim, if you don't mind," Jenny said.

But he cajoled her instead into taking a mug, saying the soft drinks were hot because they didn't take precedence when ice got short. "It's sweltering, miss, and we all needs our beer, now don't we?"

Jim's weathered shingled shack appeared to be two

rooms. Jenny could see a large woman through a torn screen door bustling around the room that apparently was the kitchen from whence the coleslaw and hush puppies came. Behind the house was a shed that had a quarter-moon hole carved into its door. To a certain extent, Jenny had understood her parents' objections to John. Her life and her experiences had changed, opened up, when she met him. They partied in beer halls, flew in airplanes, took a spur-of-the-moment trip to Denver. Things she never would have been exposed to had she married one of the boys she met in dancing classes or at the country club. Her eyes had been wet and shiny that first day when John approached her at the recently opened Curtiss-Wright Field in Oklahoma City.

"I've seen you here several times," he'd said. "Are you interested in flying, or just like to watch the planes?"

"Both," she blurted out before catching herself. "Of course, I meant the planes. No way I could fly." She giggled, and wished she hadn't been wearing these awful jodhpurs. But using the excuse of going to the stables was the only way she could manage to sneak off here to hang around watching the pilots and their planes.

"I bet I could find someone around who would be willing to teach a pretty girl like you to fly." He wasn't laughing—seemed very matter-of-fact. But a twitch around his mouth made her feel he was making fun, or playing with her. She had since learned from experience that she'd indeed been right about that twitch. Her husband, with his wickedly dry sense of humor, rarely laughed out loud, but the close observer could read his mirth or disdain in almost imperceptible facial movements.

She drew herself up that day, giving him a dismissive look. "Don't be silly. Nice to have talked to you." She turned on her heel, walked around the corner of the main hangar, climbed into her roadster, and didn't look back. She knew he was watching. She hadn't missed the fact that he'd casually ambled across the tarmac to get a view of where she was headed.

As much as she'd wanted to, she didn't go back for a week. He was handsome, older, intriguing. She'd seen him hanging around the field before. He seemed to know all the pilots. For days, she dallied with schemes for dropping by the field on her way home from school or other places in the city. She wanted him to see her in a dress. But that would give her away; she knew no one had ever seen her at the field in anything but riding clothes.

Jenny reached for one of Jim's dripping barbecued ribs and noticed Laura raptly following an animated conversation between Roy and John. They were still discussing the dangers of blacking out while maneuvering a plane through outside loops. As Jenny mopped up sauce with a flaky biscuit from her chipped plate, she thought about what Laura had said last night: that she had learned to fly because of her brother Charles. John mistakenly thought that too. After she made several more visits to the Oklahoma City airfield, he'd asked her one day why she had tears in her eyes the first time he'd spoken to her. Everyone else could believe what they wanted, but Jenny knew it was John who'd given her the courage to fly, had encouraged her, was proud of her because of her daring, and paid for and arranged for her flying lessons. He had set up a few secret lessons before they were married. Her parents never would have stood for it. But they could do nothing about it once she was John's wife. Strangely, Jenny's parents seemed to view Charles's death the way she did: he died from war, not from flying. Or perhaps she was mimicking their thinking; after all, she was only six. No, they were opposed because, as her father put it, "Aeroplanes are not a proper hobby for a young woman. Why can't you be interested in needlework, or playing the piano? We bought you that expensive horse." And they both were "simply appalled" at seeing her in pants so often.

Jenny looked across the table, the same stars always in her eyes whenever she contemplated her husband. He had given her life, romance, another world. He was a war hero. And she loved the fact that he was so indulgent, found her so amusing, was so delighted by and caught up in her accomplishment, yet didn't push. He seemed to want for her whatever she wanted.

She saw that John was in a happy mood, the sleeves of his white dress shirt rolled up. He'd removed his vest and jacket before flying with her that afternoon. "This place reminds me of Curley's—remember, Roy? Joint we used to hit in St. Louis. We had some good times there."

"St. Louis?"

Jenny frowned, straining to hear what Laura had just said. The reporter's voice was barely audible, as though she were practicing forming the sound of a new word.

"Yeah," Clem responded, "according to what I heard from my brother Stan, that's all you guys did, was have good times." He lifted a beer mug in toast. "I ended up having to go to what my parents called a *serious educational institution* after all your folderol with the Jesuits."

"Oh lordy," Jenny said. "I don't want to hear that story again about the defrocked priest who ran off with his mistress."

"All this happened at university? In St. Louis?" Laura asked.

Jim, hovering about the table, momentarily stepped in. "I got some good product come from the still, Mister Clem. You 'n yore friends like a taste?"

"Absolutely," Roy and John said in unison, and Jim hustled off toward the house.

"Yeah, I heard that story about the priest too," Clem

said with a frown. "I guess we all have. Bothered my brother, and especially my parents, because the priest was an Indian. Reinforced the notion that we're all irresponsible." He stopped and looked around at the embarrassed silent table.

Oklahoma in 1929 was loaded with assimilated, well-educated, rich Indians. Everyone bragged about humorist Will Rogers, who had billed himself on the vaudeville circuit as the Cherokee Kid, and was now Hollywood's highest-grossing star after making his first talkie. But no one ever spoke about or faced the fact that being Indian was a delicate subject no matter how rich or well educated you were. Those living on reservations were still routinely referred to in many circles as savages.

Clem dissipated the tension with a lopsided grin. "I guess I've got the wayward one to thank for getting me shipped off to Harvard, instead of St. Louis like my brother."

"Ah, Clem, I never heard that Indian part of the old scandal," John said. "Did you?" he asked, turning in the direction of Roy, who shook his head. "Nah, don't think anyone paid any attention to that."

Jim came back with a big smile as he unscrewed the lid of a huge clear jar that looked like it had previously held pickles. It now contained a liquid much paler yellow than the beer, which meanwhile had begun to develop a brown sediment that was floating in tiny particles to the bottoms of both the pitcher and the mugs.

"Like some moonshine, miss?" Jim asked Laura as he was filling up assorted jelly glasses and old mayonnaise jars and passing them down the table.

"Sure, what is it?" Laura asked.

"Made from corn I growed myself," Jim replied.

"Fine. We never see corn in New York, except in tins."

"Without cornfields, we'd never have any place for emergency landings," Jenny said with a chuckle. "Isn't that true, Roy? How many times have we had farmers running after us with a pitchfork?"

The men looked from Laura to Jenny then swiveled back to Laura again to watch as she lifted her jar to her lips. It seemed clear she was about to take a big gulp, when she got a whiff of what was coming. She looked startled, her eyes grew round, and she cut back her intake to a small sip. Even that cleared out her sinuses, judging from her facial expression and pursed lips.

"Oh my." Laura was blinking her eyes as though they stung. "Is that something akin to bathtub gin?"

Everyone laughed, including Laura.

"We Indians call it firewater," Clem said.

"So what are the stories about St. Louis?" Laura asked. "I think my mother was from there."

"You *think*?" Jenny said. "What in the world can you mean?"

Jim reached over her to set another full pitcher of beer on the table. "Anything else you folks needs?" he asked. "We got us some peach cobbler that's powerful good. Wife made it jist this morning."

"Anybody?" Roy asked, looking around the table to heads shaking no.

Jenny noticed that as Laura shook her head to the pie offer, she took another tentative sniff, then sip, of the corn liquor. Oh boy, Jenny thought, what next? She's not sure where her mother is from; she's never drunk corn liquor. We are indeed headed for a bumpy ride. I hope, at least, it means she's working up her courage to fly. Perhaps I should find out more about her. What a bundle of contradictions she is. So curious and engaged about everything and at the same time she somehow seems like a lost waif.

"Okay, everybody," Roy spoke up, "I haven't had a chance to give you a report. I spoke to Roscoe Turner and he can't join us tomorrow because he's got an upcoming event in Cleveland. But he'll definitely be with us the following day."

"What'll we do tomorrow?" Jenny asked. "Monday isn't a very good day for a show, anyway. That silly lion would have helped draw a crowd."

"Maybe you should go up in the morning and just buzz around. Might draw some attention, then we can plan to offer rides in the afternoon. Or take up anyone wanting to jump."

"Count me out on that," Jenny said. "Anyway, you'd have to be the one to take them up. You have a cabin to jump from. No way to do that from my plane."

"Isn't that how you got in trouble in the first place?" Laura asked. "Parachute jumping?"

"That was a freak accident," Roy replied. "You'll see, as soon as they autopsy that woman they'll probably find she had a heart attack."

"Who wouldn't," Laura shot back, "from jumping out of an airplane?"

"You should try it," Roy said with a sly smile. "It's very soothing to survey the landscape as you float down to earth like a swallow."

Oh lordy, Jenny thought, he's trying to seduce her every way from Sunday. I'm not sure she's got the moral compass to handle this. But not my problem—she's the one who's chosen to run around on her own and break every convention known to polite society.

C HAPTER TWENTY-NINE
CAT AND MOUSE

LAURA WAS IN HER HOTEL ROOM LATER that night thinking about preparing for bed, but kept putting it off in an anticipation she didn't quite understand. She was tipsy, she knew, maybe more than just a little. She wasn't a drinker, wasn't used to being with a group. At work, since she was the only woman other than the switchboard operators, she didn't do much palling around.

At Barnard, she had gotten on the subway and gone straight home after classes. Except for the one boy she'd met at the college mixer, she had no friends there. She and the boy, Ben, would meet for coffee once in a while at a place on Broadway near the Barnard/Columbia campuses. He was a senior literature student and she would sometimes show him her class essays. But that was it—the extent of what one might call her *intimate* relationships with men.

She changed into a clean chemise from the white flying shirt she'd been wearing all day and was running a comb through her hair when she heard a faint rap at the door.

"Who is it?" she called, but she knew. No answer, then the faint rap again.

She opened the door to see Roy, his arm extended high, leaning on the frame, a big smile on his face. Still dressed in his flying togs, his tall shiny boots, but he had changed to a red checked scarf at his throat. "Just a quick hello," he said.

"Wanted to make sure you're all right. Can I come in? Not discreet to disturb people out here in the hall."

Laura quickly nodded, although discretion was not big in her vocabulary, not a concept with which she was very familiar. The few times she'd heard her mother mention the word, it was always with a hearty laugh. "Being discreet was coined by and only observed by the petty bourgeoisie." Even though her mother was fairly fluent in French and spoke German like a native, she took great pride, and thus the big laugh, in pronouncing *petite* as *petty*.

"We had a good little talk here this afternoon about flying, parachuting, etcetera," Roy said, once he was in her room with the door closed. "Just thought we could follow up on that. Now that I've completely dispelled your fears, I'd like to see you take a jump."

"I remember," she replied. She also remembered her cheeks getting warm, the kisses he'd given her at the end of that *little talk*, as he called it. While the others were waiting in the downstairs dining room, he had stopped by "just to check," he'd said, "that you've settled in all right." Laura had finally disentangled herself. "The others must be wondering where we are," she'd said, pulling away from him. She knew Jenny would disapprove, and she'd been right. Jenny had glared at them when they'd walked into the dining room. Try as she might, Laura couldn't understand what she'd begun to call in her mind *Jenny's Rules*. She had roughly pulled Laura aside yesterday to tell her that Roy was married. The boy from Columbia, Ben, had kissed her, once or twice, as he was waiting to see her off on the subway from one of their rare meetings, but that was nothing like Roy's kisses.

Roy took a flask from his hip and a package of Camel cigarettes from his shirt pocket and put them down on the writing desk in her small standard-issue room. "If you've got a couple of water glasses," he said, "we're in business."

As Laura indicated two glasses on the top of the bureau, she fingered the gold key to her childhood diary on the chain around her neck. She had copied some of Aunt Edna's poems into the journal when she was quite young, attempting to understand the structure of poetry and the nature of love. But by the time she'd grown to her teen years, she had given up pondering where love could be or what it might mean.

Looking at Roy in his shiny boots and his rakish mustache, Laura smiled. She felt as though she'd found a home. Lines of Aunt Edna's danced from the pages of her journal: *What lips my lips have kissed / Now will the god, for blasphemy so brave / Punish me, surely, with the shaft I crave.*

Laura was way out of her depth here, and perhaps normally she would have been tough-minded and self-protective enough to realize it. But moonshine and moonlight had taken their toll.

CHAPTER THIRTY
FLYING INTO THE WIND

WHEN JENNY ARRIVED THE NEXT MORNING at the grassy area behind the courthouse where she and Roy had left their planes, she found Cheesy and Laura already there. And, thank heavens, Laura seemed totally prepared to fly. *She looks a bit green around the gills, though,* Jenny decided. *I'd better put her in the front cockpit today so I can keep a better eye on her. If she starts to throw up or do something silly, I want to know about it.*

Jenny went about checking over her plane—looking for rips, kicking the tires—not much in a mood to make conversation. But Laura seemed strangely different—giddy and talkative. *She's truly weird. Not knowing where her mother is from. What in the devil could that mean? I should find out. It's too intriguing to pass up.* She supressed a grin— *now I'll be the nosy one.*

"I've heard some strange things about this town," Laura launched in without seeming to notice Jenny's pensive mood. The reporter's manner was hyper, almost frenetic. "Some interesting stories for such a small, dusty place. So much oil money. The Indians here have the highest income per capita of any place in the world, leading to all sorts of murders."

"Oh really?" was Jenny's non-reply, as she bent under the fuselage.

"Yes. Clem explained yesterday about the headrights thing for the Osage, and the people killed for them. To get control of the money, say from a wife or her mother who would inherit."

"I think that's an old story, Laura. It was in the papers several years ago when they had a grand jury investigation."

"Old or not, it's awful," Laura snapped. "In one family alone, first one sister was shot, then another sister and her husband were blown up in their home, then their mother was poisoned at her own dinner table by a son-in-law." Getting to the end of that litany nearly ran Laura out of breath. She took a gulp, and went on. "All so he could get control of the headrights of his wife's dead relatives. The feds sent in undercover agents as salesmen, cattle buyers, because town officials were so corrupt. The Indians couldn't even control their own money, they had to have *minders*." Laura was totally out of breath, but looked at Jenny with a mystifying grin of expectation. Jenny had no way of knowing this was the grin she usually reserved for Barnes when she thought she was on to something *big*.

"Yeah, fine," Jenny cut in. "We have a show to do today. You think you're up to it? You seem a little peaked."

Laura looked at Cheesy with a slight headshake and a familiar shrug passed between them: *Not the first time we've had a story idea shot down because the editor hasn't the brains to recognize a good yarn when it's dropped in his lap.*

"Roy said I can go up with him at some point," Cheesy chimed in, "to get some shots of you gals with your stunts."

"We'll see when the fellas get here," Jenny said. "Since John and Clem decided to stay another day, they had to call their offices."

Jenny pulled her cloth helmet from the front pocket of her jodhpurs, gave a lift of her chin to indicate that Laura do the same, and hoisted herself onto the wing. As she lifted her leg over into the back cockpit, she suppressed a grin, knowing that it was harder to get into the forward hole. Then she watched Laura struggle to follow her lead. Cheesy finally had to put down his camera equipment and help the reporter. Jenny continued to grin as she pulled down her goggles and turned over the motor. I'm being simply malicious, she chided herself. What about that woman brings out the worst in me? Am I somehow jealous, as Roy suggested? But of what?

Cheesy finally got Laura settled in, then ran around to the front of the plane to crank the propeller. Jenny had to yell out to remind him to remove the chocks. As she gave him a salute of thanks, she thought that at least these New Yorkers were good for something.

Once they got in the air, Jenny relaxed. Flying was the easy part. Whether she was rolling the plane over and over in the air, or doing inside loops, it felt as though that was the way things were meant to be—natural—she didn't have to think about it.

Louise Thaden had spoken to her a few months ago about what a thrill it was to skim along very close to the ground. "If you're at a high altitude," she'd said, "you have no feeling of how fast you're going." But Jenny had countered that ground-hugging was for racecar drivers. For her, just floating along, rolling in the sky, watching the creampuff clouds going by was wonderful. She didn't understand why many of her flying friends were so hell-bent on records. Shortly after that conversation, Louise had set a women's record of 156 miles an hour, skimming only a hundred feet off the ground. Talk about feeling like you're in a racecar! That was Louise's third record: solo endurance, altitude, and speed.

Jenny came out of a series of barrel rolls and noticed

that Laura was still upright and seemed to be okay. Jenny
had completely forgotten for a moment about her passenger as they swirled around. Roy was trying to use the
reporter as some kind of goad. But Laura was the one who
was going to get burned, Jenny was sure of it. She'd tried to
warn the girl, telling her he was married, yet it didn't seem
to have worked. Roy was a womanizer, always had been.
How could Laura not see that? She must be terribly naïve
despite all her pushiness. And heaven knows, Jenny's real
loyalty was to Roy. He had taken her on as a student as a
favor to John. No one else wanted to fool with trying to
teach a young girl how to fly. Now Roy seemed to feel she
wasn't repaying his faith in her. But what was it he wanted?
She had no stomach for those endurance things. As for the
derby race from San Diego, she wasn't about to stay out
there for months, tuning up and trying out some new plane
in preparation. She wanted to be home with her husband.
Her parents were already beside themselves with what they
saw as the danger and uncouthness of it all. Besides, Roy
was some kind of glory hound—not a good idea to pin one's
hopes on any of his grandiose schemes.

Jenny gunned her engine, pulled back on the stick, and
started a steep climb, preparing for a series of inside loops.
She might let the number she would do depend on how
Laura was faring. It was possible that loops, with their steep
climbs and sharp falls, could make her passenger dizzy or
even pass out, especially since she seemed to be suffering
from a hangover.

These maneuvers, of course, carried nothing of the danger of the outside loops that Roy mastered, but still . . . If
she kept perfecting them, would that satisfy him? Was there
something really wrong with her that she didn't want to, as
Roy kept saying, *take your natural God-given gift and get
out there and show the world what you can do*?

Jenny got to the top of the arc that was going to be the
starting place for her first loop, checked her altimeter, cut
back on her throttle, swung the little ship slightly side to
side as she did a quick check of each rudder, and dropped
the plane into a deep dive. "Hang on!" she screamed into
the wind, her white silk scarf flying out behind. Watching
her altimeter closely, Jenny began pulling back slightly on
the throttle as they neared one thousand feet. She wanted
to get close enough to the ground to give any spectators a
thrill, but didn't want to give her passenger a heart attack.
The landscape below stood out in sharp relief. It was hilly
country compared to the flat, orderly plains of the Oklahoma she was used to, with its farms and fields laid out in
precise rows. At five hundred feet she could see that Clem
had arrived, could glimpse the color of his suspenders, so
she pulled out of the dive and started the climb back up. As
they rose into the cloudless blue, Laura turned toward Jenny,
a big smile on her face. Jenny couldn't hear the words, but
could read Laura's lips. *Coney Island.*

Jenny grinned back. She's got what it takes after all! I
wonder what Roy could have said on their short flight here
yesterday to get her over her fear. But he's right, she is a
spunky girl. That's what all the newspaper stories had been
saying about the women in the derby: they had guts. Actually,
they weren't all saying that. After Marvel Crosson's crash
and death on the second day, a lot of editorials screamed
that women had no place in the air. That was annoying nonsense. But as Roy and Mark Snyder kept pointing out to her,
the public didn't really trust airplanes. *If God had meant
men to fly, he would have given them wings.* How many
times had she gritted her teeth when hearing that! Perhaps
it is up to those of us who believe in flying to get out and
do our darndest to advance it. I guess that's Roy's problem
with me—he thinks I'm shirking my responsibility.

John doesn't seem to care one way or the other. Care is the wrong word, she decided. He's just easy, that's it. Whatever I want to do seems fine with him. But Laura thinks it's strange that I'm married. She seems to do whatever she wants without asking anyone. Hard to understand. How can a woman just go off on her own? Being a reporter and traveling around all over is a man's job. She really does have spunk. Does that mean she was improperly brought up, or is it just doing what she wants to do? Though I wouldn't be flying, Jenny reminded herself, if it weren't for John. He rescued me from a pretty ordinary life. In fact, all the women fliers I know are married, or have rich fathers—like Ruth Nichols and Pancho Barnes. Hmm, she thought—Amelia has a rich publicist.

As she throttled back preparing for her second dive from the top of the loop, Jenny smiled. She always smiled thinking of John. After her parents had objected to her marriage—heck, they had objected to her even dating him—John had met with her father for a heart-to-heart talk. John then took the design job with Cord auto and soon switched his enthusiasm from airplanes to cars. And the wedding was planned. That's funny, Jenny thought, she'd never quite put that together with John's growing up. But that's exactly what he'd been saying to Roy yesterday: that all his barnstorming around was no longer an adult thing to be doing. Even Wiley Post, the oil-field roustabout with only one eye and a sixth-grade education, was making serious plans to advance flying; talking about a trip around the world. But what had Roy meant by his cryptic reference to jobs for rich oilmen and what they *entailed*? Sounded as though he'd somehow been burned. She would have to ask John. As the plane dropped off into its steep dive, she wondered about when she might want to have children. Damnation, it's complicated.

What about the women in the derby? How did they

manage? Louise, she knew, was married and planning children. Her husband had sold his innovative idea to make
planes out of metal, so they were well fixed to support her
flying. Amelia was a publicity hound, or at least her publicist, George Putnam, was. Pancho Barnes seemed like some
kind of eccentric, always wearing pants wherever she went
and smoking a black cigar. Newspapers had dubbed Ruth
Nichols, a Wellesley graduate, as New York's Flying Debutante. Jenny knew Ruth and she was a lovely, modest woman,
even if she had designed and often wore an eye-catching
purple jumpsuit for flying. She was the first woman ever
to qualify to fly seaplanes and she held a transport license.
There was a thought! Even though a lot of women held a
pilot's license—Jenny knew there were over one hundred
just in the US alone—only three had transport licenses that
allowed them to carry passengers or freight. Maybe she
should think about that. She would be in heady company:
Louise, Ruth, and Phoebe Omlie, whom Jenny had never
met. All three of them in the derby. Again, guilt raised its
head. Or was it envy? They were participating, taking part,
Jenny wasn't. She was just floating, drifting around in the
sky. Even that pesky reporter threw herself into her job, ran
out and grabbed life. Getting a transport license would be
a challenge, hard work. But it would be nice to have people
look up to you, and to hold something in your hands that
proved you were the best.

Jenny suddenly realized she had to pay more attention
to what she was doing. She'd gotten so engrossed in her
thoughts that she'd almost failed to climb high enough for
her next loop. Altitude was critical in this maneuver. One
needed plenty of room going into a dive to make any necessary corrections. And, of course, you needed speed to get
the loop going.

She climbed a bit higher, and grinned. She hadn't been

so engrossed that she'd failed to notice that each time they came out of a hurtling dive headed straight for the ground, Laura had turned in her seat and given Jenny a thumbs-up as they began to climb again. Maybe I'm giving her the bug after all, Jenny thought. And maybe she's given me one as well.

C HAPTER THIRTY-ONE
PONDERING JENNY

THE BUZZING PLANE HAD ATTRACTED ATTENTION. Laura could look over its side and see activity on the field. Each time Jenny made a swooping pass, Laura strained to see if Roy had arrived. He promised last night he'd be here. But what would she do when he did? She ached to run and throw herself in his arms, even though he'd been stern in warning her against such a thing.

"We want to keep this you-and-me thing quiet," he'd said. "Jenny's a prude. Thinks people shouldn't be bedding down together before they're married."

Laura had been too woozy with love and moonshine to argue about much of anything. Now she wondered what was the point. Nothing that she could see, except appeasing Jenny. But how silly was that? Although it would be nice to make friends with her; she was an interesting girl.

Jenny had been unusually grumpy before they took off, which had made Laura nervous and giddy. She'd felt as though Jenny suspected something. But why care?

She smiled thinking that for once she agreed with her mother. "That's the way women *should* be, getting what they want and doing what they want to do," Evelyn had said when e.e. cummings and other male poet friends griped of being overtaxed by the Baroness von Freytag-Loringhoven's rapaciousness. Laura was happy that when she felt she'd found love, she had followed her feelings.

She let her mind float in the same kind of weightless, circular pattern her body was moving in as the plane spun round and round in what she was now able to identify as a barrel roll. What was it about Jenny? What was her trouble? She appeared to be daring and adventuresome, risk-taking, but she couldn't seem to free up her mind. *Free* was Evelyn's favorite word.

In a literature class in college, Laura had created havoc by declaring that she didn't understand the central premise of *The Scarlet Letter*. When she had related the school incident later at home, her mother had said, "Perhaps the apple doesn't fall far from the tree after all."

As they touched down on the small patch of grass and taxied up to the back of the courthouse, Laura could see Roy directing Jenny where to park. Jenny climbed down on her own, but Laura held out her arms for Roy to help her. As he did, he gave her a playful pat on the behind, saying out of the corner of his mouth, "Now behave yourself."

Jenny was too far away to have heard, but she nonetheless looked over and frowned. Laura couldn't resist raising her right eyebrow in a what's-it-to-you look.

A small crowd had gathered, and spectators were staring out the windows of the back of the courthouse, as well as the nearby Indian Agency building. Laura had been told the locals called this Agency Hill.

Roy pointed out the sign that Cheesy had helped him set up. It read, *Rides 50c, Jumps $1, 4 p.m.* Cheesy was now photographing it, along with a slim young man in overalls trying on a chute harness in anticipation of an afternoon jump. Roy squeezed Laura's hand and walked over to his potential customer.

Laura looked around and saw that there were several expensive cars parked haphazardly about the field—Packards, Pierce-Arrows, a Stutz Bearcat.

"I told you," she said, pointing them out to Jenny. "I bet they belong to Indians. They all have tons of money because they closed off the tribal rolls years ago, meaning there's a huge pool of oil money to be split among a small group."

Jenny shook her head. "Always on the job, huh. Don't you ever take a day off?"

C HAPTER THIRTY-TWO
PAWHUSKA

LAURA WALKED BACK TO THE HOTEL, showered, and changed into a dress. She toyed with the idea of putting on her hat. She was in a happy mood and felt like celebrating the fact that she was in love. But she decided a hat would look silly here in Pawhuska, the capital of the Osage Nation, where the headgear seemed to veer toward headbands, deerskin caps, and cowboy hats. She met Cheesy in the hotel lobby and they set off to get a bit more information and take some pictures before going to Western Union to file.

When they found the center of the little burg of a few thousand people, they discovered it was dominated by a sheer cliff that rose straight up off the main street. Atop that cliff sat the imposing Greek-columned white granite courthouse behind which Roy's and Jenny's airplanes were parked. Laura gasped.

"Doesn't look like such a steep drop when you approach it from the other direction," Cheesy said with a dry laugh.

To further emphasize the dominating aspect of the building, there were two flights of stairs leading straight up to it from the town. As the two stood gaping, a passing local informed Laura that there were 147 steps.

"It's a known fact," she said, nodding her sunbonneted head toward Laura's pad and pencil. "Folks have counted 'em." The reporter made a note of the number and thanked the woman, thinking she would count them herself later. But she was more intrigued that even in this heat, a number of people on the streets wore colorful blankets, some around the waist, others draped over one shoulder or wrapped like a shawl.

"Blankets?" she said with a puzzled look.

"So?" Cheesy responded. "They're Indians."

"Some of the patterns somehow look familiar. Maybe from a schoolbook or something. "

As they moved down the main street, both got a good laugh over the five-story redbrick Triangle Building. Several people on the street explained quite seriously that it was patterned after the Flatiron Building at the intersection of Broadway and Fifth Avenue in New York.

"You must be joking," Laura blurted out to the first person who made the comparison, a short, rumpled-looking, middle-aged man wearing a large carpenter's apron. "I'm from New York City and the Flatiron is an architectural beauty. It's probably twenty or more stories high. But this one is a squat brick."

Laura was sorry as soon as she made the smart remark. The man, who introduced himself as Charles Maxwell, the owner of Classic Hardware, was clearly embarrassed. "See, it *is* a triangular piece of land here at Main and Kihekah Avenue just like in New York," he said. Pawhuska's version was frequently referred to in the local paper as a unique architectural masterpiece. The Osages knew it as the building of a hundred lawyers, all of who seemed to be wheeling and dealing with tribal oil leases.

By way of apology, Cheesy had Maxwell pose for a photograph in front of the building with another passerby, an extremely tall Indian dressed in a buckskin jacket and beaded headband. He identified himself as Running Fast in

Tall Grass. "But," he said with a solemn smile, "several people call me Paul."

Before Cheesy could slam the first plate into his camera, a cluster of people gathered, obviously hoping to be included in the picture.

This is how it happened that the photographer, who was well known for his gritty pictures of the underbelly of Gotham, including gangsters hiding behind their fedoras, transvestites in ball gowns, and bloody corpses not yet covered by the cursory sheet, had a field day taking pictures on the sidewalks of Pawhuska for the readers of New York.

Laura trailed along as Cheesy spent an hour roaming the dusty downtown with its two-story buildings lined up along a broad, flat, treeless Main Street, and then, puffing under the weight of his camera equipment, climbed the many stairs to the town's looming attraction on the high hill. All the while a crowd followed, as though Cheesy were the Pied Piper.

He took shots of cowboys in ten-gallon hats, ladies in the very latest fashions, and Indians in an awesome assortment of just about everything, a stunning variety of dress. Indeed there were feathers, but also little pillbox caps, all manner of shirts and leather pants, and what seemed to be the running standard, soft moccasins. There was lots of spiked hair and, as always, blankets of many hues.

Suddenly, one in particular worn by an elderly woman caught Laura's eye. It had several borders of different colors around a series of children's handprints on a solid field of beige.

"Take a picture of that blanket," she said in a flash of memory. "It looks almost like one my mother has on the floor at home."

Just as quickly, her attention was distracted by a tall, beautiful young woman in a white dress that appeared to be deerskin. "Look at that elaborate beadwork!"

"Yep," replied Cheesy, never one to waste words. "Let's call the boss."

"Yeah," Laura said with a worried frown. "He's *got* to like this stuff. I can't go home right now."

Once Laura got Barnes on the telephone, she was breathless. "Such an ordinary redbrick town, with wide streets. But the array of people and dress is unbelievable. The Indians don't look like Indians, in loincloth or anything. And there are small dress shops selling expensive jewelry and frocks at outrageous prices. They say the Indians will pay anything, they have so much oil money. Except they have to buy on credit because the government thinks the Indians are incompetent and doles out cash a little at a time, or just pays the merchants when the bills come in. Doesn't seem like a very sensible system."

"You think that's your job now, writing editorials?" Barnes was yelling, as usual.

"I was just commenting," Laura replied stiffly. "You said you wanted only a little color from me that you'd fill in with the old clips from a year or so ago. You have all that about the feds investigating and sending in undercover agents and the grand jury and everything when so many Indians got killed by relatives and guardians. Somebody told me there were thirty-four suspected homicides in one year."

"Don't you read the newspapers?" The phone vibrated with Barnes's voice. "The ringleader finally got sent to Leavenworth a few months ago after a bunch of hung juries and mistrials."

"It's still interesting . . ." Laura's voice trailed off. No way to win with this lug.

"Yeah? So, I'll turn you over to rewrite. You can dictate what it felt like to fly upside down. And give 'em another piece to top off a resurrection of these old murders. But you better darn well make sure that tomorrow we have something more exciting than those barrel rolls. They're not new anymore."

"Hey, Maxine," Laura could hear Barnes shout at the switchboard, "transfer the kid to Mac!"

When Laura and Cheesy got back to the hotel, they found the others having a light lunch in the dining room.

Jenny and Roy were already sparring about whether she should make an appearance for the afternoon rides. Laura tried to catch Roy's eye but he seemed focused on the spat with Jenny. Laura knew, anyway, that he was serious about not letting on that they were in love. She couldn't envision how this was going to play out, but she trusted him to manage somehow. Besides, she would soon be back in New York, so theirs would need to be a long-distance, from-time-to-time affair. She had pangs that such an arrangement might be painful, but her mother and Aunt Edna had balanced many such loves. Edna and that major—what was his name?— who lived in Washington. Her mother had always said, "A lot of delightful poetry sprang from that liaison."

Laura decided not to fret about something she couldn't control, so she ordered a barbeque sandwich. She'd gotten addicted to them at Jim's. No such thing in New York that she knew of. Cheesy ordered grits and gravy, saying he had no idea what grits were.

"I'm glad to come along, Roy," Jenny was saying, "but you know I'm not planning to do any jumping or wing walking. That stuff is for someone else, not me. How about Laura?" She laughed and pointed at the reporter with her chin as she dug into her salad. "She took to the air this morning like an old pro, despite what seemed like a bit of a hangover."

Laura looked to Roy for his reaction.

"Could be. I've mentioned it to her. You're going to do it, aren't you, kiddo?" He smiled at Laura, but then turned back to Jenny. "You have to at least be there. It's good to have as many people around as possible. We want it to look like a crowd. Roscoe Turner said he'll be in this evening to fly with us tomorrow."

Laura opened her mouth to reply, but Jenny's response was quicker. "Oh boy," she said, "if you talked to Roscoe, he must have told you how the women finished up in the derby today. They were due into Cleveland an hour or so ago, weren't they?"

The waiter arrived with Laura's sandwich and Cheesy's grits. He took one look and blurted, "Why don't they just say it's breakfast mush?"

Roy grinned at Jenny, and Laura bit down hard on a french fry. Darn her. Yet he was the one who seemed obsessed with Jenny, not the other way around. It was painful to Laura. Why couldn't he pay more attention to her?

"You were right all along," Roy said to Jenny. "Your pal Louise Thaden won the derby. Landed first—and with the winning time—in front of thousands of screaming, adoring fans."

"Wow." Jenny's face lit up, awe in her voice. "I knew she would. Gutsy."

With nearly $25,000 in prize money at stake, nineteen pioneering women had flown out of Santa Monica's Clover Field nine days earlier. After having endured local banquets and toast masters every evening at every stop, the endurance was not quite over for Louise Thaden. Before she could park her plane after landing, she was mobbed by hundreds pouring out of the stands and had to shut off her engine for fear of harming someone. Then an official greeter encircled her neck with a wreath of red roses, thorns and all. A soft-spoken, unassuming young woman of twenty-three, who initially took a job selling airplanes to get flying lessons, Louise had diplomatically suggested her open-cockpit

Travel Air was the real winner and asked that the wreath be placed around its propeller.

Louise had dedicated her win to Marvel Crosson, who was killed when her own Travel Air crashed between Yuma and Phoenix, Arizona, on day two of the race. It was suspected that Marvel was overcome by carbon monoxide exhaust from the plane's engine. Louise luckily had made the same discovery about her own plane on a test run and flew with a jerry-rigged system of hosing to dispel the fumes. The rest of the Travel Airs in the race were modified in the same way after Crosson's crash.

"What else did Roscoe say?" Jenny demanded.

"Gladys O'Donnell was second and Amelia finished a distant third. Roscoe called her landing amateurish. She bounced all the way across the airport. Had to brake out of a ground loop before she was able to stop. Everyone was laughing, making snide remarks."

"Not surprising," Jenny said. "That Vega is way too big and fast for her to handle. Poor Amelia. She's too nice for all the stupid hoopla that surrounds her."

"Yeah," Roy said. "She wouldn't even have made third if Ruth Nichols hadn't cracked up on the last leg this morning at the Columbus airport."

"Is Ruth all right?" Jenny nearly jumped up from her chair.

"She's fine, she's fine. Roscoe said she crawled out unhurt. But a real shame. She was third place into the last day." Roy lifted his eyebrows for emphasis before imparting the next bit of information. "All the ladies with transport licenses were way out in front. Phoebe Omlie was first in the lighter craft division."

"I get your drift." Jenny could have pointed out to him that the first- and second-place winners were also flying in the open-cockpit planes that Jenny loved. Neither cooped up in an enclosed cabin that Earhart, or for that matter Roy, seemed to prefer. When Louise Thaden landed, she had jokingly referred to what she had just won as the Sunburn Derby. In an accumulated twenty hours and nineteen minutes over nine days, she had logged some 2,700 miles of sun, wind, and rain in her face.

"And Bobbi Trout had to make a dead-stick landing someplace in Indiana and busted a hole in an aileron." Roy started laughing.

"Hey, wait a min—" Laura tried to inject herself into the conversation without any luck. She wanted to tell them about the story she had written—before she'd left Cleveland to chase after Jenny—about Pancho Barnes landing on a car.

"What's so funny about Bobbi having an accident?" Jenny countered. "You have the strangest sense of humor."

"Just laughing at what Bobbi did next. You know how I admire these resourceful women. Those with spunk."

"So without the lecture, *please*. What did she do?"

"Patched up the aileron's hole with a tin can and some bailing wire and got back in the air."

"You know very well I plugged a hole in a gas tank once with a manicure orange stick," Jenny retorted. "You thought that was pretty clever at the time."

"Aileron?" said Laura. "How do you spell it?" She put down her dripping sandwich and reached for a napkin and her notebook.

"Trailing edge of a wing that you can flap up or down," Jenny replied, pushing her salad away. "Gives you lift." She turned and gave Laura a hard look. "You *really* never stop working."

"So, Bobbi didn't come in the money this time," Roy continued. "But she's already talking about doing a refueling endurance flight within the next month or so."

"Swell," Jenny said with a disdainful tone. "Sit in the air

for a day and try to connect by hose with another plane to give you fuel? Ridiculous."

Laura watched the interplay. What was it with these two? Clem had said that Roy just wanted Jenny to be a top-notch flier. And Laura agreed with that; Jenny should push herself more. Roy was right, of course. Roy was always right. And she glowed with pride at his saying he admired women with *spunk*. He'd used that very word to describe Laura to Jenny yesterday. And again last night when he'd talked to Laura about her making a parachute jump.

"Bobbi's aiming for a week in the air, not a day," said Roy. "She's asking around for another woman to fly with her so they can spell each other off."

"Stop trying to browbeat me, Roy! I'm not interested in that endurance nonsense and you know it. A week in the air? What an infernal bore!"

CHAPTER THIRTY-THREE
JUMPSUIT

LAURA STEPPED OUT OF THE PLANE into the open void as Roy had instructed her to do, and sure enough, everything was just as he had said: breath-stopping wind rush, dizzying impact, blinding sun. Tumbling, she had to tilt her head to see the sky. Then with arms outstretched, she flew like a bird. She was not afraid—she knew as soon as she opened her chute the world would slow down—but she had to count to one hundred, mustn't entangle herself in the plane. She pulled the cord and waited. It seemed a lifetime. She was racing fast toward the trees, must guide herself away. *Oops*. Now she was headed for the courthouse with its cliff on the other side. And then with a thud she was yanked upward, abruptly stopped, *bang*, another rush of wind as the chute filled. She reached up, grabbed her lines, and sat watching the landscape slowly take shape, color, and form as she focused on her surroundings and slowly descended on the breeze.

What a strange country she saw below, so foreign, another world from New York. Another world from her or her life. She couldn't imagine being from here or being like these people who were straight out of another century. But what would happen now that she was in love with Roy? She would need to come here from time to time. She wondered how often he would come to New York.

As Laura watched this astounding array of trees and bluffs and tiny dots of houses come up to meet her, she remembered Aunt Edna talking about being in love—she always seemed to be falling in and out of love—*I know a winter when it comes*. Not her mother. Her mother just *had* lovers. "Ate them alive," as she'd once heard John Reed say.

Laura smiled remembering an article about the derby entrants she'd read in a Cleveland paper: *Young, small for the most part, and pretty, these women of our century wear goggles instead of knitted shawls. They burn up distance in a way which is ridiculous. Just imagine your dear old grandmother hopping in a plane, tossing away a cigarette butt, pulling goggles over her eyes, giving the ship the gun, and heading from California to Ohio.*

Could something similar be said of her? She was young and pretty and chasing fire trucks and wayward pilots. But she didn't know any little old gray-haired grandmothers wearing shawls. She only knew women like Aunt Edna and her mother, who were poets and writers and took lovers who were painters and artists. If this was the way people outside of Greenwich Village viewed women—wearing shawls—perhaps she wasn't missing so much after all, not being versed in conventional ways.

She shifted her body and pumped her legs, trying to guide herself away from the trees around the bare plot behind the courthouse. And she *must* stay away from that sheer bluff that dropped down to Main Street. Roy had warned her about allowing herself to drift too far. Laura could now make out individual houses and buildings and streets of the town and that funny triangle building at the foot of the cliff. Arms held high, tightly gripping the ropes of her parachute, she tried to remember all of Roy's instructions. "Before you hit the ground, you need to keep your knees together, slightly bent, and prepare to run or walk as you touch down."

For the first time, her heart started thumping. There wasn't going to be any space to walk *or* run if she didn't shift herself away from those pines—*slip*, Roy had called it. But as she pulled the overhead cords first one way and then another, she overadjusted and was heading for the sheer cliff below the courthouse. Tumbling down the side of that or hitting all those steps would break every bone she had! The chutist who had fallen from Roy's plane in Atchison flashed through Laura's mind. Had that woman been given careful instructions?

When Laura finally managed to get herself lined up with the pasture, she could see Jenny, Clem, and Cheesy below. The photographer was snapping away, seeming to be everywhere at once. Clem and Jenny were moving their arms around wildly. For a minute Laura thought they were waving hi, but then realized they were signaling her to slip to her left. She took her hand from her right riser and waved back, then grabbed the lines hard and pulled the riser down to her chest to move herself away from the trees. She'd really gotten the hang of it! Roy was a perfect teacher. As the ground came at her, she could see she hadn't adjusted quite enough away from the bordering trees. She yanked hard on the riser to pull it into her chest, but a spurt of wind slipped her backward. She jerked to a stop, her knees still properly together and bent, but her feet were dangling, nothing solid beneath. She saw Cheesy still snapping and Jenny and Clem racing toward her. Their feet were on the ground, why weren't hers? Her arms felt like they were being pulled out of their sockets. She looked up and saw that her chute was caught, hanging in the low branches of a pine tree.

Geez, she thought, at least I'm not hanging upside down like that stunt pilot who crashed at the rodeo. I pray Barnes never sees this picture, but I know he will. Cheesy's camera was moving so fast, it nearly made her dizzy.

Jenny was grinning up at her, as Clem, muttering under his breath, moved around with a pocketknife, trying to cut Laura down.

"You've got guts, kid," Jenny called out. "I've never had the nerve to jump. And not a bad landing. You were slipping fine until that last gust of wind caught you."

Laura's dangling body bounced from side to side as Clem cut one cord and then another. Jenny held up her arms to break Laura's fall as the last line was severed. The two of them, both laughing, tumbled to the ground in a heap.

Clem was irate. "I don't see what's so durned funny. That Roy ought to be horsewhipped, letting you do this."

"Roy didn't *let her* do anything," Jenny said. "Laura's the one who did it, and good for her."

C HAPTER THIRTY-FOUR
THE LION'S ROAR

A SHORT TIME LATER, LAURA AND THE OTHERS were back at the raggedy field to meet the famed movie stuntman Roscoe Turner, who was joining their show for a day. Laura was exhausted and sweaty, but so exhilarated from her jump that she hadn't bothered to change her clothes. They were her badge of honor, a symbol of her accomplishment, a reminder to her lover that she could follow where he led.

Roscoe blazed in with a roar of rolling flyovers and power dives before landing in the by-now rutted grass. Sporting highly polished tall black leather boots, puttees, a waxed mustache, and something that resembled an officer's jacket, he climbed from the plane then reached back up for a lion cub. Roscoe's uniform was dotted with gold stars. Gilmore, the lion, was on a golden leash and sported a parachute strapped onto what resembled a doggie coat. Roscoe walked the lion over to a bush, where it squatted to relieve itself, then the duo moved on to Roy.

The flamboyant pilot spoke in an unhurried manner that gave Laura flash images of long, lazy days on a Mississippi River boat. His exuberance and energy belied such a vision.

He saluted. "At your service, Herr Commandant."

Roy laughed. "You old son of a gun. Your antics never change. We're expecting a whale of a show tomorrow. We've got posters around, and excitement seems to be running high."

"A spectacle it will be," Roscoe said, and gave another salute.

"So, you old blighter, I hear you didn't come in first yesterday in Cleveland," Roy answered with a grin.

"Not up to old Roscoe's standards," Turner said. "Lost the cross-country race over a technicality. And only third for the Thompson Trophy, fifty miles of speed and stunts. I'll be durned if Doug Davis wasn't flying something they were calling the Mystery Ship, and came in first. Walter Beech was smart. Purposely had that Travel Air hidden away, so the press went nuts trying to figure out what was going on. Little beauty of a monoplane, it was."

"Oh," said Laura, "that's exciting. I did a story on the Mystery Ship when I was in Cleveland. You came in third in that race? It's very prestigious, I understand. I must interview you."

"Glad to oblige, ma'am." Roscoe bowed to Laura. "So you carry your own press contingent, do you, Roy? You can bet I'll be back next year and win the Bendix and the Thompson. And who's this other lovely?" he asked, turning to Jenny. "I see my old pal John here. Hello, friend, haven't seen you in a month of Sundays."

"My wife Jenny," John replied, placing his arm possessively across her shoulder.

"Enchanted," Roscoe said, making another sweeping bow.

"She's a fine flier," Roy said, exhibiting his own possessive tone. "Sister of Charles Holmes. Ninety-fifth Aero Squadron."

"Really?" Roscoe's eyebrows shot up. "Young Roosevelt's unit. Mighty fine bunch of boys. Very few survived."

"Nor did my brother," Jenny said crisply. Her distaste

for the man many thought a buffoon was apparent on her face.

"My, my, a young lady picking up the gauntlet!" Roscoe boomed, as he gave her a hearty pat on the back.

"Hardly, Mr. Turner," Jenny said primly, shrugging her shoulder away from his hand. "I just learned through my brother what fun things boys can do, and I wanted to do some of them too."

"Hmm." Roscoe gave her a quizzical look. "They were fierce fighters, those boys. Roosevelt's downed plane had twenty bullet holes. And *he* took two in the head."

"Spare us the graphic details," John said mildly, a slight twitch appearing at the left side of his jaw.

"Of course," Roscoe said, taking a look at Jenny's pinched face. He had no way of knowing that her strained look represented disdain for what she referred to as his "circus antics" as much as sorrow over her dead brother.

"Ah," Roscoe cleared his throat and waved a leather-gloved hand at his sleek monoplane, "these Lockheeds have got the speed. Damned shame Amelia couldn't handle hers. But they're tricky beasts, just like Gilmore here. You really need to know what you're doing. Let's find food and drink. I'm famished."

They ended up back at the long table under the trees. Jenny looked around and counted, seven of them now. Her sense of foreboding hadn't abated. Laura jumping out of a plane with seemingly little instruction or worry about the risk. Heaven knows what that crazy Roscoe might add to the mix.

Out came the cold pitchers of beer, the moonshine in pickle jars, and the early announcement from Jim: "We has pecan pie today, 'sted a cobbler. Special made this morning."

The men were swapping war stories. The same tired old stories, Jenny thought. The war had ended ten years ago.

"Say, Roscoe, you've taken a long time to catch up," John needled. "While Roy and I were at the Battle of Verdun, you were working as a mechanic on dirigibles."

"Fella, you have that right," Roscoe said with a grin. "I got a slow start. My daddy wanted me to be a farmer. Used to always say: 'You'll never be worth nuthin' if you keep fooling around with things that burn gasoline instead of oats.' So, John, Roy tells me that you've turned into something of a mechanic yourself."

"Close. I'm working for Cord designing new cars."

"I'll be durned. I started out in love with cars and switched to planes. *He that sweareth to his own hurt, and changeth not*. Psalm 15:4. Speaking of the Bible, did anyone ever solve your old college mystery of the runaway man of the cloth?"

John laughed. "The priest in St. Louis? I can't believe you remember that after all these years."

"A Jesuit philosophy dean running off with a high school student he met at a lecture on Sigmund Freud?" Roscoe shook his head. "How could I forget? All the hocuspocus ingredients. So what happened?"

"I don't really know much. I just heard that he died in Germany a few years later, and the Jesuits brought his body back to St. Louis."

Laura leaned across the table to question Roscoe: "Germany? Just when was this?"

"Beats me. Ask John or Roy. It's their story."

"What did the woman look like?" she asked, turning to Roy.

"I don't know. Statuesque blonde. That's all I ever heard."

Laura put her hand to her mouth, squinted, almost seemed to be having an argument with herself. "Blue eyes?" she asked.

"Probably, if she was blond." Roy shrugged. "I never saw the woman. This happened years before I ever got to college. It was still a campus legend. The Jesuit dean who ran off with a high school kid, scandal of the decade."

"Don't you *ever* stop asking questions?" Jenny said. "Surely this ancient history can't be of interest to anyone." She'd been watching Laura's reactions to this story and found them strange. And how had she been cajoled into that parachute jump? Jenny felt sure she'd glimpsed Laura in the hall this morning coming out of Roy's room, but John had pooh-poohed her suspicions. "Don't be silly. Maybe you saw her or someone else coming from the bathroom. Darling, there *are* people in the halls in the mornings."

"Look at this." Laura was digging around in her handbag. She held up the picture of her mother and grandfather that she'd dropped in her purse as a last-minute thought before she left New York. "Could this be her?"

"I have no idea," Roy replied brusquely. "I never saw the woman. It was ten or fifteen years before my time."

After Laura insistently pushed the picture on him, he took a closer look at the fading photo in the waning light. "Good Christ," he said, "that could certainly be Father Bernard, the Jesuit. Those high cheekbones. His picture was handed around from time to time in campus beer halls."

"Father Bernard?" Laura said, her mouth open, her hand gripping the side of Jim's rough-hewn picnic table.

"Why are you asking these questions?" Jenny said impatiently.

"That's my mother. But you're wrong," Laura's tone was suddenly strident, defiant, emphatic, as she spit out the words, "the man can't be her husband, he's my *grandfather*."

Everyone at the table turned toward her in stunned silence. Jenny could hear the crickets chirping at the back of Jim's field, pots and pans clinking in his wife's kitchen. Laura looked from one to the other, blinking rapidly as though she had smoke in her eyes. She finally turned to Clem, her voice wavering. "Remember, your brother told you the story."

"That incident was around the turn of the century. The guy would be way too old to have been from around these parts." Clem's voice was soft, apologetic. "The Osage were moved here from Kansas only in 1871." He went on to explain that in those earlier Kansas days, many of the Indian children were sent to mission schools run by nuns and overseen by Jesuits. "It would be a logical step," he said, "for a boy sent off to Jesuits at a very young age to end up in one of their seminaries."

Whew, Jenny thought, that revelation took the air out of everyone's exuberance, and based on a picture that no one really recognizes. Besides, who would want to touch the hot potato of grandfather versus father? She'd known the reporter would be trouble, but this was too bizarre. She impatiently watched as the others proceeded to get drunk. Laura was downing moonshine like an old hand, but said little. She had the furrowed brow of someone trying to solve an algebraic equation in her head.

"We have a show to do tomorrow," Jenny kept warning the men as they dipped back into the pickle jar. But no one paid any attention. She said nothing at all to Laura. Not that she was rude, she just didn't have a clue what to say. She knew she should be using this opportunity to quiz Laura about her strange situation with her mother, not knowing where she was from, not being able to tell the difference between her own father and grandfather. But good gracious, how could one ask such questions? Scandalous. The poor girl. What kind of life must she have had? Jenny thought of her own stiff banker father, and how at times he exasperated her with his rigid ideas of what was proper. But she couldn't imagine her life without him. Without guidance, without a window on the larger world outside of home. Surely Laura's mother wouldn't have completely deprived her daughter of knowledge of her father? Didn't make any sense.

Staggering, most of them, they all finally climbed into Clem's Pierce-Arrow and went back to the hotel to go to bed. Laura, unbeknownst to the others, headed straight for Roy's room.

CHAPTER THIRTY-FIVE
GREAT EXPECTATIONS

"KIDDO, I DON'T KNOW WHAT TO TELL YOU," Laura heard Roy saying as though from a long distance. "You're the one who knows what your mother looks like, not me." He shrugged. "The guy *could* be the Jesuit, no way for me to know for sure. And sorry to say, if he is, he could be your father. Or he could be your grandfather, as you keep insisting. He could be *anybody*. How am I supposed to know?"

Laura was trying not to cry. Her head was spinning with the drink and the mystery. Sitting slumped on the bed in Roy's room, she could see her dejected reflection in the mirrored dressing table against the opposite wall. A man's silver-backed hairbrush resting on the table seemed to be growing from her left cheekbone, exaggerating its size, making it look square, totally blocking sight of her ear. The deformed image startled her, frightened her for a moment. High cheekbones! Who was she anyway? She must pull herself together. But she had to figure this out. Clem had said his family was embarrassed because the Jesuit was an Osage; he'd also said Laura looked Indian. Laura herself felt she looked like the man in the picture. But he must be her grandfather, she'd always believed that, had to believe that. Why was she driving herself crazy with this notion that her mother was the high school girl who ran off with the Jesuit? Because the picture was taken in St. Louis, because the time frame fit perfectly, because her mother would never tell Laura who her father was. She'd never, ever had a father, not even an image of one.

"Please tell me what you know about the Indians," she said to Roy.

"Listen, baby girl," Roy sat down beside her and put his arm over Laura's shoulder. "I think maybe you ought to go back to your own room and sleep this off. I'm not the one to deal with this kind of problem. Not my specialty."

"Then what is?" Laura looked up at him, her tears finally beginning to flow.

"Ah, geez, I don't know. But not this." Much of Roy's urbanity had suddenly skipped town, as it always did with any emotional crisis. He was out of his element. Love 'em and leave 'em, that was his style. Fly off to the next hamlet. France had been especially fertile soil, the men all off to war, and the women didn't speak your language.

Laura persisted. "John suggested that you were a pilot for a big oil company. Was that around here, when all the Osage were getting rich and getting killed?"

Roy grimaced. "It doesn't matter. I didn't enjoy it."

"When was it? Please tell me. I think it might be important."

"To whom?" Roy's words exploded. He jumped up from the bed and whirled to loom over Laura. "I see why Jenny says you're a pesky reporter. We try to have an enjoyable little fling here, and you're turning it into an inquisition. You don't know when to leave things alone."

His outburst was like a blast of cold air, a shot of ice water. Laura shook her head, clearing it.

"This is *not* to be left alone," she shot back. "I *need* to know." Her voice softened, and she reached for Roy's hand as he stood over her. "And maybe you need to tell it." She pulled him back down beside her on the bed.

Roy sat. Not only was he startled, Laura had startled

herself. It was not in her nature to take a soft approach when she was threatened, nor was it like her to have quick insight into what might lie underneath.

He took Laura's hand in both of his and smiled at her. "This has nothing to do with you, couldn't have." His voice was smooth, reassuring. "And it's no big deal, just a disgruntled time in my life."

"Please tell me," Laura said, putting her free hand up to Roy's cheek. "I want to know all I can about you."

Again startled, Roy emitted a dry laugh. "Okay," he said, squeezing her held hand. "It's two sentences and boring. I was personal pilot for a Tulsa guy named Alonso Drew, who headed up a drilling company of the same name. I didn't like being tied down, and I didn't want to be involved in some of his business dealings. That's it. So John thinks I should get a *real* job like him. Nah, not for me."

"Was it 1923, the year of most of the murders?"

"Yes, it was." Roy's voice was hard, definitive. It had the ring of confirmation of fears, although, of course, Laura had no idea just whose or what fears he was confirming. "And it didn't feel to me that Drew's hands were all that clean. A lawyer representing an Osage in an oil lease dispute was dumped off a railroad bridge in his underwear not long after Drew took him up for a ride, me piloting. It occurred to me that perhaps Drew hadn't been able to win him over with softsoap, so I bailed."

"Oh, how awful. Did you tell the police?"

"Police, what police? Are you kidding?" Roy's voice rose. It had left the confessional remorse of the moment before and was back to so-what. "The sheriff, the coroner, the local judges were all corrupt, in on schemes to cheat or kill the Indians. I didn't want any part. I had enough of fighting during the war. Better to just get out than worry about it. I consider myself a lover, not a fighter, my dear.

Now let's settle back here and forget this old history."

He gave Laura a long hard kiss, and the two of them fell back on the bed as she was protesting, "But I need to find out . . ."

Roy, indeed, did not have a highly developed social conscience, or bother to give the lack much thought. When they had joined the escadrille it was John who wanted to make the world safe for democracy. Roy hadn't wanted to be left behind, and the adventure sounded swell. Even Roy's interest in boosting Jenny had a decidedly selfish undercurrent. He was getting long in the tooth and tiring of all the running around. It would give him some status to be the "instructor" or "trainer" of a world-class aviator. Jenny could give him a new lease.

CHAPTER THIRTY-SIX
IT'S ALL OVER NOW

LAURA CAME AWAKE WITH A JOLT. Roy was stirring around, the desk lamp was on. She could smell a cigarette burning.

She smiled to herself, despite a dry mouth and a throbbing head. She had, perhaps, found some clues to her family. And she'd found her first lover. She sat up in bed, not bothering to pull the sheet up over her nakedness, and opened her arms wide to Roy, who she now saw was pacing before the open window in the small room.

"Good morning." Laura all but sang the words.

"It's early yet," he replied. "Still time to scoot on back to your room unnoticed."

"Really?" She tried to keep her voice light. "Such a hurry?"

He looked startled. "Surely you don't want to be compromised."

"Compromised?" She repeated, beginning to feel a knot in the pit of her stomach.

It all went downhill from there. Roy informed her in hushed mea culpa tones that he was married, which, of course, Jenny had already told her. And he did a mouth-open double take when Laura gave a so-what shrug, having no more reaction to such news than her mother would have had.

"How often do you ever see your wife?" Laura asked with what verged on a sly smile.

"Not a lot, but still."

"But still what?" Laura asked. "I've got to get back to New York, get back to work. Once I've questioned my mother, I hope to return here from time to time."

"Whoa," Roy said. "What is it you're expecting here? You're a grown woman. You run around the country on your own."

The room was in shadow, only the small desk lamp threw a yellow circle of light. The single fan creaked with each turn. The ordinary hotel furniture lent a shabby atmosphere: a full-sized bed, a scarred dresser, an overstuffed mohair chair. Laura noticed the carpet for the first time; it was a muddy brown with an ebony thread running through. What *had* she expected? she wondered, as she looked at her chemise lying where it had been carelessly flung on the floor. She shivered in the hot, stuffy room, a line of Aunt Edna's roiling her brain: *Oh, think not I am faithful to a vow!*

"I don't know," she said hesitantly, a frown creasing her forehead. "I don't know. I guess I thought we were in love."

"Oh my God," Roy replied. "You can't be serious."

Chapter Thirty-Seven
THE CAT'S OUT OF THE BAG

JENNY IN HER DRESSING GOWN, TOOTHBRUSH in hand, couldn't believe her eyes. Down the hall on the right, that was Roy's room! And there was Laura, bold as you please, leaving and not too gently closing the door behind her.

Jenny pivoted on the ball of her slipper-clad right foot and marched over to Laura, her bath towel flying a flag of indignation. "Are you crazy?" she exploded.

Laura didn't respond other than with a stricken look.

"Didn't your mother ever teach you anything?" Jenny demanded.

Still no response. The shoulders slumped a bit more, the head hung.

"Oh gosh," Jenny said, suddenly stricken herself. "How stupid of me. I guess that's what this is all about. A mother with no morals." Exasperated, she raised a fist of clutched facecloth and slapped it against her knee.

Laura instinctively ducked, thinking for an instant she was going to be struck.

Midwestern morality is the enemy. How many times had Laura heard that growing up? Her mother endlessly championing free love, free thought, free expression. Laura had never been able to figure out how she fit into such a system—any system, as a matter of fact. She had tried going her own way, but that didn't appear to be working out all that well either. She remembered being taken as a child to suffragette parades where Inez Milholland, a high priestess of women's rights, rode through the streets of Greenwich Village on a great white horse, Aunt Edna and her mother waving and cheering. And the cold night in Washington Square Park shortly before Laura's eleventh birthday when she had tagged along with her mother and some of her friends to the ceremony declaring Greenwich Village a "free and independent republic." Several people had shot off cap pistols and raised their flag of freedom after climbing the long spiral staircase inside the Arc de Triomphe look-alike at the bottom of Fifth Avenue. John Sloan later made an etching called *Arch Conspirators*. It showed Marcel Duchamp, long before he became infamous for drawing Mona Lisa with a beard, seated next to him, eating a sandwich. Even at that age, Laura had thought the adults were being silly. Although she did have fun chasing through the snow after the red balloons that the revelers floated down from the top of the arch.

"Well?" Jenny demanded. "Say something. Don't just stand there."

And Laura began to cry.

"Now look here." Jenny stopped for a moment, stunned. "Uh, I didn't mean anything by . . . but of course I did."

Laura looked at her, blinking, the tears continuing to roll.

Jenny tentatively patted Laura's shoulder. "Confound it! I don't know what to say."

Laura responded with a sniffle, and rubbed the back of her hand across her nose.

"Damn," Jenny blurted, startling them both. "You're a very accomplished woman, you can't just cry this way." She glanced around at the drab hallway with its threadbare runner and dim overhead bulbs. Not the place for a private chat. It was hardly the velvet carpet of the Skirvin, its every room with a private bath. "Let's go downstairs and get a cup of coffee." Laura just stood there. "Go," Jenny commanded. "I'll be down in two minutes, just have to throw on some clothes." She gave a gentle shove to Laura, who returned the gesture with a woebegone look. "Go," Jenny repeated. "I promise. I'll only take a second."

When they had settled in the dining room with coffee, juice, and biscuits, Laura wiped her tears with a linen napkin. She looked a mess. "Roy's the problem," she finally said.

"Of course he's a problem," Jenny said sharply, biting into a biscuit with honey. "But listen, Laura, I warned you about that."

"He was so sympathetic and admiring," Laura replied weakly. She hadn't touched her food, even her coffee.

"I just can't believe you're so naïve. For starters, he's a ladies' man. Always has been. Drink your orange juice!" she instructed with a bark. "Besides, he was using you to goad me into flying more. How could you not realize that?"

"You're good friends with him."

"So? Doesn't mean you can't see people for what they are." Jenny closed her eyes, a momentary vision of her own father's concern over John. That's what fathers are for, to give you a proper sense of the world, a grounding. To worry about you and give a good talking to the man you're going to marry.

"Why would I see it?" Laura asked. "I don't understand any of this. Your being friends with all these men. Your lack of aspiration is incomprehensible to me."

"So fine," Jenny snapped. "We're going to have to cut this short. I may not have any *aspirations*, as you call them, but we've got a show to do with Roscoe."

"Roy says he's going to replace us tomorrow."

"So what? He's said all along he would, as soon as he found someone."

"I don't want to leave him."

"Oh good glory." Jenny got up from the table.

"Please," Laura said, reaching up for Jenny's arm, "don't go yet. You seem to know all these things that I don't."

Jenny dropped back into her chair with a thud. "Gosh, I don't know what to say. The things I know, one just knows, that's all. Mothers teach you how to behave."

"Oh," Laura said, a startled look on her face.

"You're a mystery to me." Jenny shook her head in bewilderment. "You don't seem to know anything about how to conform to expectations. I come from a world where the rules of proper ladylike behavior are written on your soul. Modulate your voice, never carry on a private conversation in an elevator, white shoes are never to be worn before Easter or after Labor Day. Women don't smoke, or, if heaven forbid they do, they are NEVER seen doing so on the street." Jenny giggled, as though proudly sharing the secret of a wayward child. "My mother is appalled that I end up with sunburned skin because of my flying."

"I never heard of any of those rules," Laura said plaintively.

"That's not surprising from someone who doesn't even seem to know that you don't sleep with a man until you marry him."

"I sure never heard that one," Laura said with a skeptical frown. "Who made it up? It sounds like something out of *The Scarlet Letter*."

Jenny put down her coffee cup with a bang. "Your mother has always refused to tell you who your father was, hasn't she?"

Laura abruptly stood. "Wait here, please, just for a minute. Please." Her voice was pleading. "Have another cup of coffee. I'll be right back." She ran from the dining room and across the lobby, heading upstairs. She was back, breathless, in a moment, waving her faded photograph.

"This is my mother," she said, throwing herself down hard in the dining room chair and handing the picture to Jenny. "It was taken in St. Louis. Look at the inscription on the back."

"*Father Bernard.*" Jenny's voice was barely a whisper, her gray eyes round as saucers. "Oh my God. I see what you must be thinking. You always thought he was your grandfather." She stopped and tried to backpedal, seeing Laura's wounded face. "Ah, but of course, it must be some kind of bizarre coincidence."

"I don't know." Laura bit her lower lip. "I heard from neighborhood kids that she had run off with an older married man, not someone committed to some church. I always thought I wanted to know who he was. Now I'm not so sure."

"How awful." Jenny shook her head as though trying to clear it. "How unbelievably awful. But we *must* find out. I wouldn't let a thing like this go unchallenged."

"My mother has a rug on her floor that looks exactly like a blanket I saw on the streets yesterday," Laura said. "It's got children's handprints woven all over it."

"What? Are we now going to discuss interior decoration?" Jenny responded with sarcasm.

"What if I'm an Indian? You heard what Clem said about the Jesuit."

"An Indian!" Jenny was stunned by the question. But it did make a certain kind of sense. Laura just sat there staring at her as though Jenny had the answers to the questions of the universe. Jenny realized with a start that no one had ever before looked upon her as a sage. Hadn't she just complained to Roy the other day that everyone treated her like some doll? This unexpected turn was kind of a nice feeling. But would it go both ways? Jenny needed some answers herself. John had told her again last night that she could do whatever she wanted about pursuing a flying career. "But if you plan to do it, do it!" he'd said, with something close to an uncharacteristic impatience in his voice. "Make a real commitment. Get your transport license. Quit worrying about what your parents think. Who cares if they don't like to see you in slacks."

"An Indian?" Jenny repeated, trying to come back to the problem at hand. She laughed lightly. "Just hope you're an Osage, I guess. You'd be rich that way."

"Jenny, please." Laura leaned across the small breakfast table and pushed away the sugar bowl in a pleading gesture with an outstretched hand. "I don't know what to do about anything here. I've made a fool of myself with Roy, with everyone, I guess, by not understanding, by getting drunk."

Jenny exhaled, and rubbed her tongue across her front teeth. "Gee, I don't know what to say. You're treating me like I'm some font of wisdom when I can't even figure out what to do with my own life."

It was Laura's turn to laugh, and with the release, she took her first gulp of orange juice. After setting the glass down, she smiled and said, "That's easy. You're so young— what are you, eighteen? Plenty of time for a long brilliant career. Just go get that next license, and go from there."

The two of them burst into giggles.

"Funny, isn't it," Jenny said, "how when you look at a problem from the inside it looks so hard, but to someone from the outside it seems so easy? I guess that's what friends are for," she added with something close to awe in her voice.

"Please help me understand about Roy," Laura said. "I don't get it."

Jenny looked pensive for a moment, then finished off

the coffee in her cup. "Roy." She took a deep breath. "Roy's just trying to recapture his youth and somehow sees me as a way to do it. Believe it or not, he even cares about his wife and kids—just forever trying to prove something. John says he's always been that way. Living on the edge, or having grandiose ideas about himself. It's sweet and touching, but nothing anyone in her right mind would fall for."

Laura's head snapped back, as though she'd been slapped.

"I'm sorry," Jenny said, reaching across the table to pat Laura's hand. "That was a bit brutal." She paused as the waiter came to their table with a tall silver coffee pot and refilled her cup. She continued once he'd walked away. "Sometimes he acts like he's in love with himself. Maybe that's why I've been so resistant to Roy's grandiose plans for me. I've always known that his illusions about himself were nothing more than that, so I didn't want to fall for a line of patter about how great or grand I could be. And I don't like the idea that people think I'm trying to somehow regain my dead brother. I idolized him as a child, and that's what led me to the airport, but John's the one who put the idea into my head that I could actually fly."

Laura folded her napkin in a very deliberate way, staring at Jenny all the while, as she seemed to be searching for words. "Then why—"

Jenny cut her off, her voice sharp. "I'm lazy. I've got a good life. Why shake that up? Risk it all, traveling around the country to air shows?" Her tone softened. "But now John's saying Roy's right, and you're saying it too." She smiled ruefully. "That I should go for it. Get my transport license, at least. Not purposely hold myself back. You have to understand, I'm cautious, conservative. I've lived a very circumscribed life. I'm not a banker's daughter for nothing. My big rebellion was dating John, way older than me, a man of the world, all those French girls. My parents were horrified, my high school friends wild with jealousy."

Laura was mesmerized. She hadn't taken her eyes off Jenny as the pilot had picked her way through her own feelings about Roy and how he was affecting her life.

Jenny squared her jaw. "I guess I need to be making up my own mind from now on, don't I?"

"Hooray," said Laura, lifting her coffee cup in a toast.

Jenny smiled. An awkwardness moved in. Laura drank her juice, buttered a biscuit, fiddled with her coffee cup. Jenny held hers up to signal the waiter for another refill.

Finally, Laura broke the silence. "Tell me about your brother."

Jenny made a small sound that was almost a chuckle, touched her right little finger to her lips, a tiny smile creasing the corners of her eyes. "Charles? I don't know. In a funny way, I guess he was my best friend."

Laura's face lit up. "Really, a brother so much older?"

"When I was little, he would put me on his knee and read *Peter Rabbit*, and once in a while play games. But never when his friends could see. Once he said, 'Shoo, shoo, get along, little doggie.'" Jenny's words came from deep in her throat, as she frowned and puckered her lips. "He and some high school pals were in our living room, and I had tried to join and climb on his lap. His friends laughed, and I cried." She paused, took a sip of coffee, then spoke more slowly as she continued. "My father intervened that time; he heard the racket from his study and came out. But I was the one he admonished, not Charles. I think I was four. 'It's way past your bedtime, young miss. And what do you think you're doing down here with the boys? You have your own dolls and things to play with.'"

Jenny smiled now at the memory, looking into the middle distance as if searching out the details of her story. "I realized, long after Charles died, that was the summer before he was to go away to college. My father explained that Charles and his friends were deep in conversation about the growing war in Europe."

Laura sat up straighter. "That's funny. When I was a child my best friend was also an adult. My Aunt Edna would read to me and play jacks."

Jenny went on as though she hadn't heard Laura's remark. "The last time I saw him, he had come home in his uniform—shiny brass buttons, even on his epaulettes. He took me down to Klein's drugstore—I was wearing a yellow pinafore—and he bought me an ice cream cone. That was a big thing then, we usually ate ice cream with a spoon at home, but here was this special thing they were calling a waffle cone, or cornucopia. Charles explained it. He said they were first introduced at the World's Fair in St. Louis way back in 1904. That cone flashed back in my mind when I found that John had gone to college there." Jenny continued with no segue from one memory to another. "I remember looking up at Charles, he was a towhead, he was bathed in the glow from the brass and he seemed to wolf down the ice cream almost all in one inhale. Funny how things impress kids. For years after, in fact still, I guess, I eat ice cream so fast it leaves a frozen ache in my throat for several minutes."

And with no pause, Jenny returned to Laura. "Here's my advice to you, kiddo. The first thing we have to do is find out the truth about the Jesuit. Clem will do it, he's a lawyer. And that should help you get over Roy, since Clem is sweet on you."

"How do you know?" Laura asked in surprise.

"How do I know? Girl, have you not got eyes?"

Laura looked bewildered.

"Holy smoke," Jenny said. "We are a pair."

C HAPTER THIRTY-EIGHT
THE TRAIN TO NEW YORK

LAURA WAS THE ONLY PERSON TO GET on the train in Pershing—a whistle stop for the fast train to Chicago, meaning the stationmaster had to flag it down. She still had her valise and hatbox, but it felt as though everything else in her life had changed in the six days since she'd left New York. For starters, she was wearing no hat or gloves.

She made her way to the center of the car, where she found a place to herself. They would stop only once before Kansas City; she was relieved at the prospect of time alone without some seatmate chattering away. Cheesy had left for New York a day earlier, ordered back by Barnes who said he'd had "enough pictures of airplanes to last a lifetime." He let him stay only long enough to get pictures of Gilmore the Lion in flight. Her boss had warned Laura, too, that although he liked the story and photos of her parachute jump and loved the one of her dangling from the tree, he still wasn't about to pay her for traveling time, so she'd better make it home the quickest way possible.

Roy had been gentlemanly enough to see her off before Jenny and John drove her away from the Duncan Hotel. He took her hand. "It was a lovely time, my dear. But you must learn to not take these things too seriously." He had put his arms around her when she burst into tears.

As John shifted into gear, he'd turned to Laura in the

backseat and said, "Roy is careless with people." He paused for a beat then added, "Even with himself."

She had burst into tears again when Jenny hugged her as they heard the whistle of the train approaching the station at Pershing, south of Pawhuska. The Flynns had gone to quite a lot of trouble to get her there. John had had to ride back to Ponca City with Clem to retrieve his Duesenberg, then backtrack to Pawhuska instead of going on to Oklahoma City, as he'd intended. But Jenny had insisted. "After all she's been through, we can't just leave her to fend for herself," she told her husband.

"You're a special, special friend," Jenny had said to Laura, shouting over the toots and hissing of the approaching train. Laura flashed for a moment on the whistle of the ship that had sailed Aunt Edna away. She left for Paris a month before Laura's fifteenth birthday, to be a foreign correspondent for *Vanity Fair*. That's when Laura decided she'd like to be a reporter, a proper one, not freelance like her mother and her friends with no real jobs, but something solid. Laura went down to the docks to see Edna off. She had gotten there quite early to make sure she didn't miss Edna, but ended up waiting in the cold for hours, stamping in the snow trying to keep her feet warm. She went briefly inside a dusty shipping office where an electric fire was lit, but didn't stay long, worried she'd never see Edna again. The French Line's SS *Rochambeau* was at the ready, its two decks lined with waving passengers, its whistle tooting; they were about to lift the gangplank when Edna came running. Laura frantically yelled and yelled as Edna boarded; she finally turned as she got on the ship. Then, miracle of miracles, she moved right over to a deck railing and they both waved until the ship was out of sight.

As Laura had boarded the train in Pershing, Jenny said: "I'm sorry I was so mean at first, and I swear I will come to New York soon. I'm going to study like crazy for my transport license, then you can write a story that I'm only the fourth woman in the US to get one. I'm sure I'll be at Roosevelt Field often."

Laura dropped her luggage on the adjoining seat and scrambled over it to the window to return Jenny's wave. She was trotting alongside the train as it slowly picked up speed, her face melding with Aunt Edna's. Laura's tears began flowing again, her eyes red and swollen.

She opened her handbag and found an already wet and crumpled handkerchief. She must stop this. She never cried. Never. She hardly knew the meaning of tears. On the playground, a few encounters with ruffians on the street—one didn't cry, you just hit back. No emotion from Evelyn, who took pride in being what she called "self-contained." Laura wasn't sure if she liked herself better this new way or the way she was before. Good things, like making friends with Jenny, felt painful somehow. So did the dreadful suspicion that perhaps her mother had been the object of derision all these years. The woman who ran off with the priest.

The rejection from Roy was still too raw to even think about. She needed to read a magazine or work a puzzle, do *something* to take her mind away; the lost love was so painful that, just as they said in books, it felt like a stab in the heart. It took your breath away. It was even worse than the awful pain she'd felt when Aunt Edna went away. This was only the second time she'd ever lost someone. There'd really never been anyone else in her life to lose. Certainly not a father; she'd never had one in the first place.

Laura couldn't stop herself from replaying the excruciating scene in Roy's darkened hotel room, the silent movie titles floating around in her head as the melodrama unfolded to the clickity-clack music of wheels hitting rails. "What did you expect?" The words were drawn out and oval like steam puffs emerging from the villain's mouth.

Her face burning hot, not from the heat of the loco-motive but with embarrassment and pain, Laura watched herself say: "I . . . guess . . . I . . . thought . . . we . . . were . . . in . . . love." Each word emerged like a single phrase with every turn of a train wheel. As the curtain fell, the crescendo, the villain, throwing a black cape over his face. *Oh my God*, the headless miscreant replied. *You can't be serious.*

Laura stared out the window at passing scrub oak, try-ing to staunch the flow of tears with her sopping handker-chief. It *was* sort of funny that Jenny had used the exact same words as Roy: "Oh my God, you can't be serious."

As Laura was settling down and stifling her sniffles, the train began to slow to make its stop. She gasped. The scene out the window was stunning. Oil derricks as far as the eye could see. A forest of them. It looked like a child's playroom floor covered with Erector Sets.

Laura had seen quite a few derricks around both Ponca City and Pawhuska, but nothing like this. A sea of them. Wishing Cheesy were here to take a picture, she grabbed her pencil to make some notes about the strange history of the Osage wealth and death—to heck with whether Barnes said it was an old story. Besides, it actually seemed possible that she might have a personal interest in the subject, although she couldn't bring herself to think about the ramifications of that. She was trying to put it out of her mind until she could confront her mother. But this view was inspiration. She'd base her story on what Clem had told her, plus what-ever she could find in morgue clips once she got back to the *Enterprise-Post*. He'd said Congress cut off the headright allotments in January 1906. She hadn't bothered to write the date down—easy to remember, it was the month before she was born.

When she'd asked Clem how many Osage were killed

for their headrights, he replied simply, "No one will ever know."

"That sounds crazy." Laura was astounded. "Surely you can tell when someone is murdered, or even dies suspiciously?"

"Not when authorities look the other way, or are in cahoots with the killers." They'd been in Clem's mother's house. It was the day Laura had used the telephone there to call her office. She'd been somewhat distracted at the time, trying to decide if she had the nerve to go on flying with Jenny after having seen two narrow escapes that very day. As Clem told his story, Laura was surrounded with the obvious riches of the Donohue home. When she'd first met Clem he told her that his family had moved to Ponca City to get away from violence in Pawhuska.

As Laura made her notes now, she shuddered at how understated Clem's comment was. Back at his mother's house, with Laura seated in one of the straight-backed gold-leaf library chairs, Clem had explained the situation: "The federal government controls the allotments, which means there are almost more lawyers and so-called guardians in Pawhuska than there are Indians. The money is parceled out by the Bureau of Indian Affairs to these minders and they pass it on to individual Osage, or more likely their creditors. The sheriff, the coroner, the minders—none of them bother to question the death of an Indian. They say he or she was probably drunk on moonshine or peyote, or had a stroke or a heart attack."

And, according to Clem, that was that. No inquiry. No autopsy. The endless cover-ups began to unravel in 1921 when yet another so-called drunken Indian was revealed to have had a bullet in the back of her head. Within two years, the woman's sister and two others in her immediate family had died. The white man who had been married to the sister gained control of what she would have inherited from the

deaths. He and his uncle, who was the driving force behind those particular killings, were eventually indicted. But
not until the US Bureau of Investigation finally sent in four
undercover agents as salesmen, cattle buyers, and the like,
because the town officials were so corrupt. A lot of lawyers
and minders suddenly moved out of state when a grand jury
began to probe. Even so, only three cases were ever brought
to trial, and it took years to get convictions.

The train was pulling into the station, a low building of
yellow sandstone with *Santa Fe Railroad* cut into its face.
Below that on each side of the door leading into the depot,
signs read: *Bartlesville*. In Laura's mind it would forever be
Derrick Town. She could see the conductor helping several
people mount the metal stool to her car. She spread her pos-
sessions out, hoping it would discourage anyone from sitting next to her.

Clem had laughed when he'd delivered his punch line.
"The Osage insisted on buying title to the land when the
government forced them down here to Indian territory from
Kansas. God's own irony that this communal land turned
up swimming in oil, with only 2,229 people left on the tribal
rolls to share it all."

CHAPTER THIRTY-NINE
BACK IN NEW YORK

LAURA WAS EXHAUSTED WHEN SHE ARRIVED at Grand Central Terminal after nearly thirty-six hours of travel, but eager to confront her mother with her growing belief that her father had been a Jesuit priest. A redcap wheeled her luggage through to Vanderbilt Avenue, where she had stepped out of a taxi to begin this journey exactly a week ago. It was difficult for her to absorb how much her life had changed since then—a broken heart, and perhaps a scandalous father.

Her spirits sank when the cab pulled up at her brownstone on Gay Street and she saw no lights in any of the second-floor windows. It was too early for Evelyn to be in bed. Her mother often stayed away for days at a time with one of her many lovers. As Laura went up the front stoop with her hatbox and satchel, she realized she was nearly holding her breath, hoping that this wasn't one of those times.

She turned on the lights in the dark apartment, hung up her clothes, scoured the empty pantry for something to eat, and waited in the sitting room until ten o'clock. Finally, she climbed the steps to her attic room, knowing she had to be in the office first thing in the morning. Barnes had warned her about no pay for travel time.

After fraught dreams of Indians in war paint encircling her desk at the *Enterprise-Post* while she tried to hold them off with a tiny typewriter that shot out lead pencils, Laura dragged herself out of bed. It was seven in the morning and her mother still wasn't home.

Laura wearily left for work, hoping she would get a warmer reception there than she'd had at home. She got off the subway at the Park Row Elevated Terminal, across from City Hall, and walked to the old *Times* building, where she stopped in the lobby shop for a coffee. The counter boy in his white jacket and paper soda-jerk's cap took her nickel and poured her a hot brew with a smile. "Haven't seen you in a week or so. Where you been?"

"On assignment," she replied. Those words had a nice feel. Newspapers seem to come and go from Park Row, she thought. *The Times* had moved out of this building and uptown to 43rd Street long ago. Now the *Daily News* was preparing to do the same. Even so, there still seemed to be plenty of jobs in this business. Not like the journals her mother wrote for. *The Little Review* was on its last legs. *The Masses* had lasted only a few years. It was true, the literary magazines didn't seem to care whether you were a man or a woman. But still, thinking about all the newspapers located around here—there were probably fifteen—it seemed she could surely make more of a go at earning a living than her mother ever had.

When she finally got to the city room, Barnes actually seemed glad to see her.

"So, if it isn't the prodigal daughter!" he yelled as she walked in. John Riley and Mac looked up from their typewriters and smiled. When she sat down at her desk stacked high with editions of the *Enterprise-Post* that had piled up while she was away, Joe Collins, chewing on his ubiquitous toothpick at the next desk, pushed back his snap-brimmed hat and said, "So, you did pretty good, kid."

Myrtle called over from her switchboard position in the

middle of the room, "Welcome back. You got messages."

"Gee, thanks, everybody," Laura said to no one in particular. She put down her handbag, took off her hat and gloves, and set about reading the old newspapers and clearing her desk of filled ashtrays and dirty coffee cups that squatters had left behind.

When she got around to looking at her messages, she was startled to find that there were ten from Joe Bailey, that cute boy with her same name whom she'd met on the Cleveland train. And one from Clem. Joe's all seemed to say that he was in town on a story and would like to take her to dinner. Clem's just said hello. Both had left return numbers, but she decided not to answer either. She'd had enough of men for a while. Anyway, Clem was probably calling because Jenny had asked him to check about the Osage priest. But Laura felt she must confront her own mother before she could talk to anyone else about it. Besides, Jenny had said Clem was sweet on her, and she would be embarrassed to talk to him after her disaster with Roy.

The day went downhill from there. After all the exciting stories she'd written in the last week and what had felt like a warm office welcome, she was once again low on the assignment totem pole. Funny Indian expression—what made her think of that? Was she preparing herself for her heritage? Ah, nonsense.

She marched up to Barnes to ask for something better to do than a society luncheon, but he was in familiar form. "The Dow's skyrocketing, the Yankees appear headed for disaster. Got no time for your bellyaching." He looked over at the rewrite bank, which was frantically working a story on a collision between a passenger ship and an oil tanker off the coast of San Francisco. He nodded his head in their direction. "Go through the passenger list and see if any are local. Mor'n a hundred dead or missing."

After that, she got one quick assignment to check out something, which boiled down to a cat up a tree. In the afternoon, she saw Cheesy rushing through the hall to answer what fellows in the office said was a grisly police call, but he didn't even have time to wave to her.

CHAPTER FORTY
LABOR DAY WEEKEND

RIDING HOME ON THE EL, LAURA NOTICED with a jolt the familiar passing scene on Sixth Avenue. It felt as though she had been away from home for such a long time. Frequently she rode past without noticing what was beyond the train's windows, but just as often the images she was seeing were replaced in her mind by the familiarity of John Sloan paintings that hung on their own walls or those of her mother's friends: the curve in the el at 3rd Street, Village rooftops, umbrellas and flowers in the rain. The colors and brushstrokes always streaking the landscape with a feeling of night. She blinked as she stared out, riding above the shops, realizing that the colors of twilight were real, the days getting shorter as the summer receded. Would Evelyn be home when she arrived? She had to find out if the Indian priest was her father. It was crazy, didn't make any sense that she could have stumbled on it. Yet it all seemed to fit. The picture taken in St. Louis. The man identified as Father Bernard. According to Roy and John, that was the priest's name. Dean Bernard, they had called him. With the Labor Day weekend beginning, Laura feared her mother might be spending the last warm days at Steepletop, Aunt Edna's farm in Upstate New York.

She climbed down the wooden el stairs at her stop, her heart racing in anticipation of confronting her mother. As she turned the corner of Gay Street, she could see the light of a small lamp that sat near their front window. When Laura opened the door to the apartment, a recording of Al Jolson's "Toot, Toot, Tootsie!" was coming from their small radio.

"The wanderer returns," Evelyn said, looking up from her reading, an unusual and almost welcoming smile on her lips. "It's been a bit quiet around here without your banging around."

"Did you have an affair with a priest in St. Louis?" Laura demanded. She knew no other way to approach this. Evelyn would mop up the floor with her no matter what. Everything in the room was out of focus except her mother, as though the tiny lamp were a spotlight. Laura saw that Evelyn had on a new dress. She'd never before seen her wear red. The color seemed bright and shimmery in the small light that felt blinding. "Is it possible he could be my father? I thought he was my grandfather," Laura faltered, her heart racing. She was so short of breath her next words came out as a whispered gasp. "I look like him."

Laura had promised herself that she would stay calm enough to at least watch Evelyn's first reactions, judge her by *how* she responded, not by what she said. As always, she had little hope that her mother would tell her the truth. But as Laura blurted out her stream of questions in her distress, she registered nothing more than the shimmering light and the blur of Evelyn's changing facial expressions. What had they been? Fear, shock, horror, anger? Too late to ever know. Laura caught her breath, trying to collect herself—her mother's face now seemed to show only disbelief. But the book Evelyn had been reading, Nietzsche's *Beyond Good and Evil,* was lying, binding up, on the floor. How had it gotten there? Laura had been so upset she hadn't even seen it fall.

"Well?" Laura prodded.

"What are you talking about? You're behaving as

though you've gone nuts." Evelyn appeared slightly mystified, but otherwise composed.

Laura was prepared. She snapped open her purse and
pulled out the old sepia photo of Evelyn and Father Bernard. She thrust the picture at her mother. "So who's this?"

Evelyn's eyes grew wide; she moved her head back first,
and then seemed to sink her body backward into her chair,
recoiling as if from a threatening object.

Laura walked to the radio and shut off "Tootsie." The
room went silent. Only the drip of the old icebox could be
heard from the kitchen. Mother and daughter glared at each
other, Evelyn still scrunched back in her chair, Laura standing over her, hands on hips.

"Well?"

"Did Vincent give that to you?" Evelyn's tone was sharp,
but her voice was shaky.

"Yes."

"What did she say?"

"Nothing. She said I was supposed to ask you."

"Why didn't you?" Evelyn seemed to have gained her
composure, her sarcasm was coming back. "What took you
so long?"

"I'm asking you now."

"You're quite the reporter, just like John Reed, aren't
you? Digging up all that. John would have been impressed."

"Don't try to change the subject."

"You were just a tyke when John went off to Russia."

"Mother!" Laura was practically screeching. "Is this
man my father? Or was he just one more of your many lovers before I was born? You've made me believe all my life
that my father was unknown. How could you? Deprive me
of at least knowing that there was *someone*, a real person
who might have belonged to me? I was like Topsy, who just
growed—out of nowhere, like a weed." Laura was trem-

bling. She had never confronted her mother like this. She had learned at a very young age that there was no point. But why could she *never* get any kind of response or answers from Evelyn? The woman seemed to revel in torturing her. Evelyn always made her feel as though she had done something wrong. Laura was beginning to guess that her sin was in having been born.

Another long silence ensued.

Evelyn looked down at her hands twisting in her lap, then up at Laura. She reached for her Nietzsche and placed it squarely on her lap as though for support. "Your father was a fine man," she said. "Loved his religion, but our passion was too strong."

"Oh my God! You loved him? Did you? He was the only person in your life, then?" Tears were streaming down Laura's face, and she made no attempt to stop them. "Where is he now?"

"Dead. Died in Germany. There was a strong Freudian movement at the time in Munich. All sorts of brilliant minds, Otto Gross—"

"I don't care about that! But did you really meet at a lecture on Freud?"

"William James was the lecturer. He was touring the country and came to St. Louis." Evelyn's imperious bearing was returning, the font of knowledge puffing up to impart wisdom. "He really was the one who introduced the concept of psychoanalysis to America, you know."

"No, I *don't* know. But tell me about my father, my *real* father. The one I always assumed was nothing more than a blob of all the men you ever knew."

"What an utterly disgusting thing to say," Evelyn snapped. "Wherever did you come up with that?"

"It says *Father Unknown* on my birth record. You're the one who put it there." Laura was finally remembering to watch closely for telltale expressions—Evelyn was frowning, squinting, as though not quite understanding what she was hearing. Now was the time to catch her off guard.

"Tell me about Germany," Laura said in a soft voice.

The room was in shadow except for the weak front lamp. Neither mother nor daughter had bothered to switch on another light. Evelyn took on a dreamy look, and as though straining to read words written on the wall somewhere behind Laura, she began talking. Laura heard of sidewalk cafés, and famous artists and thinkers, and of the vitality of an Old World intelligentsia. Evelyn made no direct reference to her companion of those years, but by listening closely, Laura decided that references to a "Mickey" must surely have been Father Bernard.

Laura was afraid to break the spell, but finally could restrain herself no longer. "Tell me more about Mickey," she said.

Evelyn's mood changed in a flash, the dreaminess was gone, her face sagged. It was the first time Laura noticed that her mother was aging. The skin was not quite so fresh, tiny lines showed around her eyes. The severity of her pulled-back hair now revealed a bit more than the sculptured structure of her still-beautiful face.

"He was my father." Laura did not use a questioning tone. It was demanding, insistent.

"Yes," Evelyn replied crisply. "He was short and dark, like you. What else do you want to know?"

"Everything." Laura had trouble getting the word out, her voice cracking, nearly failing her.

A look of pain crossed Evelyn's face, but she seemed to square her shoulders, resigned, and then began in rapid order to tick off information as though reading from a bio. She informed Laura that Father Bernard was fluent in German, French, and Latin, and that he loved *The Katzenjam-*

mer Kids. He was a prolific writer for academic journals on Vatican murals and various aspects of church philosophy, and that his doctorate in existential philosophy had led to his early interest in Freud's teachings. And yes, indeed, he was an Osage Indian who had gone on to the seminary from mission schools.

Evelyn paused, and for an instant the dreamy tone came back, and her voice caught as she said: "He'd never had a date before he met me. I was not quite sixteen."

Laura gasped, her eyes blinking rapidly as she tried to take all this in.

Then abruptly, with no warning, Evelyn said: "Other than his interest in the Sunday comics, I don't think he'd be too interested in your work for a tabloid."

The brutal comment ended the discussion, and Laura climbed the stairs to her attic room. She sat on her windowsill overlooking the sunflowers and tomato plants winding down their summer growth in the yard below, crying over the father she had never known, and her first lover, whom she had known for only four days.

She wiped her tears and smiled ruefully at the thought that this was the scene of another parting. There had been icicles hanging from the trees and snow piled on the vegetable patch in the garden when Aunt Edna had given her the picture, and they had had their final parting as playmates. It was Laura's fourteenth birthday, two years after Edna had given her the diary. Edna had paid a surprise visit in response to a note Laura had slipped under the door of Edna's West 12th Street apartment. *I thought we would be friends forever,* she had written. *I miss you.*

Laura had included a stick drawing of a sad-faced clown, along with a line from one of Edna's poems: *I shall forget you presently, my dear.*

Edna, wearing a purple silk dress with a bright yellow

scarf beneath her drab winter coat, showed up the next day saying she'd come to celebrate Laura's birthday, and found her home alone. Evelyn was out with friends. Edna was her usual ebullient self. "So let's have a party and imagine that your mother is here. I've brought you a tea set that Bunny Wilson gave me."

Laura smiled down at the garden, remembering. They had made tea, and climbed the steep stairs to come up here. Edna'd made a flourish of setting an empty chair then slyly placing on it the picture of Evelyn in the lacy hat, saying she'd brought it along in anticipation that Laura's mother would be "out."

"I have no money to buy you a present, so I'm giving you this. But hide it, and don't ever tell your mother I gave it to you." Edna toasted Laura for her birthday with one of the fragile bone china cups, remarking dryly, "I have too much family, and you don't have enough." Edna's sister and mother were with her then, had come down from Maine to live with her. Evelyn remarked on it caustically many years later. "Look what all that cost Vincent. Not just in money, when no one had any, but in energy and emotional drain. Families are a burden—they drag you down, just as hers did."

As they parted, Edna had said: "I'm sorry, don't hate me. But my poetry is my passion. It's my life." And she was gone. They never played jacks again.

With a determined shrug, Laura came back to the present. Would her father really disapprove of her job? The heck with it; literary journals were boring. Besides, people smiled at her in the office today, finally! And where else could she find a job that allowed her to jump out of an airplane?

CHAPTER FORTY-ONE
STOCKS SOAR WHILE A PLANE CRASHES

ON THE TUESDAY AFTER LABOR DAY, the newsroom was buzzing by midafternoon with stock market numbers: volume was high, prices were soaring. That seemed like old news to Laura, stocks just kept going up, and who cared anyway. She certainly didn't know anyone rich enough to buy and sell, even though stories kept saying ordinary people were invested heavily in the market. She got excited, though, when Barnes called her over and pointed out a story off the wires that a TAT plane had gone missing en route from Albuquerque to Winslow, Arizona. There were eight people on board, three crew and five passengers.

"Just thought it might be some of your pals," he said.

"Oh, no," Laura responded, "none of them would be flying commercial." But she jumped at what she saw as her chance. After these two days back in the office with boring assignments, she envisioned bleak days ahead. "But that's a great story, boss. Send me. They'll be searching for days. This is that train-to-plane, cross-country venture that Lindbergh set up, Transcontinental Air Transport."

"Are you nuts?" he barked. "The wires'll cover it. And what makes you think you're the aviation reporter around here? If I was to send anyone, it'd be Mac. Go back to your desk and finish what you're doing. We got a paper to get out."

After a couple of false sightings and a few aborted starts, the search for the plane dragged on for days. It was reported that it had been seen at approximately the same time over both Black Rock, New Mexico, and Kingman, Arizona. *The New York Times* reported the plane had been struck by lightning and had crashed near Gallup.

The wires and the papers then settled down to stories of selfless pilots scouring for the missing plane across deserted areas of New Mexico. Laura bribed a copyboy with a nickel to give her anything new from the wires. Each time he would bring a story to Laura's desk, she would wordlessly go dump it under Barnes's nose. He ignored the silent protest so completely for two days that he not only never reprimanded the boy, but he wouldn't even put his hands on the copy Laura dropped on him, allowing it to pile up in an untouched mound of paper on the left side of his desk. The tension grew. Lindbergh and his bride of three months, Anne Morrow, joined the search.

"I don't know about that Lindbergh," Joe Collins called over from the next desk, chewing his toothpick. "He puts his pants on like the rest of us, one leg at a time."

"How original," Laura replied, but in the interest of office harmony, she had softened her tone. Joe beamed, not catching the sarcasm. Laura grinned to herself. Maybe I'm getting the hang of how to deal with these bums.

The other New York tabloids were jumping into the fray with breathless bylined accounts, and Barnes had to relent enough to motion with a nod of his head for an assistant city editor to pick up the piled-up copy from his desk and assign a rewrite man to work the story.

"I think those Ford Trimotors carry two pilots and a steward," Laura announced with authority to the room at large.

Finally, on Friday, wire stories were ecstatic with the report of a sighting. The pilot of a search plane had spotted four men waving white shirts on a high, flat mesa a hundred miles from Winslow. Rescuers on horseback had been dispatched to the scene. Laura breathed a secret sigh of relief. She would hate to see something like this set the public against flying. She had picked up Roy's zeal about furthering aviation even while the thought of him made her heart ache and her pride hurt. She would never get over what a simpleton she had been. She had forgotten for those few days in Oklahoma the lessons learned through Evelyn not to let her guard down, to be wary: *Love is no more than the wide blossom which the wind assails*. She couldn't forgive herself for behaving like such a lovesick idiot.

Then the lost plane story took another sharp turn—it was discovered that the guys on the mesa were Navajos from a nearby hogan who had never before seen a flyover and were waving their shirts in excitement at the spotter plane. Meanwhile, there were new reports of old sightings of a plane "in trouble" over both northern Mexico and southern Utah, well over a thousand miles apart. Search parties were sent to check out both. Laura thought of the Crosson woman who had been killed in the Powder Puff Derby. Marvel went missing on the second day of the race and never made it to Phoenix. *Her* crash site was found the next morning, though there were calls for the race to be cancelled. Laura worried that the notoriety over the loss of the TAT plane would set the naysayers to clamoring. She almost laughed out loud remembering the comments of the prominent oil man E.P. Halliburton after Marvel Crosson crashed: "Women have proven conclusively that they cannot fly."

On Saturday, the fifth day of the story, the search area was widened, and Barnes finally relented. He allowed Laura to work the story by phone along with the rewrite man. It had gotten too big for one person to handle. Some wreckage was spotted on the largest volcanic mountain in New Mexico. The story was changing every few minutes. The backshop was replating Page One and getting updated papers on the street nearly every hour. Laura was working the phones, poring over the continual stream of wire stories rushed over by copyboys, typing new leads. Search teams on horseback and foot began the climb up the mountain, then had to make camp Saturday night at nine thousand feet. Laura ripped that last take out of her typewriter and handed it to the waiting kid. Only then did she realize she hadn't gotten up from her chair in five hours.

Searchers resumed their climb the next day, Sunday, but couldn't find the plane. Then Lindbergh swooped in and hovered over the wreckage to spot their way. What the rescuers ultimately found, clambering over the lava, was charred remains. None of the bodies were readily identifiable, according to one early account. But another reporter wrote that the two pilots were found in the cockpit "with their left hands up before their faces as if warding off a blow."

"What nonsense, they couldn't possibly have seen that," Laura pronounced. "Yet another so-called reporter with a vivid imagination."

Stories were coming out about reporters at the site having somehow managed to hook up a portable telephone in an isolated surveyor's camp to the town switchboard in nearby Grants, and the lone operator there put them through to their papers across the country. Garbled accounts were arriving in all sorts of ways; some reports said the debris indicated the plane had been headed west when it crashed, others said it had been headed back east, the direction from whence it came. More drama ensued. A TAT official tried to block the taking of photographs and demanded the bodies be immediately removed. Armed forest rangers stepped in.

They had to wait for the district attorney to arrive. When the DA finally got there, he swore in cowboys from the rescue party to act as deputies.

The wrap-up came from Anne Lindbergh. "It seems to me," she said, "the most terrible accident in all of aviation." The comment made Laura shiver to think of the risks Jenny and Roy took every time they flew. Yet she consoled herself that their low-level flying in light planes was hardly the same as cross-country trips over high mountains.

"Wow," she said aloud, exhausted but exhilarated after finishing her shift on Sunday, "what a story." She marched up to Barnes. "See, if I'd been there, you could have relied on the information you got."

"Are you nuts? One portable telephone—you would have been trampled in the melee. Besides, it's a good thing you were here to work the extra day on Sunday, otherwise I would have had to cut your pay for all those days you missed traveling."

Laura dutifully climbed the steep el stairs and got off at the Park Row Terminal for the next several weeks, but she was miserable thinking about Roy, and dispirited about work. Her assignments were boring; nothing like the adventures of last month or the New Mexico crash. And at home, Evelyn behaved as though they'd never spoken of Father Bernard. Laura had to admit that she hadn't tried very hard after that first confrontation. An easy question here, one there, but her mother wouldn't take the bait. "So what would Dad think about such and such?" was about all Laura would venture. She was basically afraid that her mother would get angry or mean if Laura badgered her. She also didn't want her mother to start the tirade about not calling Father Bernard "Dad," the way she had always objected to herself being called "Mom." Laura couldn't decide which bothered her more, the elusiveness of her father's image or the lack of excitement at work.

Then one beautiful day in late September, as Laura was finishing up an obit, Myrtle yelled from the switchboard, "You got a call, kid!"

It was Jenny, saying she was at Roosevelt Field to discuss a business offer from Curtiss and that she planned to do the flight checkout the next day for her transport license. She'd already passed the four-hour written exam. John was there just for the in-air test and they were staying on Long Island, but Jenny could come in and spend the weekend with Laura after he left.

"I hope that grumpy boss of yours will let you come cover my trials," Jenny said, followed by her tinkly laugh. "Mark, my friend from Curtiss, says there will be plenty of reporters, but it would be special to me if you were here."

Laura, aglow with excitement that Jenny was affirming their friendship and thrilled that she had taken these first steps toward a new goal, did some quick homework before approaching Barnes about going to Roosevelt Field. She found you needed two hundred solo hours before taking the written exam. Then a grueling flight checklist that included spot and dead-stick landings, vertical figure eights, stalls, spins, loops, all kinds of dangerous-sounding maneuvers. And apparently you never quite knew what kind of critical situation the examiner would put you in to see if you could get out of it.

Laura shivered. It appeared that if you couldn't get out of it, you crashed.

Barnes cut her off before she could even tell him that only three women held the license. "Take Cheesy with you," he said, then turned back to his ringing telephone.

CHAPTER FORTY-TWO
JENNY TAKES HER TEST

WHEN LAURA AND CHEESY ARRIVED, Jenny was already in the air. Roosevelt Field was jammed with cars parked every which way around the perimeter of the right-angled flight line. The *Daily News'* plane was cruising low overhead. People swarmed along as though at an amusement park or ball game. Laura grinned to herself. Soon no more baseball to hog Page One, and with the Yankees out of contention, she had a good shot at tomorrow's front page with a story about Jenny. Probably only a home run by Babe Ruth or Lou Gehrig could knock her off.

New Yorkers were finding it hard to stomach that the Yankees, who had not only made it to the last two World Series but had won them, were falling victim this year to the Philadelphia Athletics. But Laura had learned from experience that some very good stories could get lost in the kismet of breaking events. Today's Page One was Yankee Stadium; this time for the funeral of manager Miller Huggins. Yesterday it was the amazing story of Army ace Lieutenant Jimmy Doolittle flying blind in a shrouded cockpit using only instruments. True, there was another pilot in the forward cockpit as a fail-safe, but Doolittle had done it! Aviation feats were big news.

Laura was pondering how she would write her story so that she and Jenny could knock the Yankees off Page One when she noticed Mac hanging out near the Curtiss hangar with reporters from several other papers.

"Why are you here?" she asked, rushing up to the balding reporter. "Barnes said I could do this."

"Don't worry your pretty little head. I know all these Curtiss people, including Mark Snyder, who has loaned her a plane and wants to sponsor her. You can do the interview. I'll handle the technical stuff."

"Stuff the technical," Laura said in a huff. "Doesn't he think I can do all of it?" Pretty little head, my foot, she fumed. When will these galoots ever take me seriously?

Mac answered with a grin, as Jenny swooped low and dipped her wings over the spot where they were standing.

"She's saying hello to you," Mac said. "Now you're part of the story. Cheesy's just snapped your picture. 'Our Gal Reporter Greeted by Winged Lass.' Good headline."

Laura was startled by Mac's comment. Was he making fun of her, or was he actually trying to be nice? They had all seemed to be somewhat nicer to her in the newsroom lately. She felt she never quite knew when people were being friendly—or was she antagonizing them by trying to appear too self-sufficient? She thought of Jenny. It felt as though they were becoming true friends, but she was still afraid to trust her feelings on that as well.

Laura spotted John Flynn scanning the skies, a Panama hat with a black band shading his eyes. He was pacing near the shack that sold ice cream like an expectant father in a hospital waiting room. He seemed to be talking almost to himself, hardly noticing Laura and Cheesy, who was gyrating around taking pictures of John's pacing. "She's done three stalls already. I can't imagine what that examiner wants. Probably being hard on her because she's so young and pretty."

Cheesy was gleeful. "I got a shot of hubby wearing a path in front a dat sign, *Fly for 5 bucks*."

Jenny suddenly swooped down at them, the nose of her plane rolling as she came.

"What's she doing?" Laura yelled over to John.

"A vertical figure eight." He had to shout by now—the noise of Jenny's plane so close with the background din of other planes landing and taking off was almost deafening. "Basically a couple of loops put together. The trick is staying inside a tight perimeter."

Jenny, her white scarf sailing behind, passed so close over their heads that Laura instinctively ducked.

John smiled at her discomfort. "It's a maneuver that takes a lot of control."

Cheesy was scampering this way and that, at times on one knee, at times lying on the ground.

When Laura looked back up as Jenny roared past in a fast climb, she was surprised to see a man in the front cockpit. "The inspector rides with her?"

"Sure." Laura could barely hear John's reply because he had gone back to his pacing. "He needs a close-up look."

Several of the other reporters started trotting over from hangar row, apparently alerted by Cheesy's actions that John had some importance in the spectacle. Laura, seeing them coming, leaned up on tiptoes to whisper in his ear, "Don't talk to any of these jerks. They're ghouls."

John burst out laughing. "That's the first time today I've relaxed enough to find anything funny." At Laura's panicked look, he laughed again. "Don't worry, kiddo, Jenny told me the story is important to you. What should I do, not talk to them or give them false info?"

Laura smiled. "Thanks, I've got enough trouble with a guy from my own paper here. Answer only flying questions, which they probably already know anyway. Don't answer anything else."

THEASA TUOHY

John grinned again. "Whatever you say." Then his smile faded as he squinted up into the sun.

Three reporters and another photographer came pushing through, and everyone's eyes turned to the sky. At the top of a loop, Jenny's plane suddenly seemed to be falling. As she got closer and closer, Laura realized there was no noise coming from the plane. "Her engine's conked out," Laura said, trying to control the panic in her voice. "She seems to be gliding."

"She is." John had stopped his pacing and was standing stone still. "Dead-stick landing, another test."

Even Cheesy looked like a statue, his camera dangling from his right hand. The three of them watched, clustered together in silence, as the little plane seemed to glide to earth some half a mile away. They breathed a collective sigh, and watched as the plane again rose into the cloudless sky and headed into another loop.

"Who are you, mister?" a reporter with a beak nose and a snap-brim hat demanded, turning to John.

A fellow whom Laura recognized as a *Times* reporter was more polite. "Are you the flier's father?"

Oops, Laura gloated, ask a husband a question like that! Good lesson there on how *not* to approach sources.

John turned his back on the two and addressed Laura. "You've won that round."

Jenny's plane zoomed down at them again, only to pull up at the last minute.

"Gee," Laura said, exhaling a pent-up breath, "this is painful to watch."

"I'll say," John replied. "It's worse than when I watched her first solo. Being an old hand at this myself doesn't help one bit."

The *Times* reporter tugged at John's sleeve. "Sorry to bother you again, sir, but could I ask you a few questions?"

The photographer with him was busy taking shots of John then turning to aim at Jenny when she was in range.

"You had your question," John said, turning to grin at Laura.

He walked away with Laura and Cheesy toward the infield shack and bought them ice creams, which soon began melting down their fingers as they nervously craned their necks toward the sky.

"This is taking too long." John impatiently stamped his feet and threw his cone on the ground. As he was dabbing at his sticky fingers with a handkerchief, he let out a low moan. Laura, following his pointing finger, saw a plume of dark smoke curling from the little plane.

John started out at a dead run toward the Curtiss hangar, with Laura and Cheesy close behind.

A sandy-haired man in a business suit was rushing toward them across the runway. "Mark," John yelled to him, "can you tell what the hell is going on? Have you ordered out the fire brigade?"

Laura saw that Mac was heading their way, along with several other reporters and photographers.

The bell of a fire truck was clanging as Laura turned to watch Jenny's plane drop for an easy, smooth stop practically in front of where they were standing.

A stampede of people headed to the plane. Jenny and the examiner climbed out at the same time, and he immediately stepped over and shook her hand. Laura, running by then, had gotten close enough to hear him say: "Well done. I never had a woman applicant before, so I was determined to be tough. But you came through with flying colors, if you don't mind the cliché."

John picked Jenny up and twirled her around. People continued to pour out of the hangars, everyone shouting congratulations.

Laura found herself trying to hold back tears when she gave Jenny a hug. "But what about the fire? What was it? I was so scared."

Jenny was nonchalant, shrugged. "Pooh, that happens a lot," she said. "Just a little too much throttle, have to wait while fuel burns off the engine. But the heck with that! I've got my transport license! Let's break out the champagne."

"Where?" Laura asked. "It's against the law."

"I'm way ahead of you on that," John said, giving his wife another hug. "It's on ice. Mark's planning a little party in the back room of the Curtiss hangar."

"Swell," Jenny said. "I wouldn't want this grand occasion to go unnoted. As for you," she turned to Laura, "why didn't you answer Clem?"

"Clem?" Laura looked at her as though she had a leak in her brain. The thought flashed at how startled Jenny had been a few days ago when Laura, seemingly out of the blue, had asked, "What if I'm an Indian?"

"Yes, Clem! You are the most unsocialized animal I've ever seen. I told you he's sweet on you. And rich. What girl in her right mind wouldn't follow up on that?"

Laura could feel her face getting hot. "Slightly awkward circumstances, don't you think? I was mortified about Roy."

Jenny yanked off her cloth helmet, waved it in a flourish, and linked her arm through John's. "Drum roll, please. Clem's a lawyer, you know, and he has been digging up information about how you might prove yourself eligible for your father's headright. The Indian priest *is* your father, isn't he? What did your mother say?"

"Shouldn't we talk about this later?" Laura pleaded. "Besides, I remember Clem telling me when they closed the Osage roles. It was the month before I was born."

"He'll fix it. What did your mother say?"

"Ah . . . eh, yes," Laura stammered. "But she didn't like my bringing up the subject."

"I'll talk to her," Jenny declared. "Who ever heard of a mother who would stand in the way of an inheritance? And I must say, I'm curious. I'm sure I've never met anyone like her before."

"You mean someone who had an affair with a priest?"

"Now don't get touchy. I'm sure she's had an interesting life. A different kind from anyone *I've* ever known."

CHAPTER FORTY-THREE
FEAR AND TREMBLING

IN CHEESY'S CAR DRIVING BACK to New York, Laura was in a cold sweat. She dreaded the idea of Jenny getting together with Evelyn, but there was nothing to be done about it. Jenny was going to spend a couple of days with Laura at the Gay Street apartment after John left for Oklahoma. Laura had never had a friend sleep over, even as a child, and that in itself had her in a swivet. But now Jenny's plan to confront Evelyn over Laura's father was just too much. Laura even started worrying about the rule of not wearing white shoes after Labor Day. Although she felt almost positive that her mother didn't even own a pair, she knew that with Evelyn one could never be sure of anything. Laura was in such a mumbly, distracted frame of mind that even Cheesy, who rarely took notice of anyone's mood, finally asked, "What's eating at you?" Of course, Laura replied, "Nothing." Cheesy was hardly the one to assuage her worries about whether the white-shoe thing mattered if the weather was still bright and sunny.

Lordy, she worried, using Jenny's favorite expression as all her fears tumbled through her mind, how will Miss Proper Etiquette deal with Evelyn? For the first time in her life, Laura had found a real friend, and it was all going to be ruined. She just knew it. Jenny would hate her or certainly snub her after this, and Evelyn would have a fine old time watching Laura's hopes for a new friend crumble. There was no way to stall Jenny a day, or even get home ahead of her to warn Evelyn. But what would she say to warn her? If Evelyn knew how important all this was for Laura, that would goad her even more to be mean and cynical and make fun of everything. And Jenny wanted to talk about a headright for Laura! Evelyn would go berserk. Hadn't she been vicious in telling Laura that her father wouldn't approve of her job? Laura had never understood Evelyn, and she never would. How could she explain it to Jenny, or prepare her for it? Come to think of it, Jenny could be a bit mean herself.

Laura told herself she must shake this gloom. She had to get to the office and write a good story. And the damned Yankees couldn't interfere with it. She had been so excited about Jenny's success just a short time ago, but, as usual, Evelyn was interfering even when she wasn't there.

Laura looked out at the passing parade on the Long Island Motor Parkway. Socialites whizzing past farms and fields at probably forty miles an hour in their big cars on the way to their weekend homes. Where could you see this much green except in Central Park? For Laura, it was another world, almost as strange as Oklahoma. It made her wonder what Jenny would think of the hustle and din of Manhattan. Probably no chance she'd stick around long enough to find out after Evelyn got ahold of her.

Cheesy suddenly pulled over to the side of the road.

"What are you doing?" Laura asked. She had to get back to the office. "Is something wrong with the car?"

He reached behind into the backseat of his disheveled DeSota and grabbed his camera. Cheesy claimed this car was only a year old, but Laura found it hard to believe an automobile could get so tatty in such a short time. Film, cameras, clothes, and old shoes fought for space in the rear with a blanket, pillow, and empty pop bottles. Laura had

had to shove aside all sorts of debris, including a pair of dirty socks, to get into the passenger seat.

"Gotta get some snaps here," he replied. "Battle building between Vanderbilt and Robert Moses."

Laura followed him out of the car. "What battle? That's crazy. In this bucolic place?"

"Don't you read da paper?" Cheesy was busy taking pictures.

"Oh," said Laura with a frown of recognition. "Yes. I just didn't know that's where we were. This is a new part of the world for me." The papers had been full of the scrap between the Master Builder Moses, state park commissioner, and William Vanderbilt, who had built the motorway twenty or so years before as a place to run his racing cars, and had since turned it into a private toll road. Moses had grand plans for Long Island freeways and they weren't compatible with the millionaire's private raceway.

"Hmm," Laura added, "I suppose I could work up a feature to go with your pictures: 'Battle of the Titans.' I'm so frustrated, Cheesy. After this story with Jenny, I'll be back doing obits and tea parties. Something has got to break soon."

"It will," Cheesy said, as he continued snapping pictures. "It always does. Don't pay to worry."

Laura took out her notebook and began writing today's story while she waited.

C HAPTER FORTY-FOUR
THE GREETING

LAURA WAS STARTLED WHEN JENNY stepped off the train at Penn Station to see her dressed in street clothes. She'd never seen her in anything but flying togs.

She looked chic, even sophisticated, in a mauve ensemble with pleated skirt and fabric belt low at the hips. Pale gray spectator shoes and kid gloves the color of Jenny's eyes also matched piping on the dress and the lining of her jacket.

"Wow," Laura greeted her with a hug, "you look swell. I love the cloche with the turned-up brim."

Jenny giggled. "I'm so happy to be here, and see you. You look splendid yourself."

Arm and arm the two friends walked the two blocks to the el stop at 33rd Street, Laura carrying Jenny's small satchel.

Jenny was still exhilarated and chattering away about her morning's flight and giving Laura extravagant praise for her role in pushing Jenny into taking a hand in her own future, so it took awhile to get around to the subject that was plaguing Laura—her mother.

Laura had taken the precaution of sending Evelyn a telegram from the office to alert her that they were having overnight company. They'd never had a telephone, actually few of their friends did, although a number had hall phones in their apartment buildings. Evelyn had laughed when she'd seen a news story the past March that President Hoover finally got a telephone on his desk after years of using a booth in a hall of the White House.

"With all the dirty business he's got going on, I would have thought he'd need to be on top of his clients every minute," she'd said when she saw the story. Evelyn had all sorts of reasons for disliking the conservative Hoover, not the least of which was his branding as "socialism" the proposed help for struggling farmers. "Socialism, my foot," she would frequently say, "what that prune needs is a good roll in the hay."

Laura shuddered, thinking of the possibility that her mother might raise the subject of free love with their guest.

"Jenny," Laura began to tentatively broach her subject as they settled on the elevated after paying the nickel fares for both herself and her guest, "I want to warn you that my mother is a bit what one might call eccentric."

"Good gravy, that's no surprise," Jenny retorted. "She did run off and all those other things, you know."

Laura reddened. "Yes, well, you're being polite about *all those other things*."

Jenny's laugh tinkled. "I told you before, don't be so touchy. I'm looking forward to meeting her as a grand adventure."

Thank goodness the el was rattling so that it wasn't easy to say much more. Laura was so anxious she feared she might lose the little she'd had for lunch due to nerves.

As they descended from the wooden stairs at Sixth Avenue, Laura looked around at the dirty streets and blowing debris, wishing that Jenny could see the idealized view of her neighborhood through a John Sloan painting instead of the grim and unwashed windows of the local Chinese laundry. As the rattle of the el faded, and the normal din of the fast-paced scene resumed, Laura heard a familiar and dreaded sound—a stream of high-pitched laughter and vulgarity coming from the twelve-story women's detention center.

Jenny stopped dead in her tracks. "Oh my," she said, as a particularly choice catcall rang loud and clear over the chatter of the several women leaning out the windows.

The triangle where Greenwich and Sixth avenues met was familiar ground for Laura. Right next to the beautiful Victorian Gothic courthouse was the eyesore jail. She had been hearing these catcalls since the Jefferson Market was torn down two years earlier and replaced by the facility. The beautiful courthouse and the screaming women had been in Laura's dream in Cleveland, in which Jenny was skipping rope on the P.S. 41 playground and wouldn't let Laura in. Her subconscious had been telling her then that Jenny was mean and superficial. Bringing her home and letting her into her heart was probably a terrible mistake. In the dream, Laura's mother had been yelling at her to jump from the taxi-airplane that Laura was driving into the building. For once, Mother was probably right. Laura wished she could bail out right now

"Just part of the New York street scene," she said to Jenny with a shrug. "Part of your grand adventure."

"Oh my," Jenny said again.

CHAPTER FORTY-FIVE
THE MEETING

AS THEY TURNED LEFT ONTO the block-long Gay Street, Laura pointed at her house. "That's home," she muttered.

"What a grand old place," Jenny replied. "How nice."

"We don't exactly have the entire building." Laura could hear the defensiveness in her own voice. "Our apartment is on the second floor."

After the flight of steps from the street, Laura noticed Jenny's perplexed look as they passed through the downstairs hall and climbed the inside staircase.

Evelyn was standing at the top to greet them. She must have been impressed that I sent her a telegram from the office, Laura thought.

Jenny stood erect as a ballerina on point, quickly removed her glove from her right hand, and extended it to Evelyn. She took charge before Laura could say a word. "I'm very happy to meet you, Mrs. Bailey."

Evelyn just nodded and did not remark on the fact that her name wasn't Bailey, nor was Laura's for that matter. Nor did she bother to point out that, indeed, she wasn't a "Mrs." anybody.

"So lovely to be invited to your home," Jenny cooed. "I've brought you a small house gift. A lavender sachet." She extended a small, exquisitely wrapped box. "Thank you so much for having me."

Still having said nothing, Evelyn waved the two girls into the sitting room, a small smile playing around her lips. She finally said, "Can I get you a cup of tea?"

Laura's eyes moved from Jenny to her mother, then back again to Jenny, who seemed riveted on the small, open, closet-sized space at the end of the room that served as their kitchen.

"I'd love one," Jenny said as she removed her other gray kid glove and placed the pair firmly on her lap, her back still ramrod straight as she perched on a worn-looking slouchy chair. "I've had a dusty train trip from Long Island."

Laura was truly astounded watching the two of them, as though they were on some imaginary stage. She was used to seeing Jenny in jodhpurs with her hair blowing, and her mother in her caustic, nihilist mode. Even more startling, Evelyn was already moving back from the kitchen, Edna's fragile gift pot and three tiny cups balanced on a small tray. She had prepared the tea in advance! Laura smiled to herself. Her mother's usual imperious manner seemed ideally suited to the tea ritual.

After Evelyn poured, inquired about sugar, and passed the cups around, Laura listened with wonder as Jenny began what came close to being a nonstop monologue. It was broken only occasionally by Jenny's tinkly laughter, or by a seemingly amused "yes" or "no" from Evelyn. Laura wished she had her notebook, could take notes. There was some grand life lesson to be learned here, although at this point, she had no idea what it was. But it would certainly bear further study when she had time.

"You have such a fascinating life and friends," Jenny burbled. "Just imagine, actually living in Germany."

At this, Evelyn frowned.

"I saw Edna St. Vincent Millay once on lecture. The most beautiful thing I've ever seen."

Evelyn nodded *yes*.

"You have pictures by American artists on your walls."

Evelyn replied, "Yes."

"I think that's wonderful. We are not part of really any kind of different art scene in Oklahoma City, except perhaps the Indians."

Evelyn frowned.

"So we only know to buy Old Masters, European artists." Jenny paused for breath, put her teacup to her lips, and stared hard over its rim at Evelyn for a moment, then said, "Oh my goodness, you've known all these influential people. When I was thirteen, I went with my mother on the train to St. Louis to hear Miss Millay read her poetry. Mother is on the board of the library, you know, and tried to get Miss Millay to come to Oklahoma City, but she said she was too exhausted and sick. She had been reading around the country. I remember how beautiful she was, her red hair and a blue dress." Jenny had to stop to catch her breath. "They called her the poet-girl."

Evelyn finally spoke beyond a mutter. "Apparently," she said, "Laura has told you that Vincent is a good friend."

"Vincent?" Jenny said.

"That's what her *intimates* call her," Evelyn replied. "She's the one who gave me this tea set."

Laura opened her mouth to protest her mother's expropriation of her fourteenth birthday present, but decided it would be wiser to let this strange encounter play itself out.

"Oh my." Jenny followed this with her tinkly laugh as her eyes toured the room, a wide smile on her face. "What a truly exciting life you've led!"

Evelyn responded this time with an expectant, questioning look. Good grief, thought Laura, they are playing some kind of game, and they both seem to know it, understand the rules. She looked from one to the other. What were they doing, what was the point? Were they mad at each other or were they getting along?

"So, tell me about your life in Germany, Mrs. Bailey." Not a muscle had moved in Jenny's smile.

"Of course," Evelyn replied with only the slightest hint of resignation. "That's what you came to ask."

"It must have been exciting," Jenny persisted. "Before the war. So much going on. My husband was in France, you know. In the military."

"No, I didn't know." Evelyn's face was as set as the stone wall of her answer.

Laura suddenly felt elated. It was like watching a tennis match. No, more like a wrestling contest, she decided. This dance between the two might make for a long evening, but she was fascinated to see that her mother didn't seem to have any intention of walking away. Was she in this thing to prove she could best Jenny? Or maybe she had a desire to finally unburden herself. Did she consider Jenny her social equal? Perhaps that was it.

"Oh my, yes, my husband was in France. In the Lafayette Escadrille. A flier," Jenny said brightly. "Perhaps Mr. Bailey was in the war?"

"No, he wasn't," Evelyn said with a smirk. She seemed to be taking pleasure in this. "Nor was his name Bailey. Laura made that up. Who knows why, perhaps she was ashamed of her mother."

Knowing how Evelyn hated being called *Mother*, Laura winced.

Jenny's bright smile stayed perfectly in place, only her eyes moved, momentarily searching out Laura; her body seemed to grow even straighter, if that were possible. "Isn't that interesting?" she chirped. "So what *was* his name, Mrs. Bailey? If I may still call you that for the moment. In fact, how should I properly address you, ma'am?"

Evelyn laughed out loud. It felt to Laura like the first genuine expression from anyone since she and Jenny had entered the room.

"Never *ma'am*. I couldn't bear it. It's so bourgeois Midwestern."

"So? What shall I call you?"

"My name is Sampson, Evelyn Sampson. Laura, for some strange reason, insists on referring to me as *Mother*, with no other identification, as though I had no existence aside from my relationship to her."

Jenny's intake of breath was audible. She made an almost imperceptible shift in her lumpy chair, and momentarily lowered her head to smooth out and rearrange the kid gloves, putting the bottom one on top. Laura's heart sank. The jig's up, she thought, Mom has won again. Nonetheless, she still felt a certain exhilaration. This was the first time anyone had been around to fight a battle for her since Aunt Edna.

Jenny cleared her throat. "Mrs. Sampson," she began slowly, as though picking through her thoughts, "Laura has told you, I presume, about my friend Clem Donohue, a lawyer who also happens to be Osage. He is of the opinion that, if it is true that Laura's father was an Indian, Laura may be entitled to the benefits of certain oil rights."

Evelyn's head jerked back as though she'd been slapped.

"I'm sure this is a private and painful matter that you long ago buried away," Jenny continued. "But surely you wouldn't want to stand in the way of your daughter's inheritance."

Jenny stopped speaking, and there was silence.

Laura could hear the drip of the ice in its kitchen box just as she had when she first confronted her mother with the story of the Jesuit philosophy dean. Would this time be different? Would Evelyn finally reveal more to a stranger?

Her mother seemed to have a different bearing, though. She looked confused and upset now. Two weeks ago, she had been her usual cold, caustic self.

"The intellectual life in Munich was inebriating," Evelyn broke the silence in a soft, slow tone as though she were speaking to herself. "We sat in coffee houses for hours on end, exchanging ideas with artists and intellectuals about expressionism, impressionism, humanism, Marxism. Some of those same people went on to be Dadaist leaders."

Watching Jenny's face, Laura got the feeling that her friend had no idea, nor did she care, what most of these *isms* were.

Evelyn went on, her dreamy look morphing into something hard. "These so-called free thinkers in the Village are a joke. Nothing," she almost spit the word out, "compared to Munich. People here like the baroness floating around with a stovepipe on her head. Truly a joke. No distinction between exhibitionism and true intellectualism."

The clock was ticking, the ice dripping—the only sounds in the still room. Jenny cleared her throat and rearranged her gloves again; the bottom one was back on top.

"If it hadn't been for *her*," Evelyn's explosive tone was fierce, "I wouldn't have had to leave Munich."

"*Her?* You mean Laura?"

At the mention of her name, Laura went rigid with anger. "You kept up the pretense all these years." She spit out the words. It was the first time she had spoken since she and Jenny had entered the apartment. "You pretended that you couldn't identify my father. Why?" The indignation of some twenty-odd years of emotional deprivation rose as though she would choke on it. She'd been so overwhelmed two weeks ago to find out that her mother actually knew who her father was, she hadn't had time or room for the anger to boil up.

Evelyn looked genuinely surprised. "What are you talking about? I didn't *pretend* anything. *Nichts verdrängen*, repress nothing."

"You put *Father Unknown* on my birth record. Why did you do that?"

"He is unknown to you, isn't he? And besides, he was dead. What was the point?"

Vintage Evelyn—the world revolved around her. Laura had always known how self-absorbed her mother was. She remembered that at the time of Isadora Duncan's death, she had once again come to the conclusion that her mother's lamentations were nothing more than self-dramatization. Nothing ever *really* touched her mother, Laura had decided then. And nothing since had changed Laura's mind.

Jenny, who again was busy rearranging her gloves, didn't appear to have noticed this brief exchange between mother and daughter. She turned now to Evelyn and picked up where they had left off: "Oh, no," she replied in a soothing tone, as though speaking to a child with a skinned knee. "You wouldn't have wanted to stay in Munich. In a very few years, Germany was at war."

Evelyn mustered a tepid smile. "Not for a number of years, my dear, but those were years I could have used."

"Oh," Jenny said, "you must have loved him very much to have been so empty, for life to have been so devoid of meaning."

"The philosophy of nihilism was very appealing after Mickey died. Otto Gross, a friend at the time, scrapped Freud and became a disciple of Nietzsche. And it feeds off itself."

"You seem to have managed to be a nihilist in New York as well as Germany, so what's the difference, Mother?" Laura was beginning to enjoy herself a bit, sniping at Evelyn with someone as cool as Jenny around to reduce the heat and hurt. And who knows, maybe all these revelations presaged a new phase, a new stage for Evelyn's self-drama.

"You do persist in calling me *Mother*, don't you? You look so much like your father, but are so unlike him."

"Phooey," Jenny said. "Unlike *him* is not surprising. You two are like *each other*—trying to act tough, won't express real feelings, going to fight the world when there's no fight going on."

"Phoo to you," Laura shot back. "You sit around and won't accept a challenge. Let everyone else do the hard work, while you just coast along. You could have *won* that Powder Puff Derby if you hadn't been too lazy to enter."

Jenny laughed—this time it wasn't a tinkle, but hearty. "Thanks for the vote of confidence in my flying, and you're absolutely right. Because of your example and goading by John and Roy, I've gotten my wings, and I'm going to use them."

Evelyn looked from one to the other, seemingly mystified by this exchange.

"Now, on to the business at hand," Jenny said, this time slapping both gloves against her lap as she turned to Evelyn. "Did you and Father Bernard marry? Do we have any legal proof he was Laura's father?"

"Proof?" Evelyn sniffed indignantly, straightening up to her full imperiousness.

"Of course, no offense, Mrs. Sampson. But apparently Laura's birth certificate is no help."

"Certainly proves she was born," Evelyn replied.

"So," Jenny continued, "none of your Marxist or isms friends would have cared, but surely you must have done something just between the two of you. Did Mr. Bernard know you were pregnant?"

"*Father* Bernard," Evelyn corrected.

"You called him that all the time?" The incredulous expression on Jenny's face was priceless.

"Don't be silly." Evelyn's words came out snappish, but her humor returned. Her face softened first into a wry smile, and then the earlier dreamy look settled back in. "Michael Bernard. We did, in fact, have a civil union of a sort. The church, of course, wouldn't marry us."

"Do you have a certificate?"

"I don't remember."

"You must remember. Mrs. Sampson, this is important. What about your parents? Would they know?"

"They disowned me." Evelyn's shrug was bewildered, not dismissive. "At least, I guess that's what happened. I never heard from them, even though I sent two letters and a transatlantic wire with my address. My elopement with Mickey must have caused quite a stir." Evelyn's jaw hardened. "In their rigid code, my parents had no room for lapses."

"Oh dear. You never went back?"

"What for? New York was as far into the country as I wanted to come. I could have made my way in Germany, but not with a child."

"Oh my God." Laura bit her lower lip, holding back tears. Her mother had actually wanted her! Laura had subsisted on emotional crumbs for so long that the mere fact that her mother had elected to leave Germany and not terminate her pregnancy was enough cause to rejoice. She was flooded with a strange sense of peace. Her entire life she had floated, been blown by the currents like an unfettered balloon, feeling as though she were suspended from a skyhook observing what others did, wondering what would happen if she momentarily dropped amongst them. Suddenly, she felt her feet on the ground, she knew where she was.

"I'm sorry," Evelyn said, turning to Laura with a sad smile.

"It's okay, Mother." Laura reached over and patted Evelyn's hand. "I'm fine." She'd always been the parent for the two of them. No reason to stop now.

Jenny's smile dimmed for the first time all day. "Mrs. Sampson, how awful for you to be so cut off from your parents. I would hate that."

Laura, catching her friend's concern, jumped in. "Your parents know you've decided to make a career of flying. They know you're here. And they are fine with that, right?"

"Not fine, exactly. Yet they're getting used to the idea, I think. They did have us for Sunday dinner just before I came here. They try to blame John, but they can't fool me."

"Fool you?" Laura said.

"I know they really blame themselves." The matter-of-factness of the statement startled Laura. Jenny always seemed to have such a clear-eyed, uncluttered view of the world.

Jenny went on. "They think they did something wrong with me when my brother was killed in a plane. I was so little, and they think they somehow wrongly explained his death to me, trying to tell me what war was."

Evelyn turned to Jenny. "You've had to battle your parents to do this flying that Laura tells me you do?"

"I'm afraid that until now, Mrs. Sampson, I haven't fought back as hard as I should have. I knew how they viewed my flying. They called it unladylike, but I think now that it's really more their own sense of failure."

Evelyn chuckled. "It isn't easy. Laura and I can both attest to that. I'm going to see if I can't find that German marriage certificate."

Laura stood up, threw her arms wide, and twirled in a joyous circle. "You're finally in the air, and I've finally got my feet planted!"

CHAPTER FORTY-SIX
THE NEW YORK ENTERPRISE-POST

LAURA MOMENTARILY PAUSED IN THE RUSH of morning commuters before starting down the wooden steps of the Park Row Terminal. Sunrays played with waterspray from the fountain across the way in City Hall Park. She breathed in the freshness of the morning, despite the hustle of the surrounding scene. Another gorgeous October day. She moved on down, prodded by other passengers pushing forward to their day's work.

She stopped for her usual coffee in the lobby of the old *Times* building. "Morning, Charlie." She now knew the counter boy and addressed him by name.

"What's gonna be the big news today?" he replied, bobbing his head and adjusting his paper soda-jerk's cap.

"You never know," Laura said with a laugh. "But whatever it is, I can almost guarantee I'll be stuck asking the man on the street what he thinks about it. Next time, I'll come and interview you, Charlie. What would you think about that?"

The boy looked at her over his shoulder and grinned as he moved along the counter, filling up other cups.

Laura knew she had to quit being so restless and impatient about her job, but her assignments of late had been pale compared to the excitement she'd had chasing around with Jenny and her barnstorming friends. Laura kept reminding herself that it was thanks to that trip that she had found both her father *and* her mother. Evelyn was basically her same caustic self, but a détente of sorts was slowly developing.

Laura had devised a way to ferret out information about Dad, as she'd taken to calling him, and Evelyn would generally answer. Laura would approach the subject with an innocuous question like the one just yesterday when she had arrived home from work and found Evelyn sitting on the top step of their stoop. She was taking in the fresh air and reading.

"Beautiful day," Laura began. "Was the autumn as balmy in Germany as it always seems to be in New York?"

"We were only there for one fall, the one before you were born. Mickey," Evelyn's face lit up as it always did when she mentioned his name, "loved that summer in Munich because it was so much more temperate than St. Louis."

Laura put down her purse and sat on the concrete step just below her mother.

"Why don't you take off your hat and gloves?" Evelyn snapped. "Nobody in the Village dresses up like that."

Laura obliged, smoothing out the little veil before laying the offending items on her lap. "So the weather was nice there?"

"Yes. Lovely. That was lucky. I was nearly six months along, and heavy. You were born in February." She laughed, her face taking on the dreamy look. "Mickey said I was eating too much schnitzel."

Laura's heart skipped a beat. "Mickey knew I was coming?"

"Yes," Evelyn said in a matter-of-fact manner, "he would have been happy the way things turned out. He said he wanted a girl."

Tears welled up in Laura's eyes, but she knew better

than to try to hug her mother. When she took a handker-chief from her purse to dab at her eyes, Evelyn noticed.

"Now stop that. It doesn't do any good to get emotional about these things. I taught myself that long ago. Mickey died of the flu that winter."

Laura had an agenda she was working through. Her next goal was to find out the details of how her pregnant mother had managed to get back across the Atlantic and find a place to live. That journey seemed as fraught with peril as many by destitute immigrants.

Laura left a nickel on the counter for Charlie and headed through the throngs on the sidewalks to her nearby office, mulling over what project she should next propose to Barnes. She passed a couple of newsboys touting different headlines. One was yelling about a murder in Queens, another a house fire—nothing of significance. The papers had been filled lately with news of the wobbles of the stock market, which only weeks before had been soaring. The weather was good, everyone was happy except the still-pouting Yankee fans and Laura, who wanted a new round of excitement, something to sink her teeth into. Even the World Series had quickly come and gone. The Philadelphia Athletics knocked off the Chicago Cubs in five games. The big news in that one was what the tabloids were calling a Mack Attack—named for the A's manager, Connie Mack—when in the fourth game, the A's overcame an eight-run deficit to win 10–8. Then it was back to murder and mayhem or the fortunes of Wall Street.

Laura kept suggesting ideas for long-range stories that would involve her going undercover in perhaps a sweatshop in the Bowery or an orphanage, but Barnes wasn't buying any of it. In the weeks since Jenny's visit, Laura had written a feature about Robert Moses and his parkway disagreement with Vanderbilt, but Barnes had given her only one assignment she really enjoyed—he'd sent her to Roosevelt Field when Roscoe Turner was due to set another cross-country time record. The city editor had reminded her he was doing it only because of her acquaintance with the flamboyant aviator and Gilmore, his pet lion. Beyond that was what Laura had come to dub the Barnes refrain: "We've got an aviation reporter, and you're not it."

In a rare burst of candor, Laura had even told her mother of her frustration at work. Evelyn, in an equally rare burst of what sounded almost like sympathy, had said: "Don't worry, I think your moment will come."

At least Jenny was having good luck with her career now that she had gone to work for Curtiss—demonstrating new aircraft and flying prospective buyers around. She telephoned Laura and wrote often, full of enthusiasm. She excitedly described how thrilling and different it was to have a salary, pay for her own car, buy her own clothes, get up and go to work each morning with a purpose. *No one has seen me at the tennis court in months,* she'd written in her last letter. Curtiss loved her; she was bringing in new business, giving them a high profile. In a phone call to Laura at work a few days ago, she had reported, "Buyers, even upstart airlines, look and say, 'If a tiny little lady like her can fly this crate, anyone can.'"

Laura got to the office still thinking about Jenny as she passed by Barnes, said hi, and headed for her desk. Here we go again, she thought. She could already hear what he would say when she approached him with her latest story idea. "People want happy stories, kid, not all this gloom and doom you keep promoting," he would yell before again sending her out for some silly story or for a man-on-the-street interview about whatever struck his fancy at that moment. "Listen to the radio once in a while, kid," he'd say. "Everyone's favorite tune is 'Blue Skies.'"

Laura dumped her hat and gloves on the clutter of books and papers on her desk and another familiar scene replayed. It seemed the same every day. As she flipped through the papers, commenting about the day's news, Joe Collins piped up as usual from the next desk over.

"Who you talking to, kid, the wind? People'll think you're batso, grumbling to yourself." His feet were up, snap-brimmed hat pushed back with press card stuck in its band, the forever toothpick in his mouth.

"Knock it off, Joe." But Laura had learned to say it with a laugh.

"Sure, kid. But can't everyone get on Page One." The same thing with the same big grin as though he had just invented something terribly clever.

It was like habit, repetition of a family scene, she thought. Familiar. Like her mother saying, "Conventions of the past are the enemy."

"But damnation," she called back at Joe, "I need better stories."

In the mound were her notes about the Osage murders, although she'd decided that Barnes and Jenny were right, it was an old story. The new story for her was absorbing the idea that she had a proud Indian heritage—she had spent all of her free time at the public library, reading whatever she could find. But it was a subject way too close to write about at this point. Jenny had reported that Clem was still trying to establish Laura's heritage and obtain her father's Osage headright. That would be exciting, to be accepted by the tribe, but the main thing for the moment was simply getting used to the idea of knowing where she came from. Maybe sometime in the future she would write something profound for one of Mom's little literary magazines. Now she wanted to get back to the self she knew—a wiser one, she hoped—and write interesting stories about whatever came along in

New York. This was where she belonged, she decided, and who she was. Just like most of the people in the city, she sprang from somewhere else, conceived in Munich, Germany. How about that!

"You got a call, kid!" Myrtle yelled from her perch in the middle of the room, and the telephone jangled on Laura's desk. Maybe someone's calling with a secret tip on a killer story, Laura fantasized before picking up the phone.

It was Clem! "How you doing, little lady?" Laura's heart fluttered slightly hearing the warm, reassuring voice. Perhaps Jenny was right and the interest of another man could help take away the sting from Roy's rejection. As Clem launched into some of the legal issues involved in his pursuit of her headright claim, Laura remembered Jenny's remark: "You have very underdeveloped antennae on the subject of men." Laura still didn't quite understand any of this—about sparks and chemistry, why they worked in such a strange way. She had read and reread all of Aunt Edna's love poetry, but found clues there only to the emotions that ensued after one fell *out* of love, or got hurt.

Nothing about how to develop the right instincts in the first place. Laura wouldn't have known Clem was sweet on her, if Jenny hadn't told her.

Laura had also been a bit mystified when Joe Bailey, the reporter from Chicago, had called last week saying he would be in New York in a few days and would like to take her "out to the motion pictures."

Her mind had wandered to Joe when Clem said, "I'm planning to be in New York in a few days, and I'd like to take you out to dinner."

"Lordy," Laura responded, surprised to hear herself again using Jenny's favorite expression, "what next?"

Clem sounded hurt. "I think I should explain to you in person how the headright case is proceeding. This is a long, slow process. I feel you should be kept apprised of the situation."

"Oh, of course, Clem," Laura stammered. "Sorry, I was just responding to something here in the office." There was a certain truth in that. Knowing what big ears Joe Collins had, Laura had been trying to keep her voice down while answering Clem's queries double-checking the information Jenny had already given him concerning the date of Laura's birth, where she was born, and her parents' names. The birth date was crucial, Clem said. Even though Laura was born in February 1906, a month after the tribal rolls were closed, there was a provision in the law for children born within that year.

Wow, Laura thought as she hung up the phone with a happy smile, I have so much to learn. And Jenny is a smashing teacher. I somehow have two beaus, and it feels like it's thanks to her. I never learned anything about how to deal with men from watching Mother.

Poor Evelyn, she was too young herself when catastrophe struck. Maybe repression had stunted her mother's growth to maturity, and the lack of guideposts had impeded Laura like a hunter wandering in the wilderness with no compass. She wanted to keep in mind always the lesson learned watching Jenny in action with Evelyn. That old adage about catching more flies with honey than vinegar had sprung to life before her eyes. Laura smiled, thinking about how far her friend had come too. If Jenny could put that kind of doggedness to work in pursuing a career, she would be a devil of a success.

Laura laughed to herself. I don't know if honey is the solution with Barnes and Joe Collins. But what to do? She hated the thought of having to wait forever for another story as good as Jenny stealing an airplane.

* * *

The next morning, Laura arrived at work to find the office in chaos. There were four editors screaming into telephones at the desk where Barnes usually reigned supreme. Three women at the switchboard were yanking and shoving their tangle of cords in an abstract whirl of copper and red. Laura asked several people rushing past what was going on, but no one bothered to answer until a copyboy slammed that day's paper into her hand. The wood block headline took up the entire front page:

WALL STREET PANIC
BLACK THURSDAY
MARKET CRASHES

Without taking off her hat or gloves, Laura approached the central command post, where Barnes was just another yelling editor. She tried to catch his eye with sign language and mouthed inquiries as to what she should do. After several minutes of Laura being knocked about by rushing reporters, Barnes finally put his hand over his phone's mouthpiece and moved his lips, which Laura read to say: *Man in the street.*

"What about woman?" Laura demanded.

A stub of cigar in the grip of his stained teeth, Rufus Joshua Barnes shook his head in resignation and bellowed, "Yeah, that too!"

—30—

The author's mother, Theasa Logan Tuohy, at Curtiss-Wright Field in Oklahoma City in the early 1930s with the plane in which she learned to fly, a single-engine Great Lakes Trainer.

Two grand old ladies of the flying machines inspired this book. Many of the stunts depicted herein were actually performed by Elinor Smith. She pulled off the book's opening scene of flying under all four of New York's East River bridges when she was seventeen years old. The other grand old dame was my mother, who, like Jenny Flynn, didn't view any of it as very serious. She was just in it "for the fun." She rebelled against too much stunt flying, and absolutely refused to wing walk. The seat belt in her old crate was too big to secure her ninety-two pounds, so she had to fly with a pillow behind her back. She always worried, she said, "that the pillow would slip out when I was upside down."

And then there was Christy Bradford, who, when we both were young and she was foolish, tried her hand at wing walking just for the sake of a newspaper story.

—T.T.